Pat Jarvis

DRC

OTHER BOOKS AND AUDIO BOOKS
BY TRACI HUNTER ABRAMSON

Undercurrents

Ripple Effect

The Deep End

Freefall

Lockdown

Crossfire

Backlash

Smoke Screen

Code Word

Lock & Key

Obsession

Royal Target

Royal Secrets

Deep Cover

Chances Are

Twisted Fate

DROP ZONE

A NOVEL

TRACI HUNTER ABRAMSON

Covenant Communications, Inc.

Cover image: *Venezuela Radar Map* © Bubaone, courtesy of istockphoto.com; *Soto Cano Air Base, Honduras* © Stocktrek, couresy of gettyimages.com; *Auyan Tepui on Carrao River Near Lagoon of Caniama National* © Vadim Petrakov, courtesy of shutterstock.com; *Businessman with binoculars. Over gray background.* © kurhan, courtesy of shutterstock.com

Cover design copyright © 2014 by Covenant Communications, Inc.

Published by Covenant Communications, Inc.
American Fork, Utah

Copyright © 2014 by Traci Hunter Abramson
All rights reserved. No part of this book may be reproduced in any format or in any medium without the written permission of the publisher, Covenant Communications, Inc., P.O. Box 416, American Fork, UT 84003. The views expressed within this work are the sole responsibility of the author and do not necessarily reflect the position of Covenant Communications, Inc., or any other entity.

This is a work of fiction. The characters, names, incidents, places, and dialogue are either products of the author's imagination, and are not to be construed as real, or are used fictitiously.

Printed in the United States of America
First Printing: October 2014

20 19 18 17 16 15 14   10 9 8 7 6 5 4 3 2 1

ISBN 978-1-62108-873-8

For Mom
Thank you for the gift of Venezuela.

ACKNOWLEDGMENTS

Ten years ago, Covenant Communications published my first novel. Thank you to all of the readers who have shared these adventures with me. I want to thank everyone in the Covenant family who has helped me along this journey and made this career such a joy. Thanks to Kathryn Gordon for your continued confidence and for always assigning me amazing editors. My special thanks to Samantha Millburn for always being willing to explore my crazy ideas and help me turn them into a finished product. Your efforts throughout the editing process are truly appreciated, as is your friendship.

I cannot express my appreciation enough to Rebecca Cummings for her many years of helping me discover my voice and for her continued input and guidance during the initial editing process. My thanks to Kathryn Brown and Jennifer Leigh for suffering through my first draft with me and to John Garvin, Stephanie Read, Darlene Sullivan, and Jen Leigh for carrying so many burdens when I "go dark" and disappear into my fictional world.

Thanks to the Central Intelligence Agency's Publication Review Board for your support throughout my writing career.

Thank you to my husband, Jon, for supporting me in everything I do and to my children—Diana, Christina, Lara, and Luke—for understanding my crazy schedule and for loving me in spite of it.

Finally, my thanks to Sylvia, Domingo, and Elizabeth Navas. Thank you for the gift of Canaima.

CHAPTER 1

Paige Vickers embraced the flutter of excitement bubbling inside her. Today she would find out where she would spend her tomorrows. Her personnel officer at the Central Intelligence Agency had already approved her transfer, and in two hours, she would receive her new assignment.

Her career as a psychiatric nurse had been born out of necessity, but those needs were behind her now. It was time for her to make her own choices, to choose her own path.

Paige pushed open the door to the CIA's counseling center to find Jennifer standing behind the reception desk, a clipboard in her hand. Jennifer's brown hair curled wildly around her face, her cheeks full and laugh lines beginning to form at the corners of her eyes.

The moment she saw Paige walk in, she skirted around the desk to meet her by the door as though she couldn't wait for her to walk the few steps to close the distance between them. "I found the perfect guy for you."

"No," Paige answered instinctively. This was another thing she wouldn't miss when she transferred: Jennifer's incessant compulsion to set her up on blind dates. Finding guys who shared the high moral standards she'd been raised with wasn't always easy, but at twenty-four years old, she didn't feel any sense of urgency to be in a relationship.

"You haven't even heard what he's like." Jennifer sulked. As a married woman of almost ten years, she apparently felt the need to match up all of her single friends.

"I don't need to hear what he's like," Paige insisted. "Besides, for all I know, I could get transferred out of the area."

"I still think you're crazy to go through with this transfer. You have no way of knowing where you're going to end up."

"Yeah, but we both know I can't do this anymore. I need to try something new, something away from psych units and counseling centers."

Paige could see by the expression on Jennifer's face that she was already formulating her counterarguments. "You aren't going to talk me out of it this time. This career isn't for me. I don't think it's ever been the right fit for me."

"How can you say that? You started studying nursing when you were sixteen years old. A few more classes and you can be a nurse practitioner."

"That's just it. I don't *want* to be a nurse practitioner. I want a normal life, dealing with normal people."

"We have normal people here," Jennifer said, though Paige could tell even she didn't completely believe her own words.

"Are you kidding me? What about the guy who is convinced some Iranian is after him even though he's never worked in the Middle East? Or the woman who wants us to check out every guy her daughter dates in case someone is trying to get to her through her kids?" Paige gave her a pointed look. "And that was just last week."

She reached out and took the duty roster from Jennifer. As she scanned through her appointments for the day, she was even more resolved to follow through with her plans.

"What if you hate your new job?" Jennifer persisted.

"I want to start the new year off fresh. Is that too much to ask?" Paige held up the clipboard to emphasize. "I feel like my life is getting stale here, and it's time for me to find a new adventure."

The door opened, and Paige noticed another of their former patients in the doorway. Emmitt Kemper had spent three months counseling with Paige after his daughter's death. A CIA operative with extensive training, he had gone through a battery of testing with Jennifer and their resident psychologist a few weeks before and had been deemed emotionally stable.

Emmitt's voice wavered, and his face flushed when he asked, "Where is she?"

Almost instinctively, Paige analyzed Emmitt's appearance. She sensed distress and pain in his simple question and noticed the tension in his body.

"Where is she?" Emmitt repeated, the agitation in his voice increasing.

"Where's who?" Jennifer asked.

"My daughter." Emmitt spoke as though the two women should be able to read his thoughts. His next comment confirmed his absence from reality. "I know you're hiding her from me."

Paige swallowed. So much for the man being stable . . . or safe. She knew his file well, and she knew he had killed in the line of duty before. She also knew he didn't need a weapon to do damage.

Jennifer looked at Paige, her confusion clear and a healthy dose of fear emerging. "Emmitt, we talked about what happened with your daughter. Don't you remember?" Jennifer asked.

"She's supposed to be home." He shook his head as though trying to fight against the confusion that was so clearly consuming him. Then he reached out and curled his fingers around Jennifer's arm, his grip viselike. His voice became eerily calm, his eyes boring down into Jennifer's. "Everything was fine until I came here. You took her from me."

Now Jennifer's voice trembled when she spoke. "Emmitt, calm down and let me go. We can talk about this. We can talk about your daughter."

"I'm done talking."

Paige gripped the clipboard holding the duty roster tighter as she saw the light in his eyes change, a darkness shifting over the normal pale blue. On the surface Emmitt seemed calm now, but Paige's own heartbeat picked up speed.

The muscle in Emmitt's arm flexed, and he pulled Jennifer closer. Paige knew enough about his training to see what he intended: an arm around Jennifer's throat, his other hand against her head in preparation to snap her neck. Paige didn't wait to see if Emmitt would follow through and prove her suspicion correct. Instead, she surrendered to impulse. Her arm came up, and the clipboard went flying and caught Emmitt on the side of his head.

His grip loosened enough for Jennifer to put an arm's length between them but not enough for her to break free. Paige hit the panic button on the desk and grabbed the syringe beside the button.

Emmitt shook his head, but before he could regain his focus, Paige slid the cover off the needle and quickly injected the sedative into his arm.

Jennifer pulled free as Emmitt slumped onto the carpeted floor and the door burst open with security rushing in. Paige willed her heartbeat to slow back to its normal rhythm, and she looked over at Jennifer. "When I said I wanted some adventure in my life, this wasn't quite what I had in mind."

* * *

Damian Schmitt breathed in the crisp morning air, a light breeze ruffling his dirty-blond hair and causing the manila envelope in his hand to flutter. He stared at the envelope, weighing the gravity of the moment. Inside was the answer to where he would serve his first assignment as a Navy SEAL. But it was more than just an assignment. This was his future: where he would live, the specialty training he would receive, and who he would come to trust.

He heard paper ripping as the other new graduates from BUD/S, the training program for Navy SEALs, opened their orders. Damian still didn't open his. He wanted to savor this moment.

At twenty-five, he was older than nearly everyone in his class. The other enlisted men were in their early twenties and had followed the traditional route of joining the military and then applying for SEAL training, which was difficult to get into, but unlike the others, Damian had been promised admittance to the program when he'd first been recruited as a civilian. His high aptitude scores and language skills had guaranteed him a spot in BUD/S, but completing the program and earning his trident pin had been up to him.

Six years of working in the oil industry and a year in international banking had been more than enough for him, and he was excited to start this new chapter in his life. Making it through SEAL training had been harder than he had ever thought possible, but he'd been determined. Not only had he made it, but he'd also graduated among the top of his class.

"I'm staying in San Diego," Nick, who was standing beside Damian, said excitedly. Nick Trahan had been Damian's swim buddy throughout their training, and they had become close friends. "What did you get?"

Slowly, Damian broke the envelope's seal and slid the contents free. He read through the first page, his eyes widening.

"You're not going to believe this," Damian said, his Venezuelan accent still evident in his voice even after more than a decade of living in the United States. He held his orders out for Nick to see.

"The Saint Squad?" Surprise and awe reflected on his face. "No way!"

Damian read through his orders again. Everyone in his BUD/S class knew about the Saint Squad. Several of their missions had been used as case studies on how to adapt when things didn't go as planned. Never had he expected to find himself a member of the highly respected unit.

Nick slapped Damian on the back. "You are so lucky. I never thought the Saint Squad was a possibility. I got the impression that their personnel was set in stone."

"I thought so too." From everything he had heard during his training, the Saint Squad was unique beyond its uncanny success rate. Despite its small size, the unit was more than half officers, an unusual situation in itself. Rumor also had it that the unit was still made up entirely of the original members and was closed to new personnel. Everyone said the higher-ups were so pleased with their success that they were afraid to make any changes. Apparently that was no longer the case.

Damian read through his orders again, almost expecting the words on the page to change if he stared at them long enough. Finally, he flipped through the rest of his packet, and reality hit him. This was his last day in California. Starting tomorrow, his home would be in Virginia.

CHAPTER 2

Snow blanketed Virginia, a series of storms over the holidays leaving more than a foot on the ground. Paige trudged across the icy parking lot of the CIA's training facility with her personnel officer, Fred Zimmer, walking beside her.

She wasn't sure where personnel had originally planned to send her, but they had made a change after the incident in the counseling center. That change had resulted in a transfer out of the area and into completely unknown territory.

A sense of excitement and anticipation bubbled inside her. New people. A new home. A new future. She had been waiting so long to find one for herself, one where she could try something new.

This new position would be a complete change from what she had done before. From what she'd been told, the woman who ran the training course for undercover operatives was an experienced agent who was well respected and knew how to get results. She also worked with trainees who had been carefully screened and were psychologically stable.

Fred held open the door for her, and they passed through the building's lobby and down a long hall. "Give me a minute to talk to Vanessa first," he said, slowing his pace.

Paige nodded, wondering what he could possibly need to talk to Vanessa about without her in the room. After all, from everything she had been told, this was a standard transfer. Then again, she had thought it a little odd that Fred had insisted on escorting her to the new assignment, especially when it was so far from headquarters.

Paige stood awkwardly outside the door while Fred and the woman inside greeted each other.

Then Fred spoke. "I have something for you."

"What's this?" the woman asked.

"The file for your new assistant."

The room fell silent except for the rustle of paper. Then the woman's voice carried through the open doorway. "Absolutely not."

A moment later the door closed with a quiet click. Paige strained to hear what was said but couldn't make out the muffled voices. Only a minute or two passed before the door opened once more and Fred motioned for her to enter. She passed through the office door behind him and studied the woman across the room.

She was younger than Paige would have expected, maybe thirty, but she carried an air of authority. Smooth dark skin complemented her high cheekbones, and her inquisitive eyes sized Paige up without any sign of pretense.

"Paige Vickers, this is Vanessa Johnson, your new boss."

"For the time being," Vanessa said flatly before Paige could respond. "As my last four assistants can tell you, I'm not an easy person to work for."

Paige saw Vanessa's words for what they were, simple truth and a challenge. "I don't expect any job to be easy, but if you'll explain your expectations, I'll save you the trouble of dealing with personnel anymore."

Vanessa's eyebrows lifted, and she spoke to Fred. "I think I like her already."

"I'll leave you two to get acquainted," he said with a note of triumph in his voice. "And, Vanessa, remember that Paige is Agency personnel, not military. Don't call her in during the middle of the night unless it's an emergency."

"Fine." As soon as he left, Vanessa said to Paige, "Which brings us to my first expectation. You need to have your phone with you and on at all times."

"Even after hours?"

"Even after hours." Vanessa motioned toward the door. "Because when Fred said I call people in during the middle of the night, he wasn't kidding."

* * *

"Kel, you've got to be kidding me. Brent takes leave for three days, and you pick now to tell me this?" Lieutenant Seth Johnson stared at the commanding officer of SEAL Team Eight, a man he had fought countless battles with, a man he considered a friend. A man who had clearly lost his mind. Seth's Southern drawl was barely noticeable beneath his frustration. "The squad is working great together, and now you're going to mess it up?"

Commander Kel Bennett stared back at him, clearly waiting for Seth to work through the shock of what he was asking. Changing up the Saint Squad was drastic, he knew, but he believed it was also necessary. The teams needed their new recruits to be ready for anything, and that wasn't going to happen unless they trained with men who had already seen battle, men he could trust to train these new SEALs right.

"I'm not messing anything up. I'm just giving some of our new guys the chance to learn from the best."

"Flattery's not going to work."

"It's not flattery. It's the truth. And I don't need your permission. In case you've forgotten, I'm in command. All I have to do is make this an order."

"Then why don't you make it an order when Brent gets back?" Seth asked, referring to the Saint Squad's commanding officer, whom Seth was currently standing in for.

"Brent will find out about the change soon enough. I only found out we were getting new men a few days ago," Kel said. "When I looked through the personnel files, I was impressed that two will fit exceptionally well with your squad. One of them is a Latter-day Saint, and the other was raised Catholic, but he has an aversion to drinking alcohol."

"I can appreciate wanting to throw the Mormon boys together, but we really don't need any new personnel. We're doing fine on our own."

"You have been doing fine on your own, but like it or not, the Saint Squad is expanding. You'll have to deal with it."

"Who are these guys, and when do they show up?" Seth asked, resigned.

Kel lifted a file from his desk and handed it to Seth. "The Latter-day Saint is still finishing his BUD/S training and won't report for another six weeks. The other one, Damian Schmitt, will be here in twenty minutes."

"Twenty minutes?"

A knock sounded at Kel's door.

"Come in," Kel called out, and both men turned to see an enlisted man standing in the hallway.

"I guess he's early." Kel waved him in.

The man was at least seven or eight inches shorter than Seth, around five foot ten, and Seth guessed from his build and light hair that his family originated from somewhere in Scandinavia or Western Europe.

Seth continued to study the man as he came to attention. He carried himself well enough, and his gaze was direct, something he appreciated in a man. When Damian introduced himself, Seth was surprised to hear a noticeable Hispanic accent. It was subtle enough that he couldn't quite place it, but there was no doubt this man had spent a significant amount of time south of the border.

Seth glanced at Kel, not sure what he was supposed to do now. There was a reason he was content to remain second in command of the squad. He didn't like to deal with the headaches and politics that came with being in charge.

Kel completed the introductions by motioning to Seth. "This is Lieutenant Seth Johnson. He'll be serving as your CO until Lieutenant Commander Miller returns from leave next week. I believe you have weapons training in an hour, so I suggest you settle in and then report to the firing range at ten hundred."

"Aye, aye, sir," Damian said and then disappeared back the way he had come.

As soon as he left the room, Seth turned to Kel once more and renewed his plea. "Seriously, Kel. Why the Saint Squad?"

"Because you're the best."

"I already told you, flattery isn't going to work."

Kel waved toward the door. "You'd better round up the rest of your men for weapons training."

When Seth started to leave, Kel added, "And, Seth, do me a favor and don't let Damian shoot anyone."

Seth held both hands out in surrender. "I'll do what I can."

* * *

Damian stood at the edge of the shooting range, a gun in his hand. The rest of his new squad wasn't due for another fifteen minutes, and he took this rare quiet moment to enjoy the view. In the forefront, functional buildings and snow-covered fields dominated the landscape. He had already seen the community of base housing, the airfield, and the various aircraft that utilized it.

He couldn't see the ocean from here, but the scent of salt and sea carried on the light breeze. He had dropped his gear at the temporary housing he'd been assigned, but he hoped he could find an apartment within running distance of the water.

He loved the ocean in a way few men understood. His entire life had been spent within minutes of the water, first in Venezuela and then in Houston. Not that he and his brothers had ever known what it was like to live in the high-rise condos or the beautiful homes along those coastlines. His family had always been on the outskirts of the community, using bicycles or their father's ancient pickup truck to bridge the distance between home and the beach.

A Humvee pulled up, and Damian recognized the big black man who climbed out of the driver's seat as the lieutenant he had met in the commander's office. The dark-haired man who climbed out of the seat behind Lieutenant Johnson was nearly as tall but lankier in build and a bit younger than the others.

The two men on the other side looked at him with differing expressions. The taller of the two had sandy hair, just a shade or two darker than his own, and he studied him with a look that crossed between simple curiosity and acceptance. As he followed the lieutenant toward Damian, his gait was long and easy.

The final member of the group stood around six feet tall, and his skepticism was obvious in his dark eyes and rigid posture.

Damian holstered his weapon and came to attention. He watched the men approach, flanking out in a V formation as though preparing to go to battle. They looked so connected, so unified. He wondered briefly if these men considered him the enemy.

He had been excited to get this assignment and have the opportunity to work with a squad that was so well respected, yet, now that the moment was here, he wondered if he would ever be accepted. Would he ever be good enough to be one of them? And if so, would these men ever open their ranks to let him in?

"At ease," Lieutenant Johnson said with a trace of impatience. "Damian Schmitt, meet the rest of the squad." He pointed to the serious one first. "This is Quinn Lambert. Next to him is Tristan Crowther."

Quinn offered a cursory nod, while Tristan stepped forward and offered a hand. Texas sounded in his words. "Good to meet you."

"You too."

"And the tall guy over there is Jay Wellman."

Jay also stepped forward and shook Damian's hand. "Welcome to the squad." His eyes lit with humor when he added, "It'll be nice not to be the new guy."

"How long have you been with this unit?" Damian asked, eager to find someone who could help him navigate these unfamiliar dynamics.

"Two years."

"Two years?" Damian repeated.

"You can get acquainted later. Everyone gather round. Whose turn is it to pray?" Seth asked.

Of all the things Damian had expected to come out of his commanding officer's mouth, "Whose turn is it to pray?" was definitely not on the list. Apparently, Seth noticed his confusion. "We use every tool available in our jobs. That includes asking for the Lord's guidance. You never know when it will come in handy."

"I'll say it," Tristan offered.

Everyone folded their arms, and Damian followed suit. Tristan's prayer was short and simple, asking for the Lord to watch over and protect them and to give them the inspiration necessary to perform to the best of their abilities.

As soon as the prayer ended, Seth resumed business as usual. "Go line up. It's time for some target practice." Seth motioned Damian to the shooting station on the end. "Start with your sidearm, and then we'll shift to assault rifles."

"Yes, sir."

"You don't have to 'sir' me. Call me Seth."

"Yes, sir," Damian said automatically. He quickly corrected himself. "Yes, Seth."

Seth waited for Damian to settle in and start shooting. Damian felt like he was going through evaluations all over again. After several rounds, Seth said, "Not bad. Go ahead and work on assault rifles. I'll be at the next station over."

Damian cleaned his sidearm and holstered it. He took a moment to look down the line at the rest of the squad before switching weapons. He had thought this would be like shooting practice at BUD/S, but he found it odd to no longer have an instructor standing by watching everyone's performance.

When he glanced out at the target Seth had just started shooting at, he felt a new sense of admiration. The man definitely knew how to abuse a target.

Determined to maintain a comparable level of competency, he picked up his rifle and fell in line.

CHAPTER 3

IT WASN'T THE MIDDLE OF the night when Paige's phone rang, but it was close. Four o'clock. In the morning.

Paige cleared the sleep out of her throat before she answered.

"It's Vanessa. I hope I didn't wake you, but I need you in the office in an hour."

"Okay. I'll be there." Paige took a moment to wonder why Vanessa hadn't told her to plan on coming into the office so early when they had spoken last night. Then she recognized this for what it was. A test.

She hurried across her hotel room to shower. She hoped to use her lunch hour to start searching for an apartment, but somehow, she doubted she would have a traditional lunch hour working for Vanessa.

She walked into the office at ten minutes to five to find her new boss already at her desk, her computer humming and a stack of files at her elbow.

"Oh, good. You're on time."

Paige made a mental note that Vanessa considered ten minutes early to be on time and dropped her purse on the desk in the corner of the room, the one Vanessa had assigned to her the day before.

"What do you want me to start with this morning?"

"Housing assignments." Vanessa picked up three files off her desk and held them out to Paige. "I have a new class showing up tomorrow morning."

Paige looked down at the files. "Any particular rules I need to know about?"

"Just make sure the men are in men's quarters and women are in women's quarters."

"I think I can handle that."

"The top file has all of the contact information for the housing office and some key phone numbers. You'll need to get the assignments to housing and arrange for the class members to get their keys."

"I'll take care of it."

"Great." Vanessa secured her computer and stood. "I have a training exercise I had to push up this morning because of some bad weather that's moving in this afternoon. I should be back around lunchtime."

"Is there anything else you want me to work on once I get the housing assignments done?"

"I doubt you'll finish those before I get back, but if you do, talk to security about getting your new passwords and computer access. Also, be prepared to attend my next class. You need to be familiar with what I'm teaching so you can field questions." Vanessa grabbed her coat and gloves. "See you later."

Paige watched her disappear through the door, wondering why exactly she needed to be in the office at 5:00 a.m. and what she should expect in Vanessa's class. Pushing those thoughts aside, she dropped down at her desk and began flipping through the files.

Experience told her that security would need some lead time to set up her computer access. She called the security office, not surprised when she got voice mail instead of a real person. She left a message and then moved on to the housing assignments.

One file held a class roster of only twenty names. The second file included housing diagrams of the men's and women's housing units.

Seeing the work as a big puzzle, Paige grabbed a few sheets of paper from the printer on Vanessa's desk and started making notes.

* * *

Damian stood on the edge of the rappelling wall and wondered exactly what he was doing there. When he'd graduated from SEAL training, he had thought he was ready for whatever the navy wanted to throw at him. That was before he had worked alongside the Saint Squad.

The stories he'd heard led him to expect a bunch of hardened warriors in this squad; instead, he discovered these were five family men of faith. They prayed every morning before beginning whatever activities they had planned, and they all had a noticeable respect for their wives. Even with that difference, when they went through their training exercises, they were all business.

He had trained beside them for nearly a week now. Every exercise, every obstacle was another opportunity for him to see how much he still had to learn. He didn't enjoy feeling like the weak link.

Quinn was a better shot, Tristan and Jay better swimmers. Seth was a whiz with electronics, everything from communications to explosives. Throughout each training exercise, Damian was faced with the stark reality that he was no longer the best in the class.

He had become so accustomed to being the person everyone looked to for help that he had forgotten he was far from being an expert. A gust of wind whooshed across the outdoor platform, sending the surrounding trees swaying and making the already frigid air feel colder.

"Who wants to go first?" Seth asked when he approached.

"Tristan and I can show the rookie how it's done." Quinn jerked a thumb at Tristan.

"All right," Seth said in his lazy Southern drawl. "Double-check your gear before you start your climb down."

"Already did," Quinn responded. He hooked the rappelling line to the D-ring on his harness, Tristan mirroring the action.

Moving as one, the two men positioned their feet on the edge of the wall. Trusting the lines to hold their weight, they began their backward descent.

Damian watched them use their legs to control their climbs, the two men staying even as they lowered themselves down their ropes until their feet touched the ground.

Jay stepped forward. "I'll go next."

"Damian, you go beside him. I'll be right here in case you have any trouble."

Damian nodded. This wasn't his first time rappelling, but it was odd having Jay clip in beside him instead of Nick, his old swim buddy.

The two men got into position, and Seth checked Damian's gear before giving them the okay to start.

Damian felt that familiar pitch in his stomach when he stepped off the edge and his rappelling ropes went taut. He glanced over at Jay, who gave him a slight nod to signal him to begin. Together they pushed off, catching air before swinging back against the thick wood of the wall, their boots thudding against it almost in unison.

Adrenaline rushed through him, his hands working the lines efficiently. A third of the way down the sixty-foot wall, he found himself a little ahead of Jay. They weren't as unified as Tristan and Quinn, but Damian felt a surge of accomplishment to see he was relatively in sync with his teammate.

An eerie creak above him sent a shaft of trepidation through him, and his already rapid heartbeat picked up speed. He glanced up to see his line and anchors securely intact. Then his gaze shifted slightly, and he saw Jay's anchor sag, the wood around it splintering dangerously. "Jay!" Damian shouted out, using his feet to push off the wall to swing himself closer to his teammate. He wasn't sure what he intended to do, but when a loud crack sounded, he instinctively reached out for the other man's arm.

The lines supporting Jay's weight snapped free, and he must have felt himself start to fall because he reached out too, his right hand grasping Damian's left forearm. Jay's fingers dug into Damian as the failed anchor and shards of wood hurled through the air and the ropes rained down over them.

For a moment, time stood still. A million thoughts raced through Damian's mind: the knowledge that the two lines holding him in place now had the added strain of Jay's weight, the awareness that they were both dangling more than forty feet above the ground, the sound of men's voices filled with urgency.

One voice cut through the air, drowning out the others. Seth shouted at Tristan to come to the top of the tower and told Quinn to go for help.

Quinn's response was immediate and clear. "There isn't time."

Quinn was right. Already, Damian could feel his grip on his lines faltering. He willed his mind to calm, telling himself to work through the problem. His voice was breathless when he managed to say, "I'm going to try to lower us together."

"Wait. My leg is caught in your lines." The tension in Jay's voice was obvious, but Damian sensed he was trying to logically work through this impossible scenario.

"Can you kick it free?" Damian gripped Jay's arm tighter with his left hand, the two men both struggling to maintain a solid bond.

Jay's weight shifted as he tried to free himself, and immediately, Damian's grip on his lines faltered, and they both dropped several feet. "Whoa!" Jay lifted his left hand to grab Damian's arm with both of his hands.

Damian looked down, now able to see the way his two rappelling lines had twisted and caught around Jay's leg just below the knee. When they had slipped the extra few feet toward the ground, the ropes had tangled further and tightened around Jay, preventing them from being able to slide past the obstruction.

They were trapped. If Damian tried to lower himself to the ground, he would get tangled in the line where Jay's leg was caught. He contemplated climbing up rather than trying to descend, even with the difficulty of shifting Jay so he could climb with him simultaneously. They didn't have another viable option.

"See if you can reach the line with your left hand. Maybe we can climb up instead of going down," Damian said.

Seth shouted from above. "Just hold on. I'm coming to you."

A sense of hope surfaced. Help was coming. Then logic caught up with Seth's words. Damian and Jay were dangling from the only secure anchor above. How was Seth possibly going to reach them?

He could hear Tristan pounding up the ladder toward the top of the tower, but one man wouldn't be able to secure a line for Seth to climb down. Not to mention, where would they find rope to use? Jay's lines had already fallen to the ground, and they were in a secluded part of the woods several miles from the nearest building.

Damian tried to push the negative thoughts aside, concentrating solely on holding on to Jay with one hand and the rope with his other. A minute ticked by and stretched into two, his fingers cramping, the muscles in his arms burning with the continued strain.

The rope vibrated in his hand, and he looked up at his own anchor. Was it his imagination, or was it beginning to pull free?

Doom and despair clouded over him, and he fought them back. How could this be happening? The Saint Squad was renowned for being the best, for coming up with creative solutions when faced with unbeatable odds. Now, as soon as he joined them, they would have their first tragedy? Perhaps it hadn't been a blessing for him to be assigned to the Saint Squad. Maybe, just maybe, it had been a curse.

CHAPTER 4

Paige heard the tech curse under his breath as he connected her new computer and phone. Apparently he and his tools weren't getting along, and he was being rather colorful in his language as he explained to several inanimate objects exactly what he thought of them.

Ignoring the tech's current rant at a Phillips screwdriver that had the audacity to be the wrong size, Paige sat cross-legged in front of the large dry-erase board she had secured from a supply closet down the hall. She would go out tonight and pick up some magnetic tape, but for now, sticky notes were doing the job just as well.

Using the phone on Vanessa's desk, she had already talked to housing and identified which rooms were available for the course participants. She had then used a dry-erase marker to draw a rough sketch of the floor plans of the men's and women's housing units and numbered the rooms, cross-referencing them to the current roster.

The rather large computer tech was still battling the small space beneath the desk when Vanessa entered the room at ten minutes to twelve. One elegant eyebrow lifted. "You already have IT here? How did you get them out so fast?"

"I called first thing this morning." Before Vanessa could comment, Paige motioned to a stack of manila envelopes on her desk. "I put together packets for your students for tomorrow. I included a map of the main compound, their room keys, and the first day's itinerary. Is there anything else you'd like for me to include before I drop these off at the main gate?"

"Where did you get the map and itinerary?"

"Security gave me the map, and the itinerary was in one of the files you gave me."

"Resourceful. I like that."

Another curse sounded from beneath the desk.

Vanessa smirked and appeared to be struggling not to laugh. She picked up the stack of envelopes. "Grab your coat. We'll drop these off at security on our way out."

"Where are we going?"

"We're going to grab some lunch, and I'm going to show you around the base. Then, if you're up for it, we'll spend some time this afternoon in town. I assume you don't have an apartment lined up yet."

"No, I haven't had time."

"It's a bit of a commute, but if you like the water, you might want to consider Virginia Beach."

"Is that where you live?"

Vanessa nodded.

Paige shrugged into her coat, but before she moved toward the door, she said, "There is one thing I wanted to ask you."

"What's that?"

"Any chance you can tell me ahead of time when you want me in the office for the next day? That way you don't have to call me early in the morning." Paige gave her a pointed look and added, "Or in the middle of the night."

"In the past, my assistants tended to call in sick when I gave them too much notice on our crazy hours."

"I'm a nurse. I'm used to shift work. You just tell me when you want me to be here, and I'll be here."

Vanessa studied her for a moment. "I think we may get along okay after all."

* * *

Amidst the encouraging shouts for Damian and Jay to hold on, Jay's fingers flexed, and he slipped ever so slightly, his fingers clearly suffering from cramping as well.

"Hang on," Damian muttered, not sure if his words were intended for Jay or for himself.

"We can't hold on much longer," Jay responded tensely. "I'm going to try to reach the rope and see if I can get my leg free."

Damian looked at the angle of his leg and the way the rope was looped around Jay's leg. Now that he could see Jay's leg more clearly, he realized that it wasn't just his leg that was caught; Jay's lines had tangled with his as they had fallen. Even if Jay wasn't between him and the ground, Damian wouldn't be able to rappel down safely. He would have to unclip his own harness and climb hand over hand.

"Hold on a sec." Damian tried unsuccessfully to think his way around the problem. Then he sensed someone behind him. He cocked his head around to see Seth free-climbing down the face of the tower, using the space between the wooden planks for hand- and footholds.

"Damian, I want you to swing over here toward me," Seth said, his voice surprisingly calm. "Jay, you're going to grab on to the wall, and I'll get you free. Then we'll climb the rest of the way down."

Seth made the process sound so simple despite their being forty feet above the ground with failing equipment. Damian's left shoulder was going numb from the strain of holding Jay, and he considered it a miracle that his cramped fingers were still functioning, but he knew he had to try.

"On the count of three." Seth's voice now resonated with command. He counted down, and Damian tried to think of the action he needed to take instead of the possible results of an unsuccessful attempt. Jay's hand slipped a little farther down his arm, but the look of determination and trust on his face gave Damian another dose of resolve.

When Seth called out "three," Damian piked his legs and swung them down hard to move himself toward the wall. The action put him in motion but not enough to put them within Seth's reach. He repeated the action a couple more times until Seth finally let go of one of his handholds and reached out to grab Jay's leg.

The force of their swing pulled Seth off balance, and his left foot slid free. Damian was afraid Seth was going to lose his grip completely, but somehow, Jay must have anticipated the result of Seth's actions. He reached out with one hand to grab the wall and help fight against the momentum, giving Seth the fraction of a second necessary to regain his balance.

A few grunts and barely audible instructions followed until Jay's leg was freed.

"Jay, see if you can get a better handhold on the wall," Seth said.

Jay did as he was told, first finding a solid grip with his hand and then reaching his legs out to find purchase against the wall. As soon as Jay released his arm, Damian dug his own fingers into the crevice separating one board from another, keeping himself steady while he made sure Jay had a good grip.

"Damian!" Tristan shouted from above. He didn't have time to utter any further warning before another crack in the wood sounded and Damian felt his line go slack.

In an instant, instead of Damian supporting Jay's weight, the roles were reversed. Damian's tentative hold on the wall gave Jay the split second he needed to see the equipment malfunction. He reached for Damian's free arm, holding him in place for the few seconds Damian needed to pull his feet closer to the wall and find a grip.

His breathing came in shallow gasps, but Seth was right there, calmly speaking to him, guiding him to find a second handhold. Damian clung to the wall, afraid to look down.

"Damian, look at me," Seth said.

An errant thought cut through Damian's fear as he wondered how Seth did it. How could he be so in control when they were forty feet above the ground with no safety gear, clinging to the side of a clearly faulty rappelling tower?

Then Damian remembered. Seth was trained to remain calm in a crisis . . . and so was he. He sucked in a breath and focused on the task in front of them . . . or rather below them. It was time to climb to safety.

The other two men seemed to sense that Damian's panic had subsided, and Jay said, "I'll lead the way."

"And I'll take the rear," Seth said. "Damian, work your way down. If you get stuck, holler, and one of us will walk you through it."

"Okay," Damian managed to say, hoping his voice didn't reveal his terror.

Slowly and steadily, the three men worked their way down. Minutes ticked by, and Damian suspected the other two men could have made it to the ground in half the time had they not been pacing themselves with him.

The wind picked up, the cold biting into the exposed skin on his face and through the gloves he wore. By the time Damian dared to look below him, he was only seven or eight feet above the ground.

Tristan stepped nimbly down, and Damian scrambled down the last few feet. He was so eager to feel the earth beneath his feet again, he rushed when placing his boot on his last foothold and tumbled to the ground.

CHAPTER 5

Damian couldn't say he'd ever considered what his first meeting with his new commanding officer would be like, but he was quite certain that if he had, it wouldn't have included him being flat on his back.

The lieutenant commander's dark hair was cut short and mostly hidden beneath the hat that currently shaded his eyes. From Damian's prone position, the man looked impossibly tall, but Damian guessed he might be an inch or so shorter than Seth. He wondered vaguely if there was some requirement in this unit about being tall. If so, he definitely didn't qualify. Then again, neither did Quinn, who was only an inch or two taller than his own five foot ten.

"You must be the new kid."

"Yes, sir."

Lieutenant Commander Miller stretched out a hand. Damian accepted the offered help and let the other man pull him up to stand beside him.

Seth finished his descent during the introductions and stepped beside Damian. "That's it, Brent. You aren't allowed to take leave anymore. Every time you're gone, something happens."

"Not like this," Brent countered. "Last time it was just a visit from some of our higher-ups."

"It was the president of the United States and the secretary of the navy!" Seth said.

Brent dismissed Seth's irritation with a wave of his hand and motioned toward the heap of rappelling lines on the ground. "What in the world happened?"

"I have no idea. I've never seen any of our anchors fail and certainly not two in one day."

"Did you check them before you started?" Brent asked skeptically.

"Of course I checked."

"I did too," Jay said.

"Me too," Tristan and Quinn chorused.

Brent leaned down and picked up one of the fallen anchors and studied it for a moment. Then he bent over again, this time retrieving a piece of the wood that had splintered and fallen to the ground.

His eyebrows drew together, and Damian could have sworn the color drained from Brent's face. "Seth, were we on the training schedule today?"

"Yeah, why?"

"Is anyone else on for this afternoon?"

Slowly, Seth seemed to catch up with whatever the commander was thinking. "Come to think of it, the schedule was wide open today. Tomorrow too."

"Quinn, call your buddy Larry Steinert. I think we'd better have him come over here and take a look."

"You really think we need to bother NCIS about this?" Tristan asked, stepping forward. "Seems to me we ought to be finding out who's in charge of maintaining the equipment here."

"Oh, I'm sure Steinert will look into that, but I also want him to figure out who might have it in for one of us."

"What do you mean?" Damian asked. "I thought this was an accident."

Brent held up the piece of wood and flipped it over. A half circle was still evident where the anchor had once been secured through the thick beam, but the wood around it had been gouged out so the anchor would fail when enough pressure pulled against it.

"Sabotage?"

"That's what it looks like to me," Brent said.

Behind them, Quinn was already talking on his cell phone, explaining the situation. As soon as he hung up, he said, "Larry said we need to keep the scene secure but not touch anything."

"Too late for that." Brent held up the board.

Quinn rolled his eyes. "I think he means don't touch anything else."

"Right." Brent looked around. "In that case, buddy up, spread out, and get comfortable until NCIS arrives."

Tristan and Quinn fell in step and headed for the north side of the tower. Jay and Seth moved to the southeast, effectively making a triangle from where Damian still stood.

"Looks like we have some time to get to know each other," Brent said casually. "So tell me, can you think of anyone who might want to kill you?"

The words and the easygoing way in which they were spoken caught Damian off guard. "Kill me? No, sir!"

"Just covering all our bases." Brent scratched a finger along his jaw. "If it wasn't you they were after, it must be one of them."

"What about you? Maybe someone didn't know you wouldn't be here."

"That's a possibility too."

"Tell me, sir. Does this kind of thing happen often?"

"Not usually. At least not without some kind of warning." Brent shook his head. "And don't call me sir. When we're in the field, I'm Brent."

"Yes, sir."

* * *

Paige stood in the town-house-style apartment and wavered. The location was great as far as what she wanted in a home. It was situated a short distance from the bay and within a few minutes' drive of the beach. Unfortunately, the distance to work was about twice what she had planned for.

The apartment itself wasn't terribly large. The small galley kitchen wasn't much wider than a standard hallway and was located off the main living area. The single bedroom occupied the area along the back wall of the unit. Of course, a smaller place also meant she would have less to clean. She also liked knowing there was a storage unit available where she could keep her kayak.

"What do you think?" Vanessa asked.

"It's a great place. I just don't know if I want to commute that far every day. It might be a lot easier to rent something closer to work."

"Hardly anything is close to work unless you want to live on base. And trust me, you need to have a life outside of work."

"I don't know . . ."

"The other advantage is that on the days I don't have to teach class, we can work here in Virginia Beach."

"I didn't think the CIA let people work from home."

"They don't usually, but I do a lot of training for the military as well as the CIA. Whenever I can, I conduct the military classes on the naval base. I've also been known to work out of my husband's office on base when he's out in the field."

"Your husband's navy?"

"He is." Vanessa took another look around. "You don't have to decide right now. Isn't the agency putting you up in a hotel for a couple weeks?"

"Yeah, but it would be nice to settle in somewhere soon."

"It's only four o'clock. There's a place I know that isn't far from here. Let's go grab some appetizers or something, and we can chat a little more about your schedule. It will help you decide where you want to live if you know what work is going to be like for you."

"That sounds good," Paige said, more than willing to delay going back to an empty hotel room. As they headed for Vanessa's car, Paige wondered vaguely if the complex allowed pets.

* * *

Seth led the way into the sports bar he and his squad often frequented, whether it was to take in a game together or just unwind after a tough training mission. Today definitely fell into the latter category.

NCIS had shown up thirty minutes after Quinn had called in the incident. Over the next hour, their stories were recorded and they were finally given permission to leave. Eager to put the events of the day behind them, as well as the idea that one of them might have been deliberately targeted, Jay had suggested that they all head out for a drink after work. Brent had seconded the idea.

Seth still couldn't quite believe they had all survived the encounter and considered it another in a long list of miracles his squad had been blessed with in their time together. He took a seat at a table with a view of several television screens and considered the changing dynamics of the squad now that Damian had joined them.

Though he certainly hadn't planned on indoctrinating their new teammate through a crisis, he couldn't deny that Damian had stood up to the challenge. Damian's quick reflexes had saved Jay today, and for that they were all grateful.

Brent slid into the seat beside Seth. "You do realize that if your wife saw you pull that stunt today, she'd skin you alive."

Tristan nodded in agreement. "Brent's right. You are seriously lucky Vanessa wasn't there."

Seth considered his friends' comments and recognized the truth to them. His wife might be a full foot shorter than he, but she was a force to be reckoned with, a force that, after two years of marriage, he knew better than to cross.

"The real luck lies in knowing that she won't have access to an after-action report."

"Those CIA types are tricky," Tristan said. "You never know what they have their fingers into."

"Which is why I'm glad she's out of active service and spends her time teaching now. I don't ever want to see her involved in undercover work again." Seth remembered too well how he had helped Vanessa escape from a previous deep undercover assignment.

"I have to admit, if we didn't know for sure Akil Ramir was behind bars, he'd be the first name on our list of suspects."

"I couldn't agree more," Seth said.

"Do you really think someone was targeting a member of the Saint Squad specifically?" Damian asked.

"It's possible," Brent said. Someone near the entrance caught his eye. "Well, look who's here."

Seth looked over his shoulder and saw his wife standing beside the hostess. Instantly, he turned back to the rest of the squad. He lowered his voice and said sternly, "Not a word about today." Then his features completely transformed as he stood and shifted his attention to his wife.

Vanessa crossed to him and reached out to put a hand on his arm. "What are you doing here?"

"Just grabbing a drink with the guys." Seth turned and motioned to Damian. "This is the new guy I was telling you about. Damian Schmitt, this is my wife, Vanessa."

All six men had stood at Vanessa's approach, and Damian extended his hand to shake Vanessa's. "Nice to meet you."

"You too. I hope the guys are behaving themselves."

"Yes, ma'am."

Afraid his wife might try to interrogate the new guy, Seth changed the subject and asked, "What are you doing here this time of day? I thought you would still be at work."

"I was showing my new assistant around town. She just started today and hasn't found an apartment yet."

"Where is she now?" Seth asked.

"She had to take a phone call. She'll be here in a minute."

Seth saw a pretty blonde push her way through the main entrance. "That must be her now."

CHAPTER 6

Damian turned to see the woman at the door, instantly intrigued. She was average height and wore a stylish shirt tucked into her gray dress pants. Her straight, honey-blonde hair was cut short, following her jawline, and Damian guessed her eyes were blue, although he couldn't quite tell from this distance.

She spoke with the hostess for a moment, who pointed her in their direction. The instant she saw their full table, she hesitated. She seemed to be waging some mental battle before walking toward them.

"Paige, this is my husband, Seth, and the rest of his squad." Vanessa shifted so Paige was standing right beside her. "Guys, this is my new assistant, Paige Vickers."

Vanessa proceeded to list everyone's name, beginning with Seth's and going around the table until she finally listed Damian's.

Damian watched his teammates offer cursory greetings as they were introduced, but he took advantage of his close proximity to the newcomer and reached out to shake Paige's hand. "It's good to meet you."

She looked up, and he saw her eyes weren't blue after all but a deep chocolate brown. He'd always had a weakness for brown eyes. Damian stepped clear of his seat and asked, "Would you two like to join us?"

Paige deferred to Vanessa, looking back at her with a questioning glance.

Vanessa then looked up at Seth. "Are we interrupting anything?"

"No, not at all." Seth grabbed an extra chair from the next table over and slid it in place beside his while Damian did the same. "Hey, Damian. Go ask the bartender to set us up with a round of drinks."

"What does everyone want?" Damian asked.

Brent answered for him. "Just tell him we'll take our usual. He knows us."

"Okay." Damian made his way to the bar, not sure what he thought about his squad deciding to drink at only four in the afternoon.

He wondered if his new teammates would think less of him if he opted for water instead of whatever they were planning to consume. After watching his uncle struggle with alcoholism for years, Damian had made the conscious choice not to drink. His uncle's untimely death two years ago from cirrhosis of the liver had reinforced that decision.

He put their order in and turned to see the women settling down at their table and the rest of the squad reclaiming their seats. His squad, he reminded himself. He belonged to the Saint Squad now, even if he did feel like he didn't deserve to claim the title.

The bartender set down a tray with glasses and two full pitchers, along with a double order of wings. Damian looked at the dark liquid in front of him. "What's this?"

"Root beer."

"I'm not sure this is what they had in mind. I thought they wanted a pitcher of beer."

"You're with the Saint Squad, right?"

"That's right."

"They don't drink."

"They don't drink?" Damian repeated.

"Nope." The bartender's voice was confident, and for a moment, Damian wondered if perhaps he was the butt of a prank, maybe playing into some kind of initiation into the squad. "They're all Latter-day Saints." At Damian's blank look, the bartender added, "You know. Mormons."

Damian knew a little about Mormons. He'd had a couple Mormon friends in high school and remembered they didn't drink. Still, what was the likelihood that all five men in his squad belonged to the same religion?

Resigned to the possibility that he was being duped and not seeing any way to know for sure if the bartender was serious, he picked up the tray. He prepared himself for the heckling and the laughter, but it didn't come.

Jay picked up one pitcher and started pouring. "I think this round should be on me."

Still uncertain, Damian slid into his seat between Jay and Paige. He looked at the other men at the table, wondering what would happen next. He didn't expect Vanessa to pick up on the unspoken undertones.

Her eyebrows lifted inquisitively. "Is there any particular reason this round should be on Jay?"

Seth was quick to step in. "Oh, he was just helping Damian over there feel like part of the squad in our training exercises today."

"Exactly how did he do that?" Vanessa asked.

"Just messing around. You know Jay."

Damian watched in amazement. Today on the tower, Seth had been fearless. He had climbed without reservation to help him and Jay and, up until now, had always exuded a quiet confidence. Now, with his wife staring at him, he looked like a teenager trying to hide a misdeed from his parents.

Vanessa looked over at Jay and then at Damian. "Damian, do you know what happened?"

Now that Vanessa's dark gaze was pinned on him, he could see why Seth was squirming. The woman clearly knew they were keeping something from her, and his teammates obviously didn't want the truth shared. Or more specifically, Seth didn't want his wife to know what had happened.

Damian decided this was as good a time as any to establish some trust with his new unit. Keeping his eyes directly on Vanessa, he said, "Yes, ma'am. I know what happened today."

Damian didn't expound on his answer, and after several seconds Vanessa said, "What exactly was it?"

"I guess you could say Jay drew the short straw when Seth decided I should learn more about teamwork."

"And?" Vanessa prompted.

"Now, ma'am. Please tell me you don't expect me to give all the details of a potentially awkward situation. We are in mixed company." He gestured toward Paige, deciding he could use her presence to his, and ultimately to Seth's, advantage. "Miss Vickers here is a very attractive woman. What if I want to ask her out? You wouldn't want me to embarrass myself by telling you all about my troubles, would you?"

"Maybe Paige has a boyfriend, so it won't matter anyway," Vanessa suggested.

"Do you have a boyfriend?" Quinn asked Paige.

Paige shook her head, although she looked a little uncomfortable when she answered. "No, not at the moment."

"See, Vanessa. There could be hope for them," Quinn said playfully.

Vanessa pursed her lips and stared at Damian for several long seconds. Then she asked, "You didn't shoot anyone, did you?"

"No, ma'am. I didn't shoot anyone." Damian thought back to when he had first met Seth and had overheard a similar comment after he'd left

Kel's office. Curious, he said, "Forgive me for being blunt, but why does everyone keep expecting me to shoot someone?"

"Because you're the new guy."

"Is this some ritual I should know about?"

Jay's cheeks colored slightly, and he shook his head. "Seth still won't let me forget a minor incident on my first mission."

"I gather you shot someone," Damian said dryly.

"Yeah." Seth nodded emphatically. "He shot me."

"Considering we're taught to shoot to kill, I have to say, Seth, you look pretty good for a dead man."

"It was a tranquilizer gun." Jay rolled his eyes as several of the others chuckled. "He was only out for twenty minutes."

"Jay, that doesn't change the fact that you shot me."

Damian couldn't help but smile. "If it's all the same to you, I think I'll let that little incident remain an isolated one."

"Excellent idea," Brent said.

* * *

Paige wasn't sure what to think of Vanessa and her husband's squad. One thing was certain. These men, despite their obvious physical strength, had a lot of respect for her new boss. Or perhaps it was fear. Clearly Seth was hiding something about the day's events, and his men were following his lead to keep his secret intact. Conversation conveniently stayed on safe topics, though embarrassing stories that Vanessa was already aware of appeared to be fair game.

The six men sitting around the table were unique in more ways than one. Each of them was handsome in his own rugged way, and they appeared to have very different backgrounds. If it hadn't been for the extreme differences in their appearances, Paige would have guessed that Tristan and Quinn were related somehow. Their interactions showed a familiarity that went beyond mere friendship. Even if she could look past Tristan's height and light hair compared to Quinn's average height and dark hair, Tristan's Texan drawl indicated he hadn't grown up with Quinn.

Damian was another oddity in her mind. His blond hair and blue eyes didn't quite line up with his Hispanic accent. She discovered he was a new addition to the unit and didn't miss the mixed signals about him from the squad. While several of the men appeared wary when Vanessa started questioning Damian, Jay seemed to go out of his way to include him.

Paige also hadn't miss the flicker of interest in Damian's eyes when they had shaken hands and sensed that he too felt ill at ease. When Damian was nominated to go to the bar for another round, Paige stood up as well. "I'll help you."

"I appreciate it." He pulled her chair out a little farther and led the way to the bar.

"Your unit seems like an interesting bunch of guys. How long have you been with them?"

"One week."

"That's all?"

"Yeah," Damian said. "How do you like working for Seth's wife so far?"

"It's different than what I'm used to. We were actually just looking at apartments."

"I may have to ask for your help when I start looking for a place. Maybe you can steer me in the right direction."

"Where are you staying now?"

"In the barracks." He gave the bartender their order before turning his attention back to her. "It's fine for now, but I'd like to get settled somewhere so I can bring my dog out here with me."

"What kind do you have?"

"A black lab mix. My sister is keeping him for now, but I think she's looking forward to sleeping in. Harley is pretty insistent on having his 5:00 a.m. runs."

"That's funny. I was just thinking about how nice it would be to have a dog to run with," Paige admitted. "Although, I'm usually a 6:00 a.m.–run kind of person. Of course, working for Vanessa, I may have to start running earlier."

"Having a dog to run with is great . . . unless you want to sleep in. Dogs don't understand what a weekend is."

Paige lowered her voice. "I'm not sure Vanessa knows what a weekend is either." She glanced back at their table to see Quinn and Tristan chatting, their eyes on Damian and Paige. It didn't take a genius to figure out what they were talking about. Undoubtedly, they were speculating on whether Damian was going to make a move on Paige.

"You do realize I'm going to have to ask you out now," Damian announced, his voice low.

One eyebrow winged up, and she glanced over at him. "Oh, really?"

"Really." Damian nodded toward the table. "You wouldn't want to make me look bad in front of the guys, would you?"

"I doubt you need me to impress them. I think Seth already owes you for surviving Vanessa's interrogation."

Damian wisely avoided her last comment and appeared determined to stay on track. "Seriously, what are you doing tonight? Since we're both new to the area, maybe we can go explore the city together."

Paige considered his suggestion. She was tempted for the first time in months to say yes. After all, Damian was a good-looking, intelligent guy who seemed nice enough. Yet, she wasn't sure she wanted to go on a date knowing he might be less interested in her than he was in proving himself to the other men in the room.

When he shifted beside her and leaned forward on the bar, she caught a glimpse of something she hadn't expected to see. The bulge of a gun handle in the back of his waistband.

The image of a black pistol and blood-covered tile flashed into her mind, and she battled it back. She could feel her face pale, and she swallowed before forcing herself to speak. "I don't think that would be a good idea."

"Why not?" Damian asked, clearly confused by her sudden change of mood.

The bartender set a full pitcher of root beer and the order of chips and salsa Jay had requested on the bar. Rather than answer his question, Paige picked up the chips and salsa. "I've got these."

Without another word, she hurried back to their table, leaving Damian behind.

CHAPTER 7

He was irritated and frustrated. "It didn't work."

"What do you mean, it didn't work?" the woman beside him asked, equally frustrated. "I thought you said it was foolproof."

"It should have been. I don't know how they all survived."

"Now what?" She raked her hands through her dark hair, holding it up off her neck while she considered the latest news. Letting her hair fall back down, she continued. "We have to find something to draw her out. A funeral was the perfect scenario."

"Maybe we need to stop trying to chase her and make her come to us," he suggested.

"How can we do that?"

He gave her a devious look, one she recognized well in the handsome face. "I think we need a conflict, one that will require a certain squad of Navy SEALs."

"What good will that do us?" she asked.

He slid a hand around her waist and drew her closer. "I have a feeling Vanessa Johnson will be quick to get back in the field when her husband doesn't come home."

"I assume you have a plan?" she asked, tipping her head to look up at him.

"Don't I always?"

* * *

Damian felt a sense of anticipation when he took a seat in the briefing room. There was a chance he was being sent out on his first mission. Then he saw the NCIS officer who had been at the rappelling tower the day before. In addition to the squad and him, there was also a woman wearing civilian clothes sitting beside Brent.

Larry Steinert waited for everyone to take their seats before he handed an envelope to Brent and sat across from him. "Those are the preliminary findings, but it was sabotage."

"We already knew that," Brent reminded him.

"I'm afraid there isn't much in there you didn't already know."

"Do you have any suspects?" Quinn asked.

"Nothing so far. The window of time when the damage could have been done to the rappelling anchors is pretty wide. Because of the storms and the holidays, your squad was the first to use it in nine days."

"Great," Seth muttered.

"Any idea who might be holding a grudge against you or someone in your squad?"

"I can't think of anyone who's not behind bars, at least not anyone who knows who we are." Brent turned to look at the rest of the group. "What about any of you? Jay, any chance your in-laws are coming after you again?"

Jay shook his head. "They'd go after Carina before they'd come after me. Besides, they had every chance to get at us at our wedding a couple of weeks ago."

Damian looked at Jay, confused.

Jay gave him a careless shrug. "My wife's father was part of the Chicago mob. We've had a few run-ins."

"Seriously?" Damian asked, the expressions on everyone's faces confirming the unlikely story as truth.

"I'll check that out just to make sure, but I tend to agree with Jay," Larry said. "What about the rest of you?"

Everyone shook their heads.

"Okay. Well, if anything comes to mind, let me know. Otherwise, I'll be back at my office scouring surveillance videos."

"Have fun with that," Quinn said.

As soon as Larry left the room, Brent said, "In light of what happened yesterday, we're changing our training schedule." He turned to the woman beside him. "Amy?"

"I have the new schedules right here." Amy stood and moved around the table, handing out the new schedules. "I had to bump some of your flight training up to tomorrow because of the dive schedule."

"By the way, Damian, Amy is our intelligence officer."

"And Brent's wife," Tristan offered.

Damian took a moment to process this latest tidbit of information. He looked at Brent. "So you're married to our intelligence officer, Seth's wife is CIA, and Jay's wife grew up in the mob."

"That's right," Seth answered for all of them.

"You guys are married too, right?" Damian asked Quinn and Tristan.

"That's right."

"What do your wives do? Work for the FBI?"

"Actually, my wife, Riley, trains police departments in first-responder scenarios," Tristan said. "Quinn's wife is just an artist."

"I'd like to see you say that to Taylor when she's in the room," Quinn countered, humor in his voice.

"No, that's okay." Tristan stood. "I value my life."

"Why don't you go value your life out on the shooting range?" Amy suggested.

"Great idea," Tristan agreed.

* * *

Paige walked through the town house slowly, listening to the sounds of the neighborhood, waiting for any sign of whether she could feel safe here. She liked how quiet it was and the way this particular unit was located on the end of the building.

From what she could tell, all of the units in this building were one-bedroom, which meant she wouldn't likely hear much in the way of children playing. Not that she minded kids. She just didn't want to wake up to one screaming at this stage in her life.

She looked out the kitchen window to see the parking lot and grassy area along the front walk, a few patches of snow still evident in the shade. A large oak was visible to the left, and she imagined it would provide shade during the summer months.

Beyond the parking lot, she could see more units, and in the distance, she could make out the top of the pool house. She liked knowing she would have such easy access to the water. Besides the pool, she could walk to the bay. If she wanted to visit the beach, she could drive there in less than fifteen minutes. She would also have the benefit of easy access to the freeway.

She closed her eyes and tried to imagine herself living here alone. It was easy to visualize during the day, but after dark was another matter. Determined to face her fears, she let her nightmares play through her mind. The voices rising in anger, the shouts and threats, the gunshots.

Jennifer had always talked about how well Paige related to their patients in the counseling center, but Paige had never been able to tell her it was because she knew how they felt. It might not have been her family who had lost someone that day when she'd been only fifteen years old, but she knew what it was like to hurt, and she knew what it was like to lose.

Her sister's ex-boyfriend wielding a knife, his mother holding a gun, the sound of gunshots. All of those images flashed through her mind until they merged into one: the coroner pronouncing a young boy dead.

Paige thought about how she had overreacted with Damian in the restaurant a few days earlier. She still felt bad about it, but she didn't know how to explain to him the effect guns had on her. Even throughout her training with the government, first as an intern with the FBI and then as a CIA employee, she had always managed to avoid handgun training.

Logically, she knew that just because someone carried a gun, it didn't mean they intended to use it to hurt someone. She also knew that logic didn't always triumph over emotions.

A knock sounded on the door, and Paige was pleased she didn't jump. She turned to see the apartment manager push his way inside. "Well, what do you think?"

Paige took another look around and made her decision. "I'll take it."

* * *

Damian checked over his diving gear, his mind as much on Paige as it was on the task before him. He still couldn't figure out exactly why she had blown him off at the restaurant when they'd first met, but for some reason, he couldn't get the incident out of his mind. One minute they were getting along great, and the next, it was as if someone had flipped a switch, and she acted like she couldn't put distance between them fast enough.

When they'd returned to their table, she had been friendly to everyone, even if she had been a little more reserved than when she'd first arrived. She had even been kind enough to not make an issue out of turning him down. Still, it didn't make sense.

Paige had admitted she wasn't dating anyone, and he could have sworn he had detected some interest. So why had she refused to go out with him? He hadn't even been able to find an opportunity to ask for her number.

Jay stepped up beside him and interrupted his thoughts. "Is your gear ready to load?"

"Yeah." Damian lifted his diving apparatus and carried it to the truck that would transport them to the dock.

"I can't believe NCIS hasn't found anything yet," Seth said. "It's been almost a week."

"I can't believe Damian hasn't asked Paige out yet," Quinn countered.

"He might need our help," Tristan drawled.

Damian looked over his shoulder. "I don't need any help getting a date."

"Prove it," Jay said. "We're having a little get-together at Seth's place tonight. Why don't you call Paige and see if she wants to join us."

"I didn't ask for her number."

Quinn looked over at Tristan. "Yep. He definitely needs our help."

"Maybe Paige isn't my type."

"Yeah right. Paige is every guy's type," Tristan said. When he caught the inquisitive looks his teammates sent his way, he amended his comment. "I mean, she's every single guy's type."

"Maybe Damian has his eye on someone else," Seth said.

"From what I've seen, he hasn't even noticed anyone else since he met Paige. That civilian down the hall stopped by to chat yesterday, and Damian barely gave her the time of day."

"Are you talking about the redhead with the Southern accent?" Quinn asked.

"That's the one," Jay said. "She was even hinting about whether we'd be around this weekend. I'm telling you, Damian may have missed a golden opportunity there too."

"Do you always talk about people when they're in the room?" Damian asked.

"Yep," Tristan said unapologetically. "We aren't the behind-the-back types."

"Any chance you'll listen to me when I tell you to butt out of my personal life?"

"Not really."

"Great," Damian muttered.

"We're all married," Tristan said. "You're our new source of entertainment."

"Lucky me."

"And don't even think about trying to skip out on dinner tonight," Seth added. "They'll just hunt you down and make your life miserable."

Brent walked in and ended the conversation. "Come on. Get the rest of the gear loaded. It's time to go."

Damian helped Seth secure the rest of their gear and climbed into the truck. By the time they reached the dock, he decided it was a perfect day for a dive. Even though he wasn't looking forward to the freezing temperature, at least once they were underwater, his teammates would lose their ability to talk for a while.

CHAPTER 8

Paige pulled up in front of the modest house in the suburbs of Virginia Beach. Three cars occupied the driveway and several others lined the street near the Johnsons' home. She parked two houses down, the closest available spot.

The moment she climbed out of her car, she caught the scent of grilled meat and heard the low notes of a country song. Curious, Paige headed for the house. When Vanessa had invited her over for dinner, she hadn't mentioned that she was having a party, but the number of cars indicated Paige wasn't the only guest.

She still wasn't sure what to think of the invitation. This was the first time she had ever had a supervisor invite her to dinner. Then again, she hadn't expected Vanessa to take her to look for an apartment either.

Paige lifted a hand to knock on the door, surprised when it swung open before she had a chance to follow through. Her eyes lifted to see Jay dominating the doorway.

"Oh, good. You're here."

"It sounds like there's quite the party going on here."

"Something like that." Jay stepped aside and waved her in. "I'm just going to get something out of the car. Vanessa is in the kitchen. It's through there to the left."

"Thanks." Paige walked inside, immediately self-conscious. The living room was filled with several women she'd never seen before, all of them looking over at her. The only familiar face was Tristan, who stood beside the couch, a little blue bundle in his arms.

"Paige, come on in, and I'll introduce you to everyone. This is my wife, Riley, and my sister-in-law Taylor." Tristan motioned first to the blonde on the edge of the couch and then to the redhead beside her. "Taylor had a moment of insanity a year or so ago and married Quinn."

"Ignore him," Taylor responded. "I promise you get used to him after awhile."

Tristan continued without missing a beat, now turning to the woman standing across the room. "Over there is Amy Miller."

"It's nice to meet you all," Paige said, hoping she didn't appear as awkward as she felt.

"Don't worry, there won't be a quiz on names later," Amy said with a look of understanding. "Come on. I'll help you find Vanessa. Once Tristan gets his baby in his arms, he's oblivious to just about everything."

"Can you blame me?" Tristan asked, looking down at his son.

"Not really," Amy said. For a brief moment, Paige thought she detected a note of wistfulness in Amy's voice, but before Paige could further study her expression, Amy turned and led the way into the crowded kitchen. "Look who I found."

"Paige." Damian stood from his spot at the kitchen table. "I didn't know you were you going to be here."

"Can I get you something to drink?" Seth asked, saving Paige from responding.

"Just some water would be great." Paige noticed a flash of humor in Seth's eyes and a corresponding sense of acknowledgment on Damian's face. Clearly there was some unspoken communication going on between the two men. Curiosity simmered, and she watched for more undercurrents between them.

Seth opened a cabinet and retrieved a glass. After he filled it with ice and water, he handed it to Paige. "I'd better go check on Quinn and make sure he isn't burning dinner." He turned to Damian. "Come on. You can play referee while I try to wrestle the spatula out of his hand."

Damian seemed a little reluctant to leave, but when Seth opened the door, he turned and followed him outside.

Paige looked at the various side dishes and desserts covering the kitchen table. "I'm sorry. I should have asked if you wanted me to bring anything."

"It's fine. I know you don't have a place yet," Vanessa said.

"Actually, I just signed a contract this afternoon. It's that town house apartment we looked at together." Paige motioned to the vegetables lined up on the counter. "Is there anything I can do to help?"

"Actually, you can. See those mint brownies over there?" Vanessa pulled a plastic container out of a drawer. "Put two or three of them in this."

Not sure of Vanessa's motives, Paige took the container, slid three brownies into it, and snapped the lid in place. "Now what?"

"Now you can start taking plastic wrap off of everything while I hide these." Vanessa pulled open her Tupperware drawer again and tucked the brownie container beneath several lids.

Paige chuckled. "Can I ask why you're hiding mint brownies when you can just pick one up and eat it?"

"Oh, I already had one," Vanessa said mischievously. "I just want to make sure I can have another."

"There are at least three dozen brownies here."

"Yeah, but you don't know Quinn very well. He can eat a dozen by himself."

"Just Quinn?"

"Well, my husband isn't much better, but Quinn's definitely the worst. Last time Riley made those brownies, I didn't even get one."

"Except for the ones you hid?"

"Exactly."

Paige looked out the kitchen window at the three men standing in the backyard beside the grill. She had thought Seth was joking when he'd said he was going to wrestle the spatula away from Quinn, but from the way Quinn was holding it just out of Seth's reach, Paige realized Seth was probably serious.

She couldn't help but smile, and she found herself enjoying the scene the same way she might appreciate a favorite scene in a movie. "Are they really arguing over who's going to cook?"

"More like arguing over whether the hamburgers are done." Vanessa washed her hands and moved to help Paige unwrap the rest of the dishes. "I'd never say this in front of Seth, but Quinn's actually the best of the guys at grilling."

"I can't imagine having people fighting over who gets to cook. Usually people have the opposite problem." She picked up a bowl of potato salad, unwrapped it, and set it back down. "Do you have get-togethers like this often?"

"Usually once or twice a month when the guys are in town."

"Are they gone a lot?"

"Sometimes. They've actually been home for a few months now. They all got approved for leave over the holidays because of Jay's wedding. He just got back from his honeymoon the week before you showed up."

Paige thought of Vanessa's initial reaction when she'd first arrived. "So have you changed your mind about having an assistant?"

"You changed it for me that first day." Vanessa laughed. "Do you know I pulled the same stunt on all of my other assistants and not one of them figured it out?"

The laughter did wonders for Paige, and she felt some of the knots in her stomach loosen. "Figured what out?"

"To call for tech support before dealing with the other work."

"That was just common sense," Paige said, but pleasure flushed through her at the compliment.

"Which is what I've been needing in an assistant. You're the first person who's shown up who seems to possess an abundance of that particular quality."

"I'm glad I passed the test."

"Oh, you passed all right." Vanessa crossed to her pantry and retrieved a stack of paper plates. "Have you decided when you're going to move into your new place?"

"If everything goes as planned, the movers should get here on Saturday."

"Is the government moving you?" Vanessa asked.

"More or less," Paige said. "They're packing everything up, but because the delivery is on a weekend, I'll have to unpack myself."

"If you find you need some extra help, I know where we can round up some muscle." She pointed out the window. "Or at least someone to grill some burgers."

Paige looked outside again to see Seth tackle Quinn to the ground while Damian wrestled the spatula from his hand. She laughed. "I may take you up on that."

* * *

Damian bided his time during dinner. He chatted with Quinn's wife, Taylor, about the life of an artist. He took a turn holding Tristan's son, Dixon. When it came time to play street football, he made sure he was on Quinn's team to avoid any repercussions from helping Seth dethrone him earlier as the barbecue king.

When the party started breaking up, he stayed longer than he might normally, waiting for the moment when he could get Paige alone, when he could find out what he'd done wrong.

That moment didn't present itself until she'd said her good-byes.

"Vanessa, thanks again for dinner."

"We enjoyed having you." Vanessa gave her a quick hug. "And don't forget what I said about when you move."

Paige smiled in response. "I won't."

"I'll walk you out," Damian offered as soon as Paige made a step toward the door. "I should be going too."

He thanked Vanessa and Seth before leading the way outside. "Where are you parked?"

"A couple houses down." Paige started toward a small SUV down the street.

Damian fell in step with her, noticing the way she kept her eyes on her car as though she didn't want to look at him. "I wanted to ask you, did I do something to upset you the other day?"

"No, not at all."

"Then I'm confused," Damian said, not sure why he felt the need to press the issue. "I thought we were getting along great, but as soon as I asked you out, you acted like you couldn't get away from me fast enough."

"It wasn't you, exactly."

"Then what was it?"

"It's not important." She dug her keys out of her purse and jangled them. "It's silly."

"What is?" Damian waited for her to look up at him, focusing his gaze on her. "Are you seeing someone else? Did you decide I'm not your type? What?"

Her shoulders lifted and fell as she let out a sigh. "It was your gun."

"My gun?"

"I know it probably sounds ridiculous to someone like you, but I have a fear of guns." She held her hands out apologetically. "I noticed you were carrying one, and I freaked out."

"I'm surprised you could even tell I had one."

"I've gotten pretty good at spotting them over the years."

Damian felt a sense of satisfaction to realize she had been watching him closely enough to spot his weapon. "Did you happen to notice my teammates carrying?"

"Some of them. Quinn, Tristan, and Brent all have them too. Why?"

Satisfaction bloomed into anticipation. He stepped closer. "Everyone on my squad wears a concealed weapon."

"Really?"

"Yeah, really." Damian looked over his shoulder to see if any of his teammates were watching. "Maybe we can try this again. If I promise not to take my gun with us, can I take you out on Friday night?"

Her shoulders relaxed slightly. "I guess that would be okay."

He pulled his cell phone out of his pocket. "Here. Put your number in, and I'll call you when I find out what time I get off that day."

She took the phone and added her number to his contacts. The moment she handed it back, he texted her so she would have his number as well. She unlocked her car, and he pulled the door open for her.

"I'll call you later," he said, holding onto the door until she was seated inside.

"Okay."

When he stepped back onto the curb and watched her pull away, he looked up to see four of his teammates looking through the windows, each of them giving him a thumbs-up.

Damian shook his head. He wondered briefly if any money was changing hands, but he was in such a good mood he didn't care.

CHAPTER 9

PAIGE UNLOCKED THE DOOR to her new apartment and stepped inside with a sense of new beginnings. She tugged the smallest of her three suitcases behind her and set it just inside the door, along with her purse. She glanced at her watch to see she had half an hour before Damian was due to arrive.

Since her household effects were arriving tomorrow morning, she had given him her new address. She had debated staying in the hotel one more night but decided it didn't make sense to have Damian make the long drive to pick her up only to have to get up early tomorrow morning to come back to her apartment. It wouldn't be the first time she'd crashed on the floor for a night, and she doubted it would be the last.

Returning to her car, she retrieved another suitcase and the large trash bag that contained her pillow and the bedding she had brought with her. After depositing those in the bedroom, she made one more trip for her last suitcase.

An abundance of nervous energy bubbled up inside her as she thought of her date with Damian. She still couldn't believe she'd confessed her fear of handguns, but she knew from her training that if she felt compelled to talk about it, she must be ready to face the fear. Of course, admitting she didn't like guns was a long way from talking about what had caused the fear in the first place.

Closing the door behind her, Paige busied herself with airing out her bedding and hanging up clothes. With each outfit she hung up, she wondered if she should change. Damian had said to dress casually, and she had taken him at his word, choosing a pair of jeans and a long sweater, but she caught a glimpse of her favorite scarf in a suitcase and dug it out, pleased to see it wasn't too wrinkled.

She draped it around her neck and debated changing her shoes when the doorbell rang. Her stomach jumped, and her eyes narrowed. Why was she having this kind of reaction to going out with someone she'd only met twice? Sure, he seemed like a nice guy, and he was good looking, but she also knew he might very well be taking her out just to prove himself to his buddies.

She forced herself to take her time in walking to the door, slipping her coat on as she did so. Out of habit, she looked through the window to make sure she knew who it was before she opened it.

"Hey, there. Are you ready?" Damian asked. He too was dressed in jeans and wore a leather jacket that hung open over a gray button-up.

"I think so." She picked up her purse and joined him on the front walk. "Where are we going?"

"It depends. Do you like seafood?"

"I love seafood."

"In that case, Seth suggested a restaurant not too far from here." He guided her to the small pickup truck parked next to her car. "I thought we could have some dinner and then go for a drive and check out the area a bit."

"That sounds good." She slid into the passenger's seat to find that even though the upholstery was worn, the interior of the truck was clean. Paige suspected Damian had stopped by the car wash on his way to get her, and she was flattered at the thought.

As soon as he took his seat and started the car, she asked, "How long have you been in the navy?"

"Almost a year."

"That's all?" When he nodded, she asked, "What did you do before you joined?"

"I worked in the oil industry for a few years with my father and younger brother. Then I spent a year in banking."

"Do you like the navy better than those jobs?"

"I do. I wasn't interested in living on oil rigs, and I definitely didn't want to spend my life sitting behind a desk. The navy has been a good challenge, even if I do have to carry a gun."

"Why do you have to carry a weapon?" Paige asked, hoping her voice sounded casual. "I thought most people in the military were only armed when they went into battle."

"It's actually not mandatory for most people, but someone up the chain of command decided they wanted us to stay armed. I guess there have been a few situations in the past when that decision has come in handy."

"What exactly do you do for the navy?"

Damian glanced sideways at her. "You don't know?"

"Should I?"

"I just figured Vanessa would have told you."

"No, she just mentioned that you were on her husband's squad."

Damian seemed to debate how much he could tell her. Sensing his hesitation, Paige asked, "Do you know where I work?"

"Well, yeah. Seth said Vanessa is CIA, so it only makes sense you are too."

"Which you do realize isn't exactly something you can share with people, right?" Paige said.

"I kind of figured."

"If I can trust you to keep where I work a secret, don't you think you can trust me with where you work?"

"I guess so." Damian fell silent until he pulled up to a stoplight. Then he turned to face her before answering. "I'm a Navy SEAL."

Paige had expected him to say he was in intelligence or maybe research. She even thought he might be in the military police, but a SEAL? That thought hadn't ever crossed her mind.

When she didn't respond, Damian said, "You aren't going to tell me you don't date SEALs, are you?"

"I've honestly never thought about it before. You're the first SEAL I've ever known."

"Except for my squad."

"I suppose that's true." Paige thought about her time at Vanessa's a few nights before and the afternoon when she'd first met Damian and his friends. She hadn't really thought about what they did specifically, but now curiosity blossomed. "What's it like being a SEAL?"

"So far, all I've done is a lot of training. Some of it's a bit like what you might expect from what you read about or see in the movies, but a lot of it is just basic physical training and a lot of shooting practice."

Involuntarily, Paige tensed.

"Any chance you're going to tell me why you're afraid of guns?"

"It's a long story."

"We've got time."

"It's not exactly a first-date kind of story." Paige gave him an apologetic look. "Tell me about you. Where are you from? What's your family like?"

"I'm originally from Venezuela, but my family moved to Houston when I was thirteen. I think I mentioned my dad and younger brother work on oil rigs. My older brother is living in Germany right now. He's in international banking."

"Forgive me, but you don't look like you're from Latin America. I always think of people from there as having dark hair and dark complexions."

"My great grandparents were from Germany. They moved to Maracaibo shortly before World War II and never left."

"Do you speak German?"

"I do. A lot of my dad's side of the family went back to Germany when Venezuela's government started destabilizing, and we used to visit once or twice a year," he said. "He never had enough money to buy a new truck or the bigger television he had his eye on, but he always managed to find a way to get us plane tickets."

"Sounds like family was his first priority."

"Very much so." Damian glanced over at her. "What about you? What's your family like?"

"There's not much to tell. I grew up in a little town in New Hampshire, and I have an older sister."

"How did you end up working for the CIA?"

"I guess you could say I fell into it." She was relieved when Damian pulled into the restaurant parking lot. "It looks crowded."

"I called ahead and made a reservation." He maneuvered his truck into a spot a couple rows away from the entrance. "If we don't like the food, we can blame Seth."

"Are you going to give him the credit if the food is good?"

Damian considered for a moment. "I'll think about it."

Paige felt herself relax, relieved to be on safer subjects. They walked into the restaurant, and her mood improved further. The tables were covered with newspaper rather than tablecloths, and the scent of crab and hush puppies permeated the air.

The waiters wore jeans and T-shirts with the restaurant logo emblazoned across the front, and the menus were vinyl covered. In the corner, a live band that sounded suspiciously like Rascal Flatts filled the place with noise.

Paige looked over at Damian. "This place is great."

She saw the worried expression on his face transform into an answering smile. There was no doubt about it. This place was only one step up from a dive, but if the food tasted nearly as good as it smelled, they were in for a meal worthy of a five-star restaurant.

CHAPTER 10

Damian stepped out of his truck, his feet crunching on the snow in the parking lot. He caught the scent of the ocean in the air and heard the roar of the waves crashing against the beach.

The food at the restaurant had been great, but the noise level had made it difficult to talk.

After they'd finished eating, Damian had been grateful Paige was still willing to extend their time together when he suggested they go down to the boardwalk.

He was surprised to find that the more time he spent with her, the more curious he became. Every time he asked her something, he felt like her answers spawned another dozen questions in his mind.

He took her hand when she climbed out of his truck. "Watch your step here. It's icy."

"I thought all of this snow would have melted by now."

"It is January."

"Yeah, but it always seems weird to me to see snow at the beach, especially in the South."

"Let's see how much snow is really down there." Damian tugged on her hand, leading her across the street and down the block to where they could access the wooden boardwalk that spanned the tourist section of town.

The boardwalk itself was a combination of sand and slush, but the beach still had several inches of snow covering it, except for where the tide had melted it. The moon hung low in the sky, illuminating the snow and the crests of the waves as they came in.

"I've always loved a winter beach," Damian said, staring out at the waves.

"Really? How come?"

"Actually, I love the beach any time of the year, but in the winter, it's just so peaceful."

"I agree. It's nice to not have to deal with the crowds."

"Definitely not a problem right now," Damian agreed. Her hand still in his, he guided her to the left, and they strolled past the various hotels that overlooked the ocean. "So what do you have going on tomorrow?"

"The moving truck is supposed to show up with my stuff at nine."

"Oh, that's right. Vanessa said we should stop in and help out."

"I don't know that there will be much to do. The movers will at least bring everything inside. Then it's just the joy of unpacking."

"Do you have a lot of stuff?"

"The usual. Couch, bed, table, kitchen stuff. My old place was about the same size as the new one, so it shouldn't take too long to get settled in."

"From what I understand, you won't want to take too long. Seth made it sound like Vanessa's quite the taskmaster."

"I don't mind. I like the sense of satisfaction I get from finishing something and being able to cross it off my list," Paige said. "It's a new experience for me."

"What do you mean? What did you do before?" The words were barely out of his mouth when he felt his phone vibrate. "I'm sorry. I'd better check this."

"That's fine. Go ahead."

He let go of her hand and retrieved his phone. He read the message twice, not sure how he felt about the prospect of his first mission interrupting his date. "I'm sorry. I have to go into work."

"On a Friday night?"

"My job isn't exactly nine to five."

Paige looked at him suspiciously. "Is this the kind of call that means you might be disappearing into the night for who knows how long?"

"Honestly, this is the first time I've had this happen, so I'm not sure." He put his hand on her back and started guiding her toward the pickup again. "Maybe."

They walked in silence back to his truck, both of them lost in thought. When Damian dropped her off at her apartment, he walked her to her door and waited for her to unlock it. She turned the knob and turned back to face him. "Be safe."

"I plan on it," Damian said, his thoughts and emotions jumbled. "I'll see you later."

Paige nodded and, without another word, stepped inside, closing the door between them.

* * *

By the time Damian reached base and reported where he'd been told, his frustration about his date being interrupted was completely overshadowed by an unexpected eagerness and sense of urgency. He found the rest of his squad already standing in a hangar bay, two Humvees parked inside.

"What's going on?" he asked the group in general.

"We're shipping out," Quinn answered with his usual no-nonsense tone.

"Where are we going?"

"We're heading for the helicopter that will take us out to the Truman," Brent said, waving his finger to encompass the other five members of the squad. "You're staying here."

"Why?"

"Sorry, Damian. It's a matter of experience," Brent told him bluntly. "You've only been with us two weeks. I don't feel comfortable taking you into the field yet, especially not on this one."

"What's different about this one?"

"I'm afraid it's need-to-know. Let's just say we're familiar with the target."

"This is ridiculous." Damian folded his arms across his chest. "You don't want to take me into the field because I don't have enough experience, but I can't get experience unless you give me a shot."

"Next time," Brent said before he turned to the others. "Let's go."

Damian watched the other members of the Saint Squad climb into the two vehicles, Jay and Quinn shooting him sympathetic glances. Frustration and a strange sense of loss filled him.

As he watched them pull away, he forced himself to face reality. He might be able to call these men his teammates, but he now knew how hollow those words were. They were the real Saint Squad. He was just the guy they'd gotten stuck with.

* * *

Paige stared out the window of her apartment, not sure what she expected to find in the well-lit parking lot. Part of her wished Damian would come back and tell her his message had been a false alarm. Then she wondered why she should want such a thing. After all, she barely knew the guy.

Her phone rang, and she looked down to see her mother's number displayed. She pressed the talk button. "Hi, Mom."

"How are you? Are you all settled into your new place?"

"My stuff gets here tomorrow." Paige sat beneath the window, leaning back against the wall. She fell into the comfortable rhythm of small talk with her mom, letting her bring her up to date on the happenings of the small town she had grown up in. She listened to the news about the man down the street battling cancer and the possibility of the high school basketball team making it to the state championship.

She could picture the scenes so easily, just as she remembered every detail of Main Street and the shops that lined it in the little New Hampshire town. Undoubtedly, the high school gym was busting at the seams every Friday night, and Mr. Edmonds was knee deep in fruit pies and casseroles.

Her thoughts were interrupted when her mother mentioned the one family she had tried so hard to forget. "I heard Russell is coming up for parole in July."

"That's nice," Paige said, hoping her mother wouldn't dwell on their former next-door neighbor.

"Aren't you interested in what happens to him?" she asked, her voice a little testy. "After all, you did testify at his trial."

"It wasn't like I had much of a choice," Paige replied. "Did you and Daddy decide whether you're going to take that cruise to Alaska this summer?"

"Not yet, and don't change the subject. You of all people know that talking about things can be healing."

"I also know that dwelling on the past won't change it." Paige stood and looked out the window once more. Why was it that she could help other people face their demons, but she couldn't quite put her own behind her? "I think I'm going to unpack a few more things and then get to bed. I have a big day tomorrow."

"Okay, sweetie. You take care of yourself."

"I will, Mom." Paige hung up before she added, "I always do."

* * *

"What's our mission?" Quinn asked as soon as they reached the helicopter pad.

Brent glanced behind him, still feeling lousy about leaving Damian behind. The choice had been his and his alone, but when he had talked to

Kel about the mission, he'd felt a sense of uneasiness when he'd considered taking Damian with them, one he couldn't shake until he'd ultimately decided against it.

He picked up his gear and slung it over his shoulder. "We're inserting into Venezuela. We're going after Morenta."

"The Colombian drug lord? Why would he be in Venezuela?"

"He's aligned himself with someone in one of the oil companies in Venezuela. The higher-ups are worried about the effects of his influence in an already unstable area."

"I gather we're supposed to take him alive," Seth said.

"You got it. We're after him and three of his men. CIA and DEA think Morenta is setting up new drug distribution lines through the oil industry out of Maracaibo."

"Do they really think picking up Morenta will stop that? The one thing with the drug trade is that there's always someone else ready to step in."

"Yes, but they think if we can get at least three of our four targets, they can turn them against each other and unravel the whole network. Morenta is also believed to have strong ties with two of the Mexican cartels."

"Are you sure about leaving Damian behind?" Jay asked now. "Since he's from Venezuela, he could be useful."

"Damian's family is originally from Maracaibo, and they work in the oil industry. Kel and I talked about it at length, and we decided we didn't want to take the chance that he might have to face down old friends or family members."

"Does he still have family there?"

"His maternal grandparents and several aunts, uncles, and cousins."

"You could have told him the real reason we weren't taking him with us."

"Too risky. We don't want him inadvertently telling someone we're headed into Venezuela."

Seth looked skeptical. "Is there some other reason you left him behind?"

"Just a gut feeling, the kind I can't explain."

Seth nodded. The Saint Squad had learned to trust their intuition. "Damian will get over it."

Either inspiration or unconscious logic was at work here, and Brent knew it was best to listen to it. "Eventually," Brent agreed.

CHAPTER 11

Damian barely slept, and he couldn't eat. He hated this, being left behind, not knowing what the men he had been training with for the past two weeks were facing. Clearly they weren't worried about going into battle without him. Why should they be? They had done it so many times before. But he was worried and edgy.

Brent's explanation about experience had hurt, but now Damian wondered if his commanding officer had had other motives. Had he felt Damian's skills weren't strong enough for the mission they had been assigned? Was he worried Damian would fail to perform when they were out in the field?

Admittedly, he had frozen for a brief time on the rappelling tower when his line had come loose, but he had recovered quickly enough, hadn't he?

Questions and doubts continued to plague him, and he went for an early-morning run to try to chase them away. When that didn't work, he showered and changed, deciding he might as well go help Paige move in. After all, the other guys in the squad weren't going to be available today.

The moving truck hadn't arrived yet, but anticipating the need to keep the area by the front door clear, he parked a couple spaces away. He was still fighting his foul mood as he climbed out of his truck and approached the apartment. When Paige opened the door, he saw the look of surprise on her face.

"Damian? What are you doing here?"

"I told you I'd help you move in today." He glanced down at his watch. "I'm not too early, am I?"

"No, not at all." She stepped back and motioned him inside. "I just didn't think you were coming."

"Last night didn't go exactly how I'd planned," Damian said, fighting to keep the irritation out of his voice.

"I understood why you had to leave when you did."

"That's not what I meant."

She looked at him questioningly, but when he didn't expand on his comment, she led the way into the kitchen. "I was just about to get some breakfast. Would you like to join me? I have some raspberry croissants, and there's some orange juice in the fridge."

The appetite he had suppressed during his emotional turmoil came back when faced with his favorite breakfast food. "Actually, that sounds good."

"Help yourself." Paige motioned to the plastic container on the counter and retrieved a disposable plastic cup from the cabinet by the fridge. "There are paper plates in the cabinet right above you."

Damian found them and took two plates out of the package. He handed one to Paige, trading it for the juice she offered him. He took a sip and leaned back against the counter. "I thought the moving truck was supposed to be here by now."

"It was. Apparently there was some heavy traffic, so they're running late." She selected a croissant for herself and took a bite. She kept her eyes on him as though studying some complicated puzzle. "Is everything okay? You don't seem yourself this morning."

"Should I be worried that you can tell that when we've only been out once?"

"I don't know." Her shoulders lifted. "So what's wrong?"

He hesitated, not sure he should be talking about a mission with someone outside of his command but knowing he needed to vent to someone. "My squad doesn't trust me to carry my weight. I hate feeling like I need to prove myself, but there's no way I can unless they decide to trust me."

"I'm sorry. That's rough." She took another bite and seemed to consider the problem. "Is there anything that's happened to make them not trust you?"

"You're direct," Damian said, a little surprised she wouldn't just blindly support his frustrations.

Paige looked like she understood. "Just trying to talk through the problem."

"To answer your question, no, there isn't anything I've done to show I can't do the job. In fact, I thought all of my exercises with the squad so far had gone really well."

"I assume you've already talked to Brent about it."

"Oh yeah. He's the one who doesn't trust me."

"That's good that the problem is out in the open though," Paige said matter-of-factly. "Maybe when you go to work on Monday, you can ask him what it's going to take for you to gain his trust."

"I doubt that's going to happen."

"Why not?"

"I don't think my squad will be around on Monday." He hesitated briefly before deciding to confide in her fully. "They aren't in town. They went on assignment without me."

* * *

Vanessa climbed into Riley's minivan and glanced in the backseat to see Dixon dozing in his car seat. "Thanks for coming with me. I'm sure you have a dozen things you could be doing today."

"Thanks for asking me. You know how I get those first few days after Tristan ships out. You'd think by now I would get used to it, but . . ." Her voice trailed off.

"I know what you mean." Vanessa gave her the address to Paige's apartment. "The movers should get all of the big stuff in place, but I thought we could help her unpack."

"So how's she working out? She's lasted longer than your last assistant."

"Actually, she's great. When I saw her file, I thought the personnel officer was crazy."

"Why's that?"

"She's a nurse."

"You have a nurse as your assistant? What? Did they think after you chased off the last four, you needed someone who could give herself medical treatment?"

"Ha, ha." Vanessa smirked at Riley. "I guess she wanted a change. Other than mentioning that she's used to shift work, she hasn't really talked about what she did before."

"That's interesting."

"Oh no. You aren't doing that psychoanalysis thing again, are you?" After witnessing a traumatic shooting, Riley had pursued a master's degree in criminal psychology and helped develop several classes to aid police and other first responders in similar situations.

"Sorry, it's habit," Riley admitted. "Most people in a new environment will use their past to try to make connections with their new associations."

"So far she's making connections by doing a great job. She even made friends with the guards at the front gate and has them handing out our information packets for us so we don't have to set up someone else to meet the students."

"Wow. I've been to your work. Those guards are pretty intense."

"I know." She lifted a hand and pointed. "Turn left here. Her complex is about a mile down on the right."

Riley followed Vanessa's directions and pulled up next to a pickup a few spaces down from where a moving truck was backed up to Paige's apartment.

Vanessa's eyes narrowed. The pickup looked suspiciously like the one she had seen Damian driving when he'd come to her house two nights before. "Is that Damian's truck?"

"I don't know." Riley turned off the ignition and glanced over. "I didn't notice what he was driving the other night."

"I swear it's the same one." Vanessa pushed her door open and waited for Riley to lift the baby's car seat out of the car, little Dixon still asleep inside it. She stepped up on the sidewalk and looked closer. "It has Texas license plates. Why would Damian's truck be here?"

"Maybe he was out with Paige when the call came in. Paige could have been driving and dropped him off at the base."

"I suppose so," Vanessa said, but an uncomfortable feeling started working through her. When Damian followed the movers out Paige's front door, surprise and uneasiness merged with that uncomfortable sensation.

With Riley following behind her, Vanessa walked toward Damian, who stood at the back of the moving truck. He spoke to the movers in Spanish, relaying where Paige wanted her couch.

"Damian, what are you doing here?" Vanessa asked.

"Helping Paige move in." He looked directly at her but in a way that made Vanessa certain he was deliberately not giving her the information she really wanted.

"You know that's not what I meant." Vanessa waited until after the movers had carried the couch inside before she lowered her voice and said, "The guys shipped out last night. Why aren't you with them?"

The muscle in his jaw twitched. "That's exactly the question I asked last night when I watched them drive away." He led the way into the apartment. "Paige is in the kitchen."

"This doesn't make sense that the whole squad wouldn't deploy together," Vanessa said to Riley.

"Maybe Amy knows what's going on."

"I'll call her." Vanessa slipped her phone from her pocket and dialed Amy's number. When it went straight to voice mail, Vanessa shook her head. "It looks like Amy is with them. That can't be sitting well with Damian."

"Poor guy."

"Let's go see what we can do to help," Vanessa suggested.

"Are you going to interrogate Damian to find out what's going on?"

"I don't interrogate people," Vanessa said, pretending to be insulted.

"Yeah right." Riley breezed past her. "Let me know what you find out."

* * *

Paige stood in the kitchen, amazed at how much they had already done. The movers had come and gone, and the furniture was now all in place.

Damian was currently putting her bed together, a service that hadn't been included in her move, and Riley and Vanessa were helping her finish the kitchen.

"It's almost one," Riley said. "Do you want me to call Taylor to see if she'll pick up some lunch for us?"

"That's a good idea." Vanessa lifted a plate from a box and slid it into the dishwasher. "Should we call to see if Carina wants to come over too?"

"She's at her sister's swim meet today," Riley said. "They'll be back late tonight though. She offered to help me run registration for the class I'm starting on base on Monday."

"You're teaching on base?" Paige asked.

Riley set aside an empty box and ripped the tape off another. "I run a class for the military police a couple times a year."

"Now, who is Carina?"

"Jay's wife. She was up in northern Virginia the other night, so you didn't get to meet her."

"And Taylor's your sister?" Paige asked, still trying to figure out how everyone was connected.

"That's right. She's also married to Quinn, so we usually get together when the guys ship out."

"Is this common?"

"What?"

"The way you're all so interconnected? I mean, I can understand the squad being close, but the commander's wife works with them, and the two of you conduct training at their base." Paige began unloading her silverware into a drawer.

"The squad is like a family. It's pretty much the same with the wives."

Paige glanced toward the living room, listening for any movement there. She lowered her voice and asked, "Any suggestions of what Damian needs to do to become part of the family? He's feeling a lot like a stepchild at the moment."

"Change is never easy," Riley said sympathetically.

"Does this have anything to do with why he's here and our husbands are gone?" Vanessa asked.

"You could say that," Paige said, her voice still low.

"Do you know what happened?"

"Not really. I just know he's here and he feels like he should be with them."

She heard footsteps in the living room and moved to the doorway to see Damian coming toward her. "We were just talking about getting some lunch. Are you up for that?"

"I don't know." Damian shuffled his feet uneasily. "I should probably get going."

"Oh." Paige didn't manage to hide her disappointment.

Riley stepped forward, slipping past Paige so she could check on the baby. "You know, I should probably get the baby home before he wakes up again."

Vanessa followed her into the living room. "Yeah, we should get going."

"I thought you were going to stay for lunch," Paige said.

"Sorry, I wasn't thinking about how hard it will be to help once the baby wakes up."

Paige watched Vanessa gather her purse as Riley shrugged on her coat.

"If you need more help tonight, give me a call," Vanessa told her.

"I will. Thanks for everything," Paige said, not sure what to think about their sudden change of plans.

A few minutes later, she was alone with Damian and a dozen empty boxes.

"That was strange," Damian said after Paige closed the door behind them.

"Very strange," Paige agreed. "Did you need to leave too?"

"I can stay a bit longer," Damian said, apparently changing his plans as well. "Did you want to take a break and get some lunch?"

"That would be great if you have time."

"I have time." Damian picked up both of their jackets from where they'd tossed them on the couch. He handed Paige's to her. "Come on. Let's load up the empty boxes and drop them at the Dumpster on our way out."

Paige took her coat from him. "In case I haven't already told you, I really appreciate everything you've done today."

She saw a cloud of regret in his eyes, and she hoped it didn't have anything to do with her. Picking up several boxes, she followed him outside and prayed she could find the words to ease his pain.

CHAPTER 12

Amy walked with the Saint Squad toward the flight deck. She didn't have to tell her husband how apprehensive she felt about this mission. He hadn't said the words, but she knew he shared her feelings. He hadn't even argued when she had insisted on getting permission for a situation report after they'd made their drop zone.

For years, Morenta had been a target of interest for the United States and for this squad in particular. Vanessa and Seth had firsthand knowledge of the man from an undercover assignment they had shared together, and both had expressed similar opinions of him.

He had no respect for life, and he would eliminate anything or anyone who got in his way. He was also inherently paranoid. It was this quality that made Amy uneasy now. Why would a man who went to such great lengths to ensure his personal security choose to meet with potential business associates in a regular hotel room?

Amy had gone over the intelligence reports herself and couldn't fault the sources. Several telephone intercepts supported the findings, as did local reports that included a sighting of Morenta's private plane at an airstrip outside of Maracaibo.

Everything lined up, yet she couldn't shake her uneasy feeling.

She watched the men check their weapons before they crossed to the helicopter that would take them to their destination. When a commander intercepted the men at the landing pad, they spoke for a moment and then all headed toward her. A silent prayer went through her head that they would tell her the mission had been scrubbed.

"What's going on?" she asked when Brent reached her.

"Our pilot is sick. They bumped us back an hour while we wait for the replacement to be briefed."

Amy fell silent.

As though reading her thoughts, he put a hand on her arm and leaned close so only she could hear him. "Don't worry. I'll be sure to check in."

"And you'll follow Saint Squad protocol."

"You know I will."

"Okay." Amy huffed out a breath and bit her tongue to keep from saying what she was really thinking. She knew it was taboo to express negative thoughts before sending men into a danger zone, but she suspected that if she did, she would be voicing everyone else's thoughts. She didn't feel good about this mission.

* * *

Brent used his night-vision goggles to study the terrain in the clearing and the high cliffs in the distance. Nothing about the area looked like the photos he had seen of their intended landing zone.

"Jay, check our position."

Jay checked his equipment, fiddling with it while Quinn and Tristan fanned out to make sure they were really alone.

"Well?" Brent asked impatiently.

"Something's wrong. According to this, we're fifty miles from the Brazilian border. We're over a thousand miles from where we're supposed to be."

"What?" Brent stepped closer and checked the equipment himself. "That can't be right. I verified the coordinates with the pilot myself."

"Unless this equipment is wrong, we were dropped in the wrong place."

"Seth, call in our position and verify our drop site."

"Roger that." Seth switched his comm gear to the proper frequency, and his expression changed from businesslike to irritated. "My comm gear is down."

"You've got to be kidding me."

Seth shook his head.

Without waiting to be told, Jay tried his communication gear only to find that his too was faulty. "Mine's bad too."

Quinn and Tristan checked their equipment in turn. Both men shook their heads, annoyance evident on Quinn's face, concern flickering across Tristan's.

"I have a bad feeling about this," Tristan said. "I checked my gear twice before we loaded everything on the helicopter."

"You think someone switched it?" Brent asked, already confirming that his communication gear wasn't functioning.

"That's exactly what I think," Tristan said. He looked up at the cliffs. "Unless there's some kind of jamming signal nearby."

"We're sitting ducks here." Brent looked around the clearing, where their transport helicopter had dropped them. "Quinn, take point. Head for the trees to the left. Once we take cover, I want an equipment check. Let's see what works and what doesn't."

Quinn took his position, and the five men spread out, alert for any movement around them. Using the darkness for cover, they headed into the jungle.

Five hundred yards into the depths of the trees, Brent chose a small clearing to reassess their situation. He signaled Tristan and Jay to take up guard positions opposite him, the three of them creating a triangle. Seth and Quinn began taking inventory, checking their own gear first.

After they finished, Quinn traded places with Tristan, and Seth headed toward Brent.

"Well?" Brent asked.

"Someone did mess with our gear. All of the communications gear was sabotaged, and our emergency transponders are missing."

"You think someone deliberately dumped us here in the middle of nowhere and made sure we wouldn't be found?"

"That's exactly what I think." Seth took a guard-like stance so Brent could check his own gear.

Sure enough, his emergency beacon was missing, and he could see where someone had taken a knife to his comm unit. "This is insane. Who would have been able to access all of our gear and then manage to leave us so far away from our target?"

"I don't know. Everything was secured and stowed this morning when we went to our briefing. Only the flight crew would have had access to it," Seth said. "The only equipment we checked out after we stowed the rest of our gear was our weapons."

"Which means we have to assume everything in our vests could be compromised. Even food and water."

Seth nodded. "And since we're supposed to maintain radio silence, it could be days before anyone realizes we're missing."

"Not exactly," Brent said.

"What do you mean?"

"Amy cleared it for me to check in as soon as we made our landing site. When that doesn't happen, you can be sure she'll start digging." Brent was suddenly grateful that his wife had come aboard ship with his squad. They had been there only one night to prep the mission, but after an intelligence error a couple years earlier, they rarely left Amy behind.

"If Amy's expecting a sit rep, we should probably stay near the drop site. As soon as she questions the pilot, she'll know where we are."

"Unless he's the one behind all of this," Brent said. "Think about it. He had complete access to our gear after it was loaded, and he is the one who dropped us off at the wrong site."

"He also wasn't originally scheduled to fly us. It's possible he slipped something to our original pilot so he could take the flight," Tristan said.

"In which case, we're wasting our time if we just wait here."

"We'll give it twenty-four hours. If someone doesn't show up to get us by then, we have to assume we're on our own to get out of here." Brent walked over to Tristan, who was putting his combat vest back in order. "Tristan, you and Quinn sweep the area to make sure we're really alone out here, and see if you can find a freshwater source. Jay can set up camp while Seth sees if there's any way to get a message out."

"Got it."

As soon as Tristan and Quinn disappeared into the foliage, Seth voiced the thought that was burning in the back of Brent's mind. "What do you think? Who would want us stranded out here? And why?"

"I wish I knew."

* * *

He waited in the shadows of the cargo hold, pleased to find himself alone. The hatch opened, the light from the hallway illuminating the outline of the man he was waiting for. The helicopter pilot walked inside and turned in a circle. The lieutenant's voice was low when he called out, whispering his name.

Stepping forward, he too kept his voice low. "Were you successful?"

He jumped slightly at the sound of the voice, but he recovered quickly. "Yes, sir. I dropped them right where you told me, and their communication gear is all disabled."

He smiled at being called "sir." The pilot was around thirty, around the same age as he was. Leave it to the military guys to be polite, even when betraying their fellow servicemen. "And you're sure there's no way they can get a message out?"

"Positive. That whole area is nothing but wilderness except for a couple of primitive native tribes. Even those are a good forty miles from where I dropped them."

"Excellent."

"Now, about my payment. You said the other half would be wired to my account as soon as I completed my part of this."

"I'll take care of it before the day is over." When the pilot turned to leave, he reached into the back of his waistband. "Oh, and one more thing, Lieutenant."

"Yes?" The lieutenant started to turn but didn't get the chance to fully face him before a knife stabbed him between the ribs in his back.

"Never turn your back on people unless you know you can trust them." He stabbed the pilot a second time, this time making sure he pierced the heart. Straightening, he wiped off the blade and let it clatter to the floor.

After a quick detour to change his clothes, he crept along the edge of the fantail, made sure no one was around, and dropped his bloodstained clothes and gloves into the water below.

In the darkness, he couldn't see the tightly wound bundle hit the water. He was a little disappointed not to have the satisfaction of watching the evidence against him sink into the depths of the ocean. But he indulged himself for a minute or two, staring out into the darkness and checking off yet another item on his mental list of tasks to accomplish along his road to success.

Just another few steps and everything he wanted would be within his reach.

CHAPTER 13

Amy read over the communication report, her sense of uneasiness growing. After her squad had left, she had followed her normal routine and taken a nap during the time they would be traveling under radio silence. She then spent the next two hours in CIC, the Combat Information Center, waiting for her squad to check in.

The radio silence had prevented her from having any updates beyond following the aircraft on the ship's instruments. She was surprised when she arrived in CIC and found that the helicopter's transmitter had stopped working shortly before it had cleared Venezuelan airspace and dropped below radar.

The mission plan had called for the helicopter to evade detection by local military forces, but she hadn't anticipated a malfunction in the signal that would normally allow the navy to track it. Her nerves had strained when the time of its expected return came and went without contact. The silence had continued for more than an hour longer than anticipated until the helicopter popped back up on the ship's radar.

The pilot reported that he had successfully made the drop, but Brent hadn't reported in. This fact rolled through her mind repeatedly. Based on the time the helicopter had returned, Brent should have messaged her over three hours ago. Even if they'd had to secure the area before radioing in, she should have heard from him by now.

Since they had discussed his following Saint Squad protocol, she knew he wouldn't have sent the message back with the pilot. He would have sent it himself, along with an inserted code to verify it was really him or another member of the squad sending it.

So why had the pilot said everything had gone according to plan when clearly it hadn't?

For an hour and a half after the helicopter's return, Amy waited in CIC for some kind of signal, but it never came. She wasn't one who was prone to cry foul unnecessarily, especially knowing many people in the military weren't fond of the presence of civilian intelligence officers aboard ship. When her concerns continued to eat at her and she could no longer justify any reasons that the communication delay had taken so long, she sought out the ship's executive officer.

"Commander Dunnan, I think we may have a problem."

"What's that?"

"The captain gave my squad permission for a sit rep after insertion, but I haven't received one."

"The pilot said everything went off without a hitch."

"With all due respect, sir, you've worked with my squad before. If it had gone off without a hitch, we would have heard from them by now."

The commander fell silent for a moment, processing the logic of her words. He turned to the duty roster and spoke to a seaman nearby. "Seaman, go track down Lieutenant Coswick and have him report to CIC."

"Commander, I think he was the one who got sick. There was another pilot who replaced him."

The commander amended his order. "Find out who the pilot was and get him up here."

"Yes, sir."

* * *

Brent sat on a large rock and used his flashlight to study his mission map. It didn't take long to confirm what he'd suspected—the map was useless. They had been dropped outside of the area the map covered.

He looked up when Quinn and Tristan entered the campsite.

"We have good news and bad news," Tristan said.

"I'll take the good news first," Brent said. His men's easy manner already told him what he most needed to know. They hadn't found any discernable threats in the area.

"I caught breakfast." Quinn held up a lifeless iguana by its tail.

"There's also a fresh spring a half mile inland," Tristan added.

"What's the bad news?"

"We're boxed in. There isn't any sign of life out there, and it looks like we're surrounded by steep cliffs," Tristan said.

"We'll be able to tell more when the sun comes up."

"Who wants to take the first watch?" Brent asked, fully intending to follow procedure even if they didn't anticipate any problems through what remained of the night.

"I'll do it," Quinn offered. He held the large iguana out to Jay. "Let me know when breakfast is ready. Then we can switch off."

"Way to get out of cooking, Quinn. I thought you were supposed to be the barbecue king," Brent said.

Quinn grinned. "I don't see a grill."

Jay took the offering and wrinkled his nose. "I don't know how to cook iguana."

"If you do it right, it's supposed to taste like chicken," Seth told him.

"How about you come help me do it right."

"Tell you what. I'll go find you a nice stick to roast it on."

While Quinn took up watch, the other men alternated between helping and heckling as Jay prepared their meal. The scent of roasting meat filled the air. Brent took an appreciative sniff, and his stomach grumbled. Then his whole body tensed when Tristan suddenly jumped up and drew his knife. Brent sprang up as well, searching for the threat, even as Tristan's knife left his hand and went spinning through the air.

Across from him, Jay used his flashlight to illuminate the tree where the knife had landed. All of them relaxed as soon as they saw he had hit his target.

"A spider? Really, Tristan? I think it's time you get over this fear of arachnids."

"Take a closer look." Tristan shuddered. "It's huge!"

"Oh, for heaven's sake," Brent holstered his sidearm. "I thought you saw someone out there."

"While you're up, will you grab my knife for me?" Tristan asked, holding his ground.

"I'm pretty sure the spider is dead. It's not going to hurt you."

"Yeah, but you're closer," Tristan said with a weak grin.

Quinn stepped out of the shadows from where he had been standing watch. It didn't take him long to figure out what had caused the commotion. He shook his head and crossed to where Tristan's knife had speared a ridiculously large spider's abdomen.

He grabbed the handle, pulled it free, and wiped the blade on his pants before handing it over to his brother-in-law. "Looks like it's your turn to stand watch."

"Thanks," Tristan said, clearly referring to the return of his weapon.

When he moved to take a watch position, Brent called after him. "Hey, Tristan. We only want you to wake us up if you find something deadly out there. Spiders don't qualify."

"I'll make sure I remember that if I see a venomous one crawling on your face."

"If that happens, do me a favor and don't use your knife."

* * *

Paige sat at the kitchen and laced up her shoes with a sense of uneasiness. What had she been thinking? Agreeing to go on a 5:00-a.m. run with Damian had seemed logical enough when they had talked on the phone yesterday. She went running most mornings anyway. Then she had remembered what he did for a living. How in the world was she going to keep up with a Navy SEAL?

The knock on the door startled her, and she glanced out the window to see Damian standing on the doorstep. She opened the door. "I didn't hear you pull up."

"I ran over here."

"You ran here so we could go running together?"

"You said last night you normally run three or four miles. It made sense to add a few on either end."

She stepped outside and closed the door behind her. "Are all Navy SEALs so dedicated?"

He stiffened. "Can't say I know the answer to that. I haven't met very many."

"I'm sorry. I know work must be tough to talk about right now."

"It's okay. It's hard not to think about it, especially not knowing what I'm supposed to do with my squad out of town."

Paige fell into step with him as he started out at an easy jog through the darkness. "Do you know anything about what you're doing today?"

"I just know I'm supposed to report to Commander Bennett's office at oh eight hundred."

"Who's Commander Bennett?"

"He's the commander of SEAL Team Eight." They turned the corner and headed toward the bay. He glanced over at her. "Is this pace okay for you?"

"It's fine, thanks." Paige didn't doubt he normally ran much faster when he was by himself, but she appreciated having someone by her side as they traversed the unfamiliar streets. When they turned a corner to reveal the dark water of the bay stretched out in front of them, she renewed that sentiment in her mind.

Lights from nearby buildings shimmered off the water, but the beach area in front of them was eerily quiet. Water lapped quietly along the shore, and in the distance, she heard the rumble of an engine.

Damian must have heard it too because he slowed his pace for several steps and then held up a hand, signaling her to stop.

The rumble grew in intensity until Paige saw the lights of a helicopter, the craft's silhouette just visible in the first fingers of daylight.

It hovered over the open water, and Paige thought she saw several splashes below. After the fourth splash, she realized what was happening. "Are those people jumping out of the helicopter?"

"Yep."

"Why would someone want to jump out of a helicopter into freezing cold water?"

"Training. You'd be safe to bet they're SEALs," Damian said, his voice oddly devoid of emotion.

"This is the kind of stuff you do for training? Jump out of perfectly good aircraft?"

"Pretty much."

"Sounds crazy to me."

"Oh, it is," Damian agreed without hesitation.

"Then why do you do it?"

"Because we never know what kind of situation we'll find ourselves in." Damian motioned toward the water. "We practice making night drops with full gear to be sure we can do it right when it really matters."

"You mean when you're dropping in behind enemy lines somewhere."

"Yeah, that's exactly what I mean." Damian kept his eyes on the men now making their way to shore. "Believe it or not, most missions for Navy SEALs are below the radar. They go in, get whatever information they need, and they get out, ideally without anyone ever knowing they were there."

Paige noticed his use of the word *they* instead of *we*, and she understood the thoughts behind it. "Don't do that to yourself. You're one of them. This one mission doesn't change that."

Damian shifted his attention to her now, an odd expression on his face. "Do you always do that?"

"What?"

"Read people's minds?"

"Sorry. It's an annoying habit of mine."

"You have an uncanny way of seeing right to the heart of things." He glanced out at the water again and then turned back the way they'd come. "Ready to head back?"

"Sure."

CHAPTER 14

Damian knocked on Commander Bennett's open door. Three weeks before, he had stood in this exact same spot with a combination of excitement and determination. Now he felt only dread.

His determination to prove himself worthy of the Saint Squad had not yielded the desired results. Because of that, his excitement about his future here had been completely extinguished.

"Come on in." Commander Bennett waved him in and motioned for him to take a seat. "I know you can't be thrilled about being here when your squad is out in the field, but I promise as soon as they get back, we'll brief you with the reasons you were left behind."

"I got the impression Lieutenant Commander Miller didn't feel I was up to the task."

"Your abilities weren't called into question. It was more a matter of inherent knowledge for this particular mission. This isn't the first time the Saint Squad is going up against this particular target. Let's just say I had hesitations about sending in a seasoned squad, let alone a rookie."

Damian knew the commander's words were meant to appease him, but they didn't erase his feelings of inadequacy. "What would you like me to do while the rest of the squad is in the field?"

"Today you're going to meet with NCIS and walk their investigators through the incident at the rappelling tower."

"We already did that right after it happened."

"I know, but they haven't turned up any leads on who might be behind the sabotage, and they want to go over the details one more time. That will be at ten hundred. The rest of your time will be spent primarily working on a project for me." Kel stood up and handed him a thick file and a single sheet of paper. "That page on top is the schedule for when some of the other squads will be taking in target practice. I want you to work that in every day, along with your PT, but the rest of the time, I want you reviewing that file."

"What's it for?"

"A drug dealer named Morenta from Colombia. Rumor has it he's left his villa near Cali. I want you to see if you can confirm that."

"Isn't this a job for intel?"

"It is. Intel has already given me their report, and it was compelling enough to send the Saint Squad into the field."

"Then why do you want me to do the job again?"

"To see how you think . . . and to see if there's anything intel missed." Kel settled back in his chair. "One of the secrets behind the Saint Squad's success is their ability to process raw data. It isn't uncommon for them to help Amy analyze reports before missions."

"Did they help on this one?"

He shook his head. "We weren't given enough time. That's why I'd like you to take a second look."

"Okay, I'll do what I can." Damian stood.

"And, Damian?"

"Yes?"

"Don't assume you're wrong if you don't agree with the analysts. I want you to tell me if you find anything that would prove Morenta's location one way or another."

"I'll do my best."

* * *

Damian checked out the training schedule Kel had given him and debated for several minutes whether he should go to the shooting range at his first opportunity or put it off as long as possible. It wasn't that he didn't enjoy being out at the range. He just didn't look forward to the questions. How did he explain that his squad was in the field and he had been left behind, especially when he didn't have any injury preventing him from being with the rest of them?

Knowing he wouldn't be able to concentrate with that scenario hanging over his head, he opted for the first available time slot, deciding he would have just enough time to get his range practice in before meeting with NCIS.

Thankfully, the squad he joined had already lined up when he arrived, allowing Damian to avoid the pesky questions he didn't want to answer. He found the lieutenant in charge, introduced himself, and chose a station on the end.

After checking over his weapon, he lined up with his target, squeezed the trigger, and wondered what the rest of his squad was doing right now.

* * *

Amy paced back and forth across the boardroom her team had been assigned when they'd first arrived on board. After a half-hour search, the seaman had returned with the news that he couldn't locate the pilot. A page went out over the shipwide communications system, but it went unanswered. Now security was combing the ship, and Amy was stuck waiting for news.

As minutes ticked by, she repeatedly checked for updated intelligence reports on her husband's mission, on Morenta, or on the area in general. The only news was that there was no new news. She used her intelligence access to check other cable traffic in the area, including Colombia. Again, she found nothing.

She tried to think of anything that would have caused her squad to fail to check in, but only two reasons came to mind: one was that something had happened to them after the pilot had dropped them off, and the other was that Brent had forgotten. She supposed it was possible. After all, she hadn't mentioned that she expected a communication to anyone besides her husband. She hadn't thought she would need to. He had never forgotten before.

She tried to fight against the fear that was causing worst-case scenarios to fester in her mind, but one single thought continued to eat at her. These men were the best at what they did. If they were in trouble, somehow, one of them would have figured out a way to get a message through.

After what felt like forever, the door to the boardroom opened and the captain entered. Since she normally dealt with the XO, his presence alone was enough to send another wave of trepidation crashing over her. "What's wrong?"

"Still no word from your squad, but we found the pilot."

"What did he say?"

"He didn't say anything." The captain's eyes met hers when he added grimly, "He's dead."

"Dead? What happened?"

"He was stabbed. He had changed out of his flight gear, but the doctor thinks he was killed within an hour of returning to the ship."

Apprehension pierced through Amy at the unexpected news. She remained silent for a moment while she absorbed this new fact. "Is there anyone else who would be able to verify that the Saint Squad made it in okay?"

"I'm afraid not." The captain shook his head. "We did check to make sure none of their homing devices were active. Other than that, all we would have is the pilot's word."

Amy knew the mission well, and she also understood military procedure. "Since they're scheduled for extraction tonight, I guess we're proceeding as planned."

"That's right." He gave her an understanding look. "Hopefully the lieutenant commander just got focused on the mission and neglected to call in."

"Hopefully." Amy's jaw set. "But if that's the case, the doctor had better be ready for another casualty because my husband is going to pay for making me worry."

The captain's lips curved up slightly. "I'll let you know if we have any contact."

"Thank you, Captain." Amy watched him go, but as soon as she was alone, she picked up the phone and requested a secure line. The navy might be bound by procedures, but that didn't mean she had to sit idly by.

As soon as the line was available, she made her call. "Kel, I need your help. And I think we may need Vanessa's help too."

* * *

Paige sat across the room from Vanessa and watched her tension level increase exponentially. Vanessa said very little, but obviously, whatever the person on the other end of the line was telling her wasn't good news.

She hung up and seemed to take a moment to settle her emotions. Then she said, "I want you to drop what you're working on and pull up everything you can find on Morenta."

"Who's he?"

"A Colombian drug lord." Vanessa sat at her desk and started typing on her own keyboard. "I especially need anything you can find that ties him to Venezuela. Any properties he owns there, business alliances—anything."

"I'll do what I can. When do you need it by?"

"Yesterday." The printer on Vanessa's desk started humming, and Vanessa stood. "I'll be back in an hour. I'll need everything you've got by then."

Paige watched her boss snatch the paper off the printer and rush out of the room. Not sure what to think about Vanessa's uncharacteristic sense of urgency, Paige started a database search with one hand and picked up her phone with the other.

She called the Latin American operations desk at headquarters and requested everything they had on Morenta. Then she made another call to the intelligence analyst over that region. Forty-five minutes later, she printed off the reports she had received and organized them into a folder. She was retrieving the final report from the printer when she saw a familiar name.

Andrea Kemper, the deceased daughter of Emmitt Kemper.

Stunned to see a connection to her previous job, she began reading. Even more shocking than seeing the woman's name in a new context was the report that the woman's body had never been recovered after a drowning at sea.

How was it that Emmitt had never mentioned that detail? He had talked about his daughter's skills incessantly, her knowledge of firearms, her ability to disguise herself so she could hide in plain sight. Obviously, not having a body to bury could make it difficult to find closure and even cause someone to cling to the possibility that their loved one was still alive. His previous behavior suddenly made a little more sense.

She glanced through the analyst's report, her sympathies and suspicions stirred. According to the woman's file, she had served undercover in Colombia, working as a low-level employee for Morenta. Was it possible her true identity had been discovered? Had Andrea been killed by the man Paige was now researching?

Or was it conceivable that Emmitt's daughter was still alive? Morenta was reported to be ruthless to his enemies. He not only killed anyone in his way but also went after their families. Could she have faked her own death to protect herself and her family from this drug lord? Possibilities clouded Paige's mind.

Remembering that Vanessa had also asked about connections between Morenta and Venezuela, Paige glanced through Morenta's known property holdings and associations. Nothing flagged for Venezuela. In fact, in the psych profile from a few years earlier, the analyst specifically mentioned his paranoia and how specific he was when traveling outside of Cali.

Paige was still browsing through the data in front of her when Vanessa came back in. "What do you have?"

"A lot of information but no ties between Morenta and Venezuela. From what I've read so far, I find it unlikely he would travel there."

"Why do you say that?"

"The psych profile indicates he's paranoid in nature. Venezuela is in a state of unrest, and security is not easy to come by. Those two situations make it highly doubtful Morenta would go there. He also appears to have a very strong network throughout Colombia and parts of Central America and Mexico. I don't see any advantage of him trying to make ties in Venezuela."

"What if he were trying to use the oil industry as a new source of distribution into the United States?"

"That would certainly garner a reason for him to be interested but not enough to visit the country personally. My guess is he would bribe Venezuelan officials to come to him in his villa in Colombia or have them meet him at a neutral site where he feels he could maintain control."

Vanessa fell silent and then held out a hand. "I'll take whatever you've got."

Paige handed it over to her. "Do you want me to keep digging for more information, or should I get back to work on the schedule for next week's class?"

"Actually, I need you to set up an appointment for me. I may need to drive up to DC later today." Vanessa handed Paige a slip of paper with a name and phone number.

Paige goggled at the information in front of her. "You want me to call the deputy director of operations?"

"That's the number for his secretary, Maryanne. Tell her I need a meeting today, whenever Warren is available."

"And if she asks what it's regarding?" Paige asked. She knew CIA culture put everyone on a first-name basis, but she didn't know what to think of the easy way the DDO's name rolled off Vanessa's tongue.

"Just tell her I need more information on Venezuela."

"They said they sent over everything they have."

"You and I both know better than that. There's always something in the need-to-know category, something everyone isn't privy to."

"What if she says no?" Paige asked.

"She won't say no."

Vanessa was right. The secretary didn't say no. In fact, she seemed to know exactly who Vanessa was without any kind of explanation.

"When is Vanessa available?" Maryanne asked.

"She said anytime today, but it will take her a few hours to drive to headquarters."

The woman put her on hold for a moment, presumably to check her boss's calendar. When she came back on, Paige was surprised again by the response. "Tell Vanessa that Warren will meet her at the training center in two hours. We'll give you an update of when he'll need transportation from the helicopter pad when he gets closer."

"I'll tell her," Paige managed to say despite the unexpected answer. She hung up and relayed the information to Vanessa. When her boss seemed to take everything in stride, Paige wondered exactly what Vanessa's background was within the agency to be able to reach into the upper echelons of management so easily.

Though it took a few moments for the facts to process through her mind, Paige found a new understanding of why Vanessa had been selected to teach field operatives. She wasn't just well read in undercover tactics. She was well experienced.

CHAPTER 15

Vanessa stood at the edge of the helicopter pad, dread curling in her stomach. If the deputy director of operations was flying to the training center to talk to her, something must be very wrong.

She thought of Amy's concerns and the shock of finding their husbands' pilot had been murdered. The only real comfort she could cling to was the knowledge that the pilot had indeed made it back to the ship after dropping them off.

She had seen these men in action. So had Amy. They were not the types to be forced to do anything against their will. In fact, one of their specialties was hostage rescue.

The only conclusion for the helicopter making it back safely to the ship without them on it was that they had gotten off voluntarily. So why was Warren Harris making a special trip of nearly two hundred miles to talk to her when they had access to secure phones?

He climbed out of the helicopter, its blades ruffling his short, graying hair. If the extra few pounds around his middle were any indication, Warren's workload still kept him chained to a desk and out of the gym more often than not.

"Warren, you didn't have to fly down here. I would have come to you."

"I didn't want to wait that long." He motioned to her car. "I assume you have somewhere secure that we can talk."

"Yeah." Vanessa slid behind the wheel and waited for him to take the seat beside her. They were both silent on the drive from the helicopter pad to her building, and Vanessa could feel the tension rising as they made their way to the conference room she had reserved.

Warren took the seat across from her and spared her from asking for the real reason he was here. "I have a mission for you."

Vanessa's jaw dropped, and it took her a moment to recover. "Warren, I just called to get the latest intel on Venezuela. I wasn't volunteering to go back into the field. You know I don't do that kind of work anymore."

"You're the only one who can do this particular job."

"Don't start with that kind of talk again. We both know there are plenty of good agents out there. I've trained a decent number of them."

"Yes," Warren agreed, "but you're the only one who's ever seen Morenta, the only one he's ever seen."

"So?"

"So we need someone on the inside."

"What's going on here? I just heard my husband was going after Morenta, and now you're sitting here telling me you want me to do the same." Vanessa leaned forward, her elbows resting against the table. "Was the Saint Squad unsuccessful in apprehending him?"

"We picked up some chatter. Supposedly, Morenta was tipped off that your husband and his squad were coming after him. Indications are that Morenta's men were waiting for them, and the Saint Squad was captured."

She swallowed hard, trying to choke down the implications of what Warren had just said. "All of them?"

"We aren't sure. The only intel we have is an intercepted phone conversation." Warren hesitated before adding, "We also know the pilot of the helicopter that transported them was murdered after returning to the ship."

"I already heard about that," Vanessa admitted. "Do you know who did it?"

"Not yet. They're just beginning their investigation."

"Has the navy at least tried to make contact with the Saint Squad?"

"Not yet. They don't want to take the chance that someone made that phone call to deliberately throw us off. It's possible Morenta's men know the SEALs are there and are trying to intercept a communication."

"So what's your plan?"

"I want you ready to travel. If the Saint Squad doesn't make the rendezvous tonight, we'll send you in to make contact with Morenta."

"What would my cover be? I only saw the man from a distance, and I'd honestly prefer to keep it that way."

"We think we can get him to come to you. You'll travel as Lina Ramir," Warren said, referring to a previous alias she had lived under for more than a year. "Lina's family had some dealings in Maracaibo, which is near where we think Morenta is staying. We think that as soon as he sees you're there, he'll make contact."

"Why would he care about Lina? Her entire family and most of the people who worked with them are in prison."

"Yes, but we're going to plant the rumor that you're starting up the family business again."

"You want me to pose as an arms dealer?"

"That's exactly what I want you to do."

Vanessa contemplated his proposal. Finally, she said, "Okay, I'll do it, but under one condition."

"What's that?"

"You give me forty-eight hours in country before you plant the rumor that I'm running guns. That will give me time to see if I can find my husband and his squad."

"The easiest way to find your husband is to find Morenta."

"Maybe, but I'd like the chance of finding him without throwing myself into the same trap he might be stuck in. I'm not any good to him or his friends if I'm a prisoner too."

Warren fell silent, then said, "I'll do what I can."

"What do you mean you'll do what you can? You're in charge. It's your decision," Vanessa said firmly. "Make it happen."

"You never were an easy one to give orders to, you know that?" Warren nodded his assent. "Get ready to go, and I'll get your travel arranged. If your husband's squad doesn't make contact, you'll fly out first thing in the morning."

"There's one more thing. I'm not waiting to fly down there until tomorrow. I'm leaving today."

He shook his head. "I'm not sending you into an unstable country until we have a reason."

"I know, but I can at least be en route. Send me to Aruba or Curacao. I can insert from there," Vanessa said. "We both know I can't fly straight from the U.S. to Maracaibo anyway."

"Okay, you win. I'll take care of your travel arrangements." He stood. "You'd better go pack."

Vanessa stood as well. "Who's going to be my contact point?"

"With the possibility of a leak, you're stuck with me."

"I'd also like to bring my assistant into the circle of confidence."

"Any particular reason?"

"I already have her looking at reports, but I'd like to have her work at the naval base and act as our liaison," Vanessa told him.

"I don't know . . ."

"Warren, you know how valuable it is to have an assistant you can trust. We both know you'd be lost without Maryanne keeping your schedule organized and all of your intel where you can find it. I need what you have, and Paige is capable of giving it to me."

"Yes, but Maryanne has been working for me for five years," Warren countered. "Your assistant is brand-new."

Vanessa told him what she knew would sway him. "I trust her, Warren."

"If you feel that strongly about it, go ahead. Just make sure she understands the concept of need-to-know." He opened his briefcase and pulled out a thick manila envelope. "Here's your clean cell phone and the latest phone intercepts on Morenta. If you think of anything else you need, give me a call."

"Thanks." Vanessa held up the envelope and started for the door.

"Hey, Vanessa?"

"Yes?"

He shuffled his weight slightly like he wasn't quite sure what he wanted to say. He looked at her. "I hope you find him."

Vanessa nodded. "I hope I don't need to."

* * *

Seth stood at the edge of the river and looked at the surrounding jungle. Upriver he could see cliffs spearing up above the foliage, but behind him all he could see was a thick tangle of trees and undergrowth. He had spent over an hour trying to put together a communications unit out of the pieces of all five of the broken ones. Unfortunately, one of the key components was ruined in all of them.

"What do you think?" Brent stood beside him, his eyes also sweeping the area.

"I think our pilot took a left when he should have taken a right."

"I agree. How in the world did he get the wrong coordinates? There's no way anyone could be this incompetent."

"I don't think its incompetence. It has to be sabotage. All of our transponders are missing, all of our communication gear is busted, and we're a thousand miles away from where we're supposed to be."

"What would anyone have to gain by dumping us out here in the middle of the jungle?"

"Maybe Morenta paid someone off to keep us out of his way."

"Maybe."

Quinn stepped out from behind a thick palm tree. "I think you guys need to see this."

Curious, Seth and Brent followed Quinn along the water until the river curved around to the left and widened. Quinn pointed at the high cliffs in the distance. "Look familiar?"

"Not really," Seth admitted.

"Here. Try looking through these." Quinn handed him his binoculars.

With the image magnified, Seth could now see the white water cascading in a tall, narrow waterfall over the high cliff.

"That's Salto Angel," Quinn said. "Angel Falls. The longest waterfall in the world."

"Which is located where exactly in Venezuela?"

"On the western side of the country near Brazil and Guyana. In other words, this confirms we're on the exact opposite side of the country from where we're supposed to be."

"We're going to have to find a way to hike out of here," Seth said.

"That's the other thing." Quinn paused. "Based on the location of the falls, we're in the western part of Canaima National Park. It's filled with plateau mountains and is only accessible by air."

"There's got to be some way out."

"I came here once after I finished my mission in Caracas. There's an airstrip for bringing in tourists, but from the angle we are to the falls, we're probably a good fifty miles from there. If we watch for planes coming in, though, we should be able to track what direction to head."

"Set up a rotation for lookouts today. If our ride doesn't show up tonight, we'll head for the tourist area."

"That's another thing."

"What?"

"I'm not sure there are flights every day. It may take some time to figure out which direction we need to go."

"In that case, I suggest you do what you can to get your bearings. We can try to head in the general direction until we have a fixed point to focus on."

"I think this would be a good time for all of us to pray for some extra inspiration," Quinn said. "But I'll do what I can."

CHAPTER 16

"I don't understand." Paige watched Vanessa. At Vanessa's instruction, she had followed her back to her home and now stood in her bedroom taking notes while Vanessa packed a suitcase. "I canceled next week's class like you asked me to, but why do you want me to work at the naval base until you get back?"

"You'll be the liaison between the CIA and the navy. We've found from past experience that we work better together in tense situations when we have people working side by side rather than trying to figure out who has the information we need. You'll also communicate with Warren if I run into any problems. If you ever can't get in touch with him right away, call Maryanne."

"Maryanne? His secretary?"

"That's right. She understands the situation well, and you can have her relay information if Warren is ever unavailable."

"I feel like everyone else knows a whole lot more about what's going on than I do," Paige said.

"Not really. Warren and Maryanne have some historical knowledge you aren't privy to, but they are among the very few people at CIA who know my full case file. Warren assigned me to my first long-term assignment. Maryanne was hired on as his assistant while I was undercover, so she ended up in the circle of need-to-know."

Vanessa held up two shirts, studied them briefly, and then packed one and hung the other back up in the closet before she continued. "After you drop me off at the airfield, I want you to report to Commander Kel Bennett. He's the commander for SEAL Team Eight."

"It's already two o'clock. Do you want me to go over today?"

"Yeah. He's going to need some of those intel reports."

"Why didn't you call and give him the information yourself?"

"There are some things I'd rather not discuss on the phone, and I don't want him to have all of this until I'm already en route." Vanessa didn't wait for Paige to question her motives before adding, "Kel Bennett used to command the Saint Squad. He won't want me going after his squad, and I'm not going to waste time convincing him that I'm their best option."

"Does the commander know I'm coming?"

"He will," Vanessa said. "As soon as he finds out I'm going after the Saint Squad, I'm sure he'll want your help."

"Vanessa, I appreciate the trust you seem to have in me, but I'm not an analyst. I don't know what you expect me to do."

"I expect you to be my eyes and ears while I'm away. When I call in, I expect you to have answers to my questions, and if you don't know them, find them."

"I'll do the best I can."

"That's what I wanted to hear." Vanessa closed her suitcase and zipped it shut. Hefting it off her bed, she set it upright and then crossed the room and opened the top drawer of her nightstand. She retrieved a key and a cell phone from inside and handed them to Paige. "Use this cell phone to contact me. Never use yours. I don't want my clean phone to be connected to anyone from the agency."

Vanessa proceeded to give Paige the phone number to program into the memory.

"What's the key for?"

"It's my spare house key. If there's ever a time you lose contact with me or have an emergency, come over here and call the number that's programmed into my phone under number seven."

"Wouldn't it be easier for me to just write down the number?"

"That's not how it works. If you call from any number other than here, the person on the other end won't answer."

"And who would I be calling?" Paige asked.

"A friend. After you make the call, you'll go on a little shopping spree, and my friend will give you further instructions."

"You definitely live an interesting life."

"Hopefully, we won't have to use any of the precautions Seth and I have put in place." Vanessa closed her fingers around the handle of the suitcase and added, "My husband tends to be a little paranoid."

"It sounds like he has reason to be."

"I guess we'll see soon enough. Let's go."

* * *

"Did anyone find anything?" Amy asked as she entered the boardroom.

"Maybe," Commander Dunnan said. "We did find a few traces of blood near the scene and more near the fantail of the ship."

"Was anyone seen there last night?"

"One of the night watchmen said he saw movement in that area but couldn't say who it was."

"Does he know when?" Amy asked.

"He said it was only about forty-five minutes after the helicopter returned." Commander Dunnan handed her a preliminary report. "He also said it looked like a man, and he wasn't wearing a uniform."

"A civilian?"

"That's right, but it's possible he changed his clothes to throw everyone off in case he was spotted."

"If it was someone in the military, we'll have a hard time narrowing it down." Amy rolled this latest information over in her mind. "How many civilians are on board right now?"

"That's the thing. Besides you, we only had five civilians on board when the pilot was murdered. Three of them were working together upgrading our communications software."

"And the other two?"

"They were preparing to leave the ship. They hopped a COD twenty minutes before the body was found," he said, referring to the carrier onboard delivery aircraft that were used to transport people to and from the ship.

Amy hadn't considered that the murderer could have possibly left the ship so quickly. "Who were they?"

"Derrick Hazelwood and Terrance Gunning. Gunning was only aboard ship that day. Hazelwood was here for six days helping with maintenance on our F-14s."

"What was Gunning here for?"

"I'm honestly not sure," Commander Dunnan said. "He was cleared by someone in the Pentagon. My guess is he was with intelligence."

"I'll check it out. Thanks."

"Let me know what you find."

"I will." Amy waited for him to leave and then picked up her phone. She tried to take the direct route by calling Vanessa, surprised to find that Vanessa didn't answer her call.

Resigned to follow normal procedures, she logged on and sent several e-mails to various contacts within the intelligence community, requesting information on Terrance Gunning. She tried to get comfortable in her chair despite the worry eating at her. Answers would come eventually, and she was determined to wait at her computer until they arrived.

* * *

"Everything is going as planned."

"What's happening with the SEALs?" Morenta asked the woman beside him.

"My guess is they're sitting around waiting for someone to show up and get them, assuming they're still alive."

"I thought I made it clear that I wanted an assurance that they're dead."

"If the poison in their food doesn't get them, the jungle will. They're more than fifty miles from the closest village. There's no way they'll be able to find their way out of there," she said. "They'll die eventually, but it will be slow and painful. I thought you'd like that."

"Don't underestimate them. These are the same men who ruined years' worth of planning the last time we crossed paths," Morenta said.

"Even if they don't eat their food and can find their way to the airport, they won't be able to leave Canaima without us knowing about it."

"Maybe you should consider a challenge for them that goes beyond trudging through the jungle."

"What kind of challenge?" she asked.

"Perhaps one that would include dodging bullets from a Venezuelan fighter plane."

"How would the pilots find them?"

"Like you said, they're probably sitting around waiting for their ride."

* * *

Damian spent three unproductive hours with NCIS at the rappelling tower, going over every detail of that terrifying day the week before. According to Larry Steinert, the lead investigator, NCIS was still trying to identify everyone who had come onto the base in the two weeks prior to the incident, but because of the holidays, it was unlikely they would be able to use that resource to identify any suspects.

Steinert also confirmed that the only fingerprints found on the damaged area of the rappelling tower belonged to Brent, who had picked up a piece of it. The lack of other physical evidence suggested the culprit wore gloves, but little else was known about his or her identity or motive.

After NCIS dismissed him, Damian stopped at the mess hall for lunch before returning to his office. Already, he was dreading the paperwork Kel had assigned him. The idea of reading someone else's mission reports and debriefings set him on edge. He should be in the field right now, not reading about what others did.

He stopped to check in with Kel but found he wasn't in his office. He continued down the hall to the office he shared with Tristan and Quinn. His teammates' desks were evenly spaced and faced the door; his own desk was shoved into the corner next to the printer table. He sighed. His office was just one more reminder that his team had yet to make room for him.

He unlocked the vaulted safe where he had secured the file Kel had given him. Taking the file to his desk, he flipped it open and started reading. What he had expected to be boring paperwork instantly caught his attention. This wasn't just any case file. It was one of his own squad's mission reports from several years earlier, or rather, it was from the original Saint Squad.

Kel had been in command of the squad at the time, and Jay had not yet joined them. The mission had been for Seth to make contact with a CIA operative in the Dominican Republic, a woman he had known previously. Damian started to lean back in his chair to get more comfortable only to bolt upright when he saw the name of the operative: Vanessa Lauton. Could that be Seth's wife?

Damian was completely engaged in the reports when a knock sounded. He looked up to see Paige standing in the doorway.

"Sorry to interrupt."

Damian stood and dropped the file on his desk. "Hi, Paige. What are you doing here?"

"Apparently we're going to be working together. Kel said I should take one of the desks in here."

Before Damian could question her further, Kel walked in. "Oh, good, Damian, you're back." He closed the office door and motioned for everyone to sit. Paige set her purse and the files she carried on Tristan's desk and lowered herself into Tristan's chair. Kel wheeled Quinn's chair closer so he was sitting between Damian and Paige.

"We've got a situation, and you are two of the few who will have access to all of the information."

"What's going on?" Damian asked, noticing some tension in Kel's voice.

"We have intel reports of a phone conversation between Morenta and one of his men that indicates they have captured the Saint Squad."

"Captured? No way." Damian shook his head.

Kel didn't give his opinion, but Damian could tell by the expression on his face that he wasn't sold on this intel either.

"Where was their insertion point?" Paige asked.

"Thirty miles inland of Maracaibo, Venezuela," Kel said. The muscle in his jaw tensed before he added, "The pilot who dropped them off in Venezuela was murdered shortly after returning to the ship, so we don't have anyone who can verify their status when they inserted."

"Their pilot is dead?" Paige asked incredulously.

"I'm afraid so. If the Saint Squad really is missing, I have to think the two situations are related."

"Kel, you've known them all a lot longer than I have. Do you think there's any way the whole squad could have been captured?" Damian asked.

"Not unless they were surrounded the moment they were dropped off. Even then, it's unlikely," Kel admitted. "My concern is the report that the transponder on the helicopter stopped functioning right before it entered Venezuelan airspace. The navy has no way to verify if they were even dropped at the correct coordinates."

"What are we going to do? Has anyone tried communicating with them?"

"Brent was supposed to check in after landing, and that never happened. Right now, we're hoping that when the helicopter goes in to extract them tonight, this will all prove to be a false alarm."

"But you want us to be prepared in case it isn't," Damian surmised.

"Exactly. It's already getting late, so for today, just familiarize yourself with the file. I want you both here tomorrow at oh six hundred. If they don't make the rendezvous, we have to come up with some options."

"Got it."

"And make sure you get some sleep tonight. If things don't go well, it will be a long day tomorrow."

CHAPTER 17

Amy wasn't surprised that the CIA was the first to respond to her inquiry about Terrance Gunning, but the source of the phone call she received stunned her.

Warren Harris, the deputy director of operations, called personally to give her the man's background. "Terrance Gunning was in the navy for six years. He left the military and began working as a civilian contractor for naval intelligence four years ago."

"If he's only worked for the navy, I'm surprised the CIA has any information on him."

"He applied to work for us when he left military life, but he didn't make it through our initial screening."

"May I ask why?"

"His foreign language skills were limited to Spanish, so professionally, he wasn't a good fit. At the time, we weren't looking for specialists in Latin America. Personally, his debt level was higher than it should have been, and his psych profile showed some areas of concern."

"Like?"

"I guess you could call it the James Bond syndrome. He had a glorified view of what CIA life is like, and his spending habits indicated image was his priority."

"Do you have any idea why he was aboard the *Truman* yesterday?"

"I don't. One of my people contacted the Pentagon, and no one seems to know who actually authorized his travel. We think he may have managed to put in a ghost travel order."

"Meaning he authorized it himself."

"Exactly," Warren confirmed. "He also hasn't been to work since leaving the ship."

"Does anyone know where he is?"

"Negative. My people checked the GPS signals on his phone and car to find both were at his apartment, but when I sent someone over there, he was nowhere to be found."

"Great," Amy muttered.

"I'll let you know if we find anything else out."

"I did have one more question for you."

"What's that?" Warren asked.

"Have you heard from Vanessa Johnson lately? I tried calling her, and she's not answering."

"I'm afraid she's going to be out of touch for a few days."

"I see." Amy understood the unspoken message. "Thank you for all of the information. Please let me know if you locate Terrance Gunning."

"I will. Same goes for you."

Amy took down his number, hung up the phone, and did the only thing she could think of. She prayed for everyone she cared about to return safely home.

* * *

"Do you think they're all right?" Paige asked after an hour of silently reviewing files.

"I think so." Damian hoped he sounded more confident than he felt. He thought back to Kel's explanation of why he had been left behind and the way the commander had said he had been worried about the mission. He was now starting to believe that maybe it wasn't his skills that had been called into question. Maybe it really was the risk level of the assignment. At the moment, that idea was more unsettling than his original impression that he'd been found wanting.

Damian looked up at the clock on the wall. "We should probably call it a night. Did you want to go out and grab something to eat?"

"I think I'm too nervous to sit in a restaurant right now," Paige said. "I was thinking about ordering in. Do you want to come over, and we can call in some Chinese food?"

Damian thought about it for a minute, a little surprised at how quickly he had come to expect he would spend his free time with Paige. "That sounds good. I could use something to keep my mind off all of this."

"I know what you mean." Paige gathered the papers she had been working with and put them into file folders. "Do you have a vault in here where we can secure the classified documents?"

"Yeah, over here." Damian opened the second drawer of the vaulted safe beside his desk and secured his documents as well as hers. "It will take me a few minutes to lock up. If you tell me what you want, I can call in our order and pick it up on my way over."

"I like anything that doesn't have bell peppers in it."

"Why would anyone put bell peppers in Chinese food?"

"I have no idea, but some people do." Paige slipped the strap of her purse over her shoulder. "Just order a couple of things you like, and we can share."

"Okay. I'll meet you at your place in about a half hour."

"Sounds good. Thanks." Paige left the office, and Damian finished securing everything in the room. He looked at his teammates' desks. Though they had only been together for a short time, he could almost hear Tristan telling him with that Texan drawl not to worry or Quinn teasing him about how he shouldn't be standing around thinking about them when he had a chance to go out with a beautiful woman.

Damian tried to take the imagined advice, but somewhere in the back of his mind, he heard a whisper of one more thing they would expect him to do. He crossed the room to close the door Paige had left open, folded his arms, and offered a heartfelt prayer.

* * *

Paige waited for Damian. There were still boxes to unpack and clothes to put away, but she couldn't seem to focus long enough to do anything beyond setting the table.

The images of what Damian's squad could be going through right now kept running through her head, frightening images of torture and even death. She didn't know these men well, but she didn't have to for those possibilities to leave her uneasy. She also couldn't shake the guilty feeling of relief in knowing Damian was still here safe and sound. Although *sound* was a relative term. Clearly, the uncertainty of his friends' fate was wearing on him.

She looked over at the clock on the stove to see he was already fifteen minutes late. Now a new set of emotions crept through her. Had he decided he didn't want to be around her tonight?

Three more minutes passed as she paced back and forth across her apartment. Her stomach growled, reminding her that in the confusion of getting Vanessa ready to leave, she had missed lunch.

She was debating eating a snack when she finally heard Damian's truck pull up outside. Even though she knew it made her seem anxious, she met him at the door, pulling it open as he came up the walk. "I was starting to get worried about you."

"I'm not the one you need to be worried about."

She heard the remorse in his voice and found she couldn't begin to imagine the anguish he must be feeling right now. She stepped aside to let him in and followed him to the table, where he set the paper bag of Chinese food.

Determined to be positive for Damian's sake, Paige waited for him to set the food out. When he turned, a troubled expression on his face, she followed instinct and stepped forward, slipping her arms around his waist.

She saw the surprise on his face but noticed he didn't hesitate to encircle her with his arms and return the hug. He pulled her tightly against him as though the gesture of comfort was a lifeline he had been grasping for without knowing it.

A combination of emotions took her breath away. She caught the lingering scent of Chinese food on his clothes, felt the stubble on his chin rub against her hair, and couldn't stop the unexpected ripple of pleasure at finding she fit so well in his arms. Contrasting those sensations was the tangible worry in the air.

"I'm sorry everything is so unsettled right now. You have every right to be worried," Paige said softly.

"I thought you were going to tell me not to worry and that everything will be okay."

"I hope everything will be okay. I pray it will, but worrying is normal, and I doubt you'll be able to stop no matter what I say."

Damian shifted back slightly so he could see her face. "I'm sorry I was late."

"It's okay." Her lips curved slightly. "I was just worried about you."

His own lips twitched into the beginnings of a smile. "Come on. Let's eat while it's still hot. I'm sure you're going to tell me I have to keep up my strength."

"That sounds like something I would say." She took a step back and let her arms drop back to her side.

Damian pulled a chair out for her and waited for her to sit before taking the chair across from her. "You know, I'm never quite sure what to expect when I'm around you."

"You don't know me very well yet."

"That's true, but I'm starting to realize that I want to."

"I'd like that." Paige watched Damian open the cartons of Chinese food and dish some out for both of them. When their eyes met again, she gave him the words she felt he needed to hear. "We are going to find them."

"You're right. We are." Damian gave her a determined look. "Whatever it takes."

* * *

A light rain drizzled down on the five figures perched on the edge of the landing zone. The cloud cover hid any moonlight that might have otherwise illuminated the wide clearing.

"Do you think anyone will show up?" Quinn asked from his position beside Seth.

"Only one way to find out." Seth glanced at his watch. "Five more minutes. Even you can wait that long, Quinn."

"We've already waited twenty-four hours."

Seth heard the rumble of an engine and lifted his binoculars. "I hear an aircraft."

"Commercial flights don't come into Canaima at night," Quinn said optimistically.

"Our guys would come in dark. I see lights."

"I agree," Brent said, shifting to stand beside them.

"It's your call, Brent. What are your orders?"

"Stand fast. Let's see what happens."

The helicopter closed the distance, slowing a half mile before reaching the clearing. A beam of light swept out over the landing zone.

"Something is not right," Seth said.

The words were barely out of his mouth when gunfire burst through the air, strafing the five forms in the clearing, punishing them until there weren't any left standing. Bullets continued flying through the air for several more seconds, an exclamation point on the pilot's determination to make sure the men were dead. Then, as quickly as it had appeared, the helicopter circled and headed back the way it had come.

"Well, that was overkill," Brent said, stepping out from behind the boulders where his squad had taken cover.

Strewn across the clearing were the shredded clothing and palm leaves that had been stuffed into them to make it appear as though the squad was standing by the landing zone.

"I guess it's safe to say they weren't here to pick us up," Tristan said.

"Good thing they didn't get close enough to notice it wasn't us standing out there," Seth added.

"Salvage whatever you can of your spare clothes," Brent said.

"Not much chance of that." Jay lifted a shirt that had been shredded by the bullets.

"Better your shirt than you," Seth reminded him. "The good news is that whoever was after us thinks we're dead."

Tristan kicked a coconut on the ground. "Yeah, but we're still trapped out here in the middle of the jungle."

"Not for long," Brent said firmly. "Come on. Let's head back to camp and get some sleep. We'll set out at first light."

CHAPTER 18

Vanessa read the encrypted message on her cell phone, the message confirming her fears. Her husband was missing.

She refused to consider the possibility that she wouldn't see him again but rather relied on a combination of hope, prayer, and uncertainty to push her forward to prepare for her flight.

She had to leave Vanessa Johnson behind when she walked out of this room. She would be Lina Ramir, as she had been when she had first seen Morenta.

Her hands trembled slightly as she looped a scarf around her neck. She took a moment to harness her emotions, reminding herself to have faith that Seth would be okay when she found him. Not finding him wasn't an option. She knew it, and so did Warren. She would either come back with Seth, or she wouldn't come back at all.

With one last check in the mirror to make sure her transformation was complete, she picked up her purse and rolled her suitcase to the door of her hotel room.

A car was waiting for her when she exited the building, and Vanessa let the driver see to her bag. Then, with an air of arrogance and wealth, she slid into the backseat and tried to pretend she didn't have a care in the world.

* * *

"I don't care what you think I need to know. I want it all," Kel said into the phone. "And I want it now."

Damian and Paige stood just outside his office, both torn over whether to enter.

"Don't just stand there," Kel said, slamming his desk phone back onto the receiver. "Come in."

Damian led the way but waited for Paige to claim a seat before sitting beside her. "I gather things didn't go as planned last night."

"You're right. There wasn't any sign of them at their designated rendezvous point. When he didn't see them, the pilot who tried to pick them up broke radio silence but didn't receive a response."

"What about their emergency signals? Were any activated?"

"Not one."

"This really doesn't make any sense." Damian shifted forward in his seat and rested his arms on his knees.

Kel studied Damian and Paige, then said, "I've been working on a theory I want the two of you to help me explore."

"What's that?" Damian asked.

"I think I already mentioned that the ship wasn't able to track the helicopter that dropped them off because the transponder wasn't working properly."

"What about it?"

"Let's assume it was switched off deliberately and that the pilot was murdered to keep him from talking."

"You think the pilot took them somewhere else," Damian said, following Kel's logic.

"I had Amy work with the flight crew of the helicopter. They verified that there weren't any bullet holes or any evidence of a firefight."

"So you think the Saint Squad made the drop thinking they were at the right location and then were captured?"

"I'm still not convinced on the captured part. I think if Morenta really had them, we'd be hearing demands by now. Besides, I'm sure they prayed before they left on this mission. I'd like to believe the Lord is looking out for them."

At Paige's confused expression, Damian explained, "They're all Mormon. They have this thing about praying every morning before they do anything else."

"All of them?" Paige asked, clearly surprised.

"Actually, I am too," Kel said. "That's how the squad got its name. *Saint* comes from 'Latter-day Saint.'"

"I never realized that," Paige said.

Kel changed the subject and handed Damian a rolled-up map and a handful of notes. "I want you to look over this map and project a range of where the helicopter could have dropped them in the time he was off our radar. Remember, we can't be certain he even dropped them in Venezuela. It could have been at one of the nearby islands or even a neighboring country."

"Do you have the specs on the helicopter, positions, and time it was off grid?"

"It's all in there. I know you haven't lived in Venezuela for a long time, but I also want you to see if you can narrow down other locations within range that could have been mistaken for their drop site."

"Actually, I traveled there a lot the year before I joined the navy."

"Even better. I know it's a long shot, but maybe if we can find out how Morenta is tied to Venezuela, we can pinpoint where they might have been dropped off."

"I'll do what I can." Damian stood.

"Is there anything in particular you want me to work on?" Paige asked, also standing.

"I guess just keep reviewing the intel reports we already have. What we really need is an updated psychological profile on Morenta to see how likely it is that he's the one behind all of this. Unfortunately, that will take time, and that's one thing we don't have a lot of."

"I can do it," Paige said, although she didn't sound too confident in the assertion.

"A psych profile?" Kel asked. "Do you have any experience with that kind of thing? I thought you were a nurse."

"I'm a psychiatric nurse, but I also interned with the FBI during college. Two of those summers, I worked in profiling."

Apparently pleased with her answer, Kel said, "In that case, that's where you can start. Both of you get to work."

Damian led Paige down the hall to his office. As soon as they were inside, he said, "I didn't know you were a psych nurse before you came here. Why the change of careers?"

"After four years of trying to help people work through their problems, I realized it was starting to wear on me. Dealing with mental illness and trauma is emotionally exhausting."

"You don't look old enough to have worked as a nurse for that long."

"I started when I was nineteen. My high school had a nursing program, and I took summer classes at the community college starting when I was sixteen. With all of that, it didn't take me long to finish my credentials."

"I didn't realize you were one of those overachiever types."

"I'm not really. I just like understanding what's going on around me." Damian heard the undertones of some hidden meaning in her words, but she shut the door on the conversation when she said, "We'd better get to work."

Damian unrolled the map and pasted it on the huge whiteboard on the wall near the door. He stared at the country of his birth and considered Kel's theory and the possible reasons behind why someone would want to capture or strand the Saint Squad. The more he thought about it, the more confused he became.

"This doesn't make any sense," he said. "First someone tries to kill one of us, and now my teammates are either lost or captured? I think I'm a curse for this squad."

"You aren't a curse," Paige began, but then her mind must have caught up with the rest of his comment. "What do you mean someone tried to kill you?"

Damian hesitated, realizing he had said too much.

"Don't start holding things back now." She put her hands on her hips and took a firm tone Damian wasn't used to hearing from her. "We need all of the pieces on the table, and you know it."

Damian dropped into his seat. "There was a training accident a couple weeks ago. In fact, it was the day I met you."

"That's what you were all hiding from Vanessa." Her eyes flashed with the connection, but Damian was pleased that condemnation didn't accompany it.

"Yeah. Seth didn't want her to know about it."

"Why not?"

"I'm not sure. I guess he didn't want to worry her." Damian lifted both hands helplessly. "I'm the only guy on the squad who isn't married, so I'm afraid the whole husband-wife thing is pretty foreign to me."

"I know what you mean," Paige said. "What exactly happened that day we met? I gather if you think someone tried to kill one of you that it wasn't really an accident."

"No, it wasn't an accident. NCIS agrees that it was sabotage, but they don't have any idea who was behind it." Damian proceeded to tell her about the events of that day, leaving out his complete terror when he thought he and Jay were going to plunge forty feet to their deaths.

Paige listened intently. When Damian finished his account, Paige asked, "If someone wanted to target one of you, why use sabotage when there would be no way to be sure who the victim would be?"

"Maybe they just wanted someone to die, and they didn't care who. It could have been some sort of revenge."

"Maybe," Paige conceded, looking like she was trying to wrap her mind around a motive. She set her oversized purse down on her desk. "I think you're right on one thing."

"What's that?"

"None of this makes any sense."

* * *

"Are you sure you know where you're going?" Seth asked as he followed Quinn through a particularly dense section of jungle.

"Well, no, Seth. I don't," Quinn retorted. "In case you've forgotten, we don't have a map, and we're in the middle of a jungle."

"Just asking," Seth said.

"Ignore him." Tristan fell into step beside Seth. "You know he gets grumpy when he's hungry."

"Quinn's always hungry."

"Not always," Quinn said, the banter apparently taking the edge off his frustration . . . or at least distracting him from his never-ending hunger. He held his compass in front of him and veered slightly to the left. "Maybe we should try to find the river and follow it to the tourist area. It will take longer, but at least we'll know where we're going."

"Hey, quiet down, you two," Brent called out, raising his hand to silence them.

Everyone stopped. The silence was the first thing Seth noticed. No longer did he hear the chatter of birds in the trees or the movement of the various animals inhabiting the area. Then the rumble of a helicopter sounded in the distance.

"You don't think that's our friends from last night, do you?"

"I don't think so." Brent looked up, but the dense evergreen trees above them made it impossible to see the sky, except in tiny patches. "Jay, get up one of those trees and see what's out there."

"How come I'm always the one who has to go up a tree?" Jay said, but he moved to the nearest one and started shimmying up the branches.

No one answered his question. They simply waited until he'd made it high enough to report. "It looks like a recreational craft, probably a tourist helicopter."

"Where's it headed?"

"Looks like an overflight of the falls." Jay hooked an arm around the tree trunk and kept his eyes on the sky.

"I hate to do this to you, Jay, but stay up there until you can see where it lands. That's where we're heading," Brent said.

"Okay."

"Tristan and Quinn, go see if you can round up some food for us."

"I already took care of that," Tristan announced. He opened up his pack and held up a pineapple.

"Where'd you get this?"

"We picked them this morning when we went to fill up our canteens."

"Them?"

"I have one more, and Quinn has a couple in his pack," Tristan said. "After what happened last night, I figured you wouldn't want us to start a fire if we could help it."

"You were right about that." Brent tossed the pineapple to Seth, who drew his knife and cut away the skin of the pineapple. He then sliced it into chunks and handed everyone a section, reserving one for Jay.

"Hey, it looks like it's landing."

"Can you figure out coordinates?"

"A direction at least." Jay waited another minute before beginning his descent. Once his feet were on the ground, he said, "I think we're only about thirty or forty miles from where it landed."

Seth heard the hesitation in Jay's voice. "But?"

"The terrain isn't going to be easy to cross. We'll have a river in our path, and there's a nasty-looking mountain a couple miles from here."

"At least we know what direction we're heading," Tristan said.

Jay accepted the wedge of pineapple Seth handed him. "I don't suppose any of you brought any climbing gear, did you?"

"I'm afraid not. Just some rope." Brent took a step in the direction Jay indicated. "We'll figure out a way around, one way or another."

"As long as it doesn't involve me climbing any more trees."

CHAPTER 19

"The commander of SEAL Team Eight has been digging," Terrance said, concern in his voice.

"Let him dig," Andrea said calmly.

"What if he finds something that leads back to us?"

"He won't. I've made sure there's nothing to find. Since we tricked Morenta into going after the Saint Squad for us, all clues will lead back to him."

"This is a dangerous game you're playing."

"You know I tend to live on the edge." Andrea gave him a sultry smile. "That's what you love about me."

"Yeah, but I'm starting to look forward to this all being over." Terrance raked his fingers through his hair. "It was bad enough when we had to deal with Rodrigo. I rather hoped Morenta would never learn our names."

"Rodrigo's nothing more than Morenta's watchdog, but you can bet anything that if one of them knows, the other one knows too. Neither of them has a clue what we're really up to." Andrea gave him a smug look. "Don't worry. It won't be much longer now."

* * *

Paige jotted down notes from the various files she read on Morenta, everything from his business associates to his favorite foods. She had come prepared today with a purse full of office supplies, expecting to spend most of her time analyzing data. It didn't take long for her to decide that getting inside the mind of a drug lord wasn't a place she wanted to be.

Her various colored sticky notes were arranged across the desk she now knew to be Tristan's, each color representing a different aspect of her subject's life, from his family and business dealings to his favorite foods and travel patterns.

On his side of the room, Damian muttered to himself in Spanish as he worked through the mathematical equations to figure out the range of the helicopter two nights earlier. He had clipped the map to the front of a large whiteboard, along with a photo of what the real landing zone looked like.

When Paige had too many sticky notes on her desk to organize them easily, she stood and started hanging them in the empty space on the wall beside her. A picture was beginning to take shape in her mind, but she had even more questions now than she did before she had started.

"Have you found anything that ties Morenta to anywhere in Venezuela?" Damian asked.

"No, nothing." She watched Damian pick up a string, fix it to the point on the map where the helicopter's transponder had stopped working, and tie a pen to the other end of the string. "What are you doing?"

"Establishing our search area." Damian took the cap off the pen and stretched the string out, using it to guide him as he drew a thick red circle on the map. He took a step back and stared. "We're going to need more clues than what we've got so far. There's way too much area to cover here."

"Am I reading this right? Does that take in all of Venezuela?"

"Almost, along with parts of Colombia, Guyana, Brazil, and at least a dozen islands in the Caribbean," Damian said, frustrated.

Discouragement seeped into Paige's voice. "That's a lot of area to cover."

"Exactly."

"Wait. You said part of the search area is in Colombia, right?"

"Yeah." Damian pointed at the upper tip of the country.

"That's where Morenta's from. Maybe they were dropped off there."

"It's possible," Damian admitted. He looked at the photograph of the landing zone and then back at the map. "You know, if we assume that the squad got off the helicopter voluntarily, we would be able to eliminate the islands. They might not know exactly where they were heading while en route, especially if they were going over their mission on the way, but they'd be able to tell if they were inserting onto an island."

"Are you sure? Some of those islands are pretty good sized."

"I know, but their flight plan was supposed to take them over land for a good hour. Even though they were supposed to insert only thirty miles from shore, in order to avoid detection, they were supposed to go inland and then circle back to the drop zone. None of those islands are large enough for them to be over land for that long, and someone would have noticed if they were over the ocean the whole time."

"That makes sense."

Damian set the string and pen on his desk. "I'm going to go tell Kel what I have so far. I'll be back in a minute."

"Okay." Paige turned back to the blue, orange, yellow, purple, and green sticky notes now decorating the wall.

From all reports, Morenta was ruthless in every aspect of his life. He demanded complete loyalty from his family and employees, and disobedience was dealt with severely, often fatally. His motivations appeared to be money and power, and he equated respect with fear. Everything so far confirmed the information Paige had read in the last psych analysis on him.

She thought of the mission reports she had reviewed from when the Saint Squad had previously crossed paths with the man. When Damian came back into the office, Kel was right behind him.

Kel took one look at the sticky notes on the wall and asked, "What's all this?"

"The beginnings of a psych profile." Paige leaned back against her desk. "Do you think Morenta could have set up some elaborate plan to lure the Saint Squad to him so he could get even with them? They did interfere in some of his smuggling routes a couple years back."

"I saw that too," Damian said, "but I don't know how he would gain access to the Saint Squad's identities."

"It's possible he did," Kel said quickly. "He was working with an arms dealer at the time, a man named Akil Ramir. I was shot when we were making an extraction, and we think Ramir saw a newspaper article about my injury. It's possible he shared the information with Morenta."

"We're working with too many what ifs," Damian said.

"I agree. That's why we need the psych profile, to figure out if Morenta is really capable of fixating on revenge."

Paige felt that uncomfortable burning sensation in her chest, the same one that always came when she knew a wrong analysis could be life altering. She looked at her notes again and tried to let her training and experience overcome her fears. "From what I've gathered so far, he runs his organization using fear as a main motivator. I suppose if he feels he's being seen as weak, it's feasible he could strike out for revenge."

"You don't sound convinced," Kel said.

"That's because I'm not," Paige admitted. "Even if he managed to find out the identities of the squad, I have a hard time believing he could recruit multiple people to carry this off. If he didn't have any problem with the pilot being murdered, why wouldn't his people just shoot down the helicopter in the first place?"

"Good point," Kel conceded.

"The other question is whether or not their disappearance has anything to do with what happened at the rappelling tower," Damian said.

"It's possible, but I don't see a connection," Kel said. "NCIS still hasn't found a viable suspect, much less a motive."

"We were talking about that," Damian said. "Why try to kill someone that way when you can't be sure who your victim will be?"

"Maybe they were trying to disable the squad so they couldn't go on this mission," Paige suggested.

"I don't think so." Kel shook his head. "If they couldn't go, we would have sent another squad."

Paige considered this information. "What would Morenta or anyone gain if someone on the Saint Squad died or was seriously injured?"

"I don't know. When I was injured, the squad was in the middle of a mission, the same mission that shut down Morenta's drug routes into the U.S. A new person was assigned, and they kept doing their jobs."

"Could the sabotage at the rappelling tower have taken out more than one person in the squad?" Paige asked.

"Maybe two, but like Kel said, the squad would still be able to keep functioning. Worst case, Kel would assign a couple of people from another squad to stand in."

"For whatever reason, it looks like whoever detoured them on this mission needs them alive," she concluded.

"You think they're trying to get information from them rather than go for revenge?" Damian asked.

"They wouldn't be very good candidates," Kel said. "Navy SEALs are trained to be mentally tough. They wouldn't be easy to break down."

"And why would they try to kill someone one week and then capture them a week later?" Damian asked.

Kel leaned back against Quinn's desk. "Maybe the two things aren't related after all."

"Or maybe it isn't someone on the Saint Squad who's the target," Paige suggested.

"What do you mean?"

"Could someone be using the Saint Squad to draw someone else out into the open?"

"Like who?"

"I don't know." Paige shrugged. "Someone who would come to a funeral for a squad member or to the hospital if someone was injured."

"And someone who would go after them if they got caught behind enemy lines." A sense of urgency filled Kel's voice. "Do you have a way to get in touch with Vanessa?"

"Vanessa?" Paige asked. "Why would someone use the Saint Squad to get to her?"

"Because she was deep undercover when I met her, and she's been out of the game since then. The only way to find her without having direct access in the CIA would be to get to her through her husband."

"Or her husband's friends," Paige said, her understanding growing. She pulled out the secure cell phone Vanessa had given her so they could communicate and called the number. "It went straight to voice mail."

"She won't turn on her phone until she's ready to call you," Kel told her. "Leave a message. Tell her she's the target."

Paige left the message, the color draining from her face. As soon as she hung up, she asked, "What happens if I can't reach her in time?"

"Pray that you can."

CHAPTER 20

Vanessa felt eyes following her the moment she stepped into the airport terminal in Maracaibo. Her training prevented her from reacting to the knowledge that she was being watched, but her mind raced. How could anyone know she was here? Why would anyone even care?

Vanessa had changed planes and identities several times on her way to Aruba, the most recent switch occurring in Panama City. Even though she had adopted her old alias Lina Ramir for this most recent flight, it was doubtful anyone would be able to track her down that quickly. She had purchased her ticket at the airport counter, and the flight had been less than an hour long.

She pulled her carry-on behind her, debating whether she should keep walking through the terminal or duck into the restroom, knowing she would be trapped.

She kept walking, her eyes casually scanning the area. It took her several sweeps of the terminal to identify the problem. The woman dressed as a custodian caught her eye. For a brief moment, Vanessa saw her watching her beneath lowered lashes as she went about changing the liner of a trash can. The action itself was innocent enough, but Vanessa sensed an awareness in the woman that piqued her suspicion.

Not seeing a lot of options, Vanessa headed for customs. She studied the other passengers, choosing to stay close to a family of five, the three children all under the age of four.

Anticipating that they might need some help to get through the checkpoint, Vanessa dug her passport out of her bag and got into the line, which was still six people deep. As she did so, she shifted her body so she could check out the custodian.

Her heartbeat quickened when she saw that the woman was no longer visible, even though the trash bag she had just emptied was still tied up and sitting on the floor beside the can.

The line moved, and Vanessa indulged in another quick sweep of her surroundings. Again, she didn't see the woman anywhere.

Vanessa reminded herself to stay calm. She was in a public place with plenty of people around. All she had to do was be smart and not let herself get cornered.

The woman in front of her juggled the baby on her hip so she could dig for her passport. Unable to easily retrieve her documents, she shifted the diaper bag to her husband, who was forced to let go of their two-year-old's hand. Almost as though he'd been waiting for the opportunity, the little boy tried to dart away as soon as his hand was free.

Vanessa spoke in Spanish when she scooped him up. "Hold on there. Your mama won't want you running off."

The little boy gave her a mischievous grin and pointed at the window, despite a sippy cup in one hand. "Plane."

"Yes, that's a plane."

The woman turned to see her son in a stranger's arms. "Oh, I'm so sorry."

"It's okay." Vanessa didn't release him. Instead, she motioned toward the customs agent. "You have your hands full. If you want, I'll hold him until we get through customs."

The woman clearly debated for a second, but when her infant started squirming, she gratefully accepted the offer. "Thank you. I appreciate the help."

The woman's husband looked understandably protective of his young family, and instead of letting Vanessa fall into line behind him, he and his oldest son shifted behind Vanessa so she was flanked by the two parents.

Vanessa handed her passport over to the customs officer and took advantage of being concealed so she could look around for the custodian again.

Her heart sank when she noticed the woman standing beside two policemen. Her training could help her keep from getting cornered by another civilian, but taking on two armed police officers wasn't likely to end well. Even if she could escape them, she would undoubtedly end up in the public eye.

From where she stood among the throngs of people in the customs lines, she could stay hidden by the crowds. Once she passed through, she would be easy to spot.

She had to change her appearance somehow, at least long enough to slip past the custodian and police.

The toddler in her arms pointed at the planes again, and once more, she noticed the cup in his hand. She jiggled him on her hip slightly and heard liquid sloshing against the lid.

Taking another quick survey of her surroundings, she saw the boy's mother still had her attention on the baby, but the father was watching her closely.

Rather than try to distract him to put her plan in play, she took the opposite approach. "Are you from here?" she asked the father.

"No. We live in Mexico. We're here to visit my wife's parents."

"I'm sure they must be excited to see their grandchildren."

"Very much," the man replied politely, though he still seemed wary.

Keeping her eyes on the father, she put one hand on the cup as though keeping the boy from flailing it around. While continuing with the small talk, she slowly managed to unscrew the lid.

When the customs officer finished reviewing their documents, Vanessa reached out to retrieve hers, deliberately spilling the contents of the boy's cup all over her shirt and jacket. From the scent, she guessed it was apple juice.

"Oh no." Vanessa said the words quietly enough that it didn't draw too much attention to her. "I'm sorry. The cup spilled."

"You're drenched. I am so sorry." The mother turned to face Vanessa. "I don't know how that happened."

"It was just an accident." Vanessa continued forward a few feet so they could get out of everyone's way.

"What can I do to help?" the mother said.

"I think if I can just get my other jacket out of my bag, I'll be fine."

The husband stepped forward to help too, taking his son from Vanessa so she could shed her scarf and sweater. Ignoring the wetness that had seeped into the plain white T-shirt she had worn beneath her sweater, she pulled out a black jacket and slipped it on. She then dug out another scarf and used it to tie back her hair.

Wrapping the soiled clothes in a wad, she stuffed them into her suitcase, zipped it closed, and stood up. "Thanks for your help."

"Thank you for yours. I'm really sorry about your clothes."

"It's fine. Really." Out of the corner of her eye, she saw the police and the custodian woman searching the crowd. She deliberately kept walking with the young family, positioning herself so the man was between her and the people she was trying to avoid.

Her mind was spinning with possibilities of how anyone would know she was here and why they would be looking for her. Only Warren and Paige knew she was coming to Maracaibo, and only Warren had access to her full travel plans. Knowing she could trust her long-time agency associate, where could the information have leaked?

Had she been too quick to trust her new assistant? Surely no one could have managed to plant someone that close to her, especially not coming through a medical office, but doubt niggled in the back of her mind.

It was almost as if someone was expecting her to come, but how could that be? She hadn't even known she would be here until first thing this morning. Had it not been for the message that Seth was still missing, she would have turned around and gone back home to Virginia.

She continued toward baggage claim despite having all of her own luggage with her. Never comfortable with spending idle time in airports, she had packed everything she needed in her carry-on and in the large shoulder bag she had used as her personal item.

With her free hand, she pulled her cell phone out of the back pocket of her jeans. She noticed she had a voice message, but she ignored that, instead switching to the camera function. As she turned the corner away from customs, she reversed the camera and used it as a mirror so she could see the custodian over her shoulder. Vanessa snapped several photos, pretending to try to get reception in the crowded airport.

Once out of sight, Vanessa said her good-byes to the young family and headed for the airport exit.

She noticed a man with fair skin and light-brown hair heading for the same exit, and she slowed down. From the brand of his jeans, she guessed he was likely American, and at the moment, Vanessa preferred not to be near anyone from her own country.

To her dismay, he also slowed down. She was too close to the door to change direction now without being obvious. They reached the doorway at the same time, and the man bumped into Vanessa in the same way she might if she was trying to pickpocket someone or plant a tracking device.

She made a mental note to check her clothes for anything that didn't belong. Then the man spoke to her in a low voice. "Vanessa Johnson? I'm your contact. Welcome to Maracaibo."

She reminded herself not to react and call this man's bluff. She didn't have a contact here in Venezuela, and even if Warren had sent someone to meet her, no one would have ever used her real name in a foreign country.

"Where's my usual contact?" Vanessa asked quietly.

"I don't know. I just got a call telling me to pick you up." He continued forward, keeping pace with Vanessa. "I have a car parked right outside."

Vanessa wasn't about to get in a car with this man, but she certainly couldn't afford to draw the attention of the local authorities.

"Where?"

"Over there. Down at the end." He motioned to a plain hatchback parked behind a string of taxis.

Vanessa played along, already going over possible outcomes in her mind. When they reached the car, the man made it abundantly clear that he had never been to any of her training classes. He pulled his keys out of his pocket and turned his back to her when he unlocked the passenger side.

Vanessa took advantage of the opportunity, turning in a quick circle and connecting her elbow with the back of the man's head. He dropped forward, one arm catching on the open car door as he fell halfway into the passenger seat. Vanessa leaned over him, feigning concern in case anyone was watching.

Setting her suitcase to the side, she slipped her arm around the now unconscious man and managed to sit him up in the passenger seat. She then picked up the keys he had dropped and slipped them into her pocket. No reason to make it easy for him to follow her.

She retrieved her phone and used the camera to take a photo of the man. After closing him in the car, she put her hand back on her suitcase and rolled it forward to the nearest taxi, glancing back long enough to make a mental note of the license plate number and the make and model of the vehicle.

When she reached the taxi, she debated only a moment about whether she should go to the hotel she was registered in. Assuming someone could track her there, she opted for her backup plan.

Always cautious, she asked the taxi driver for his suggestion on where to stay. He gave her a couple of choices, and after a brief discussion on the location of the ones he'd suggested, she opted for the hotel nearest the city center.

Though she would have liked to check her clothes and purse for tracking devices, she didn't want to give the cab driver any cause to take special notice of her. Instead, she pulled out her cell phone to look at the photos once more. When she did, she again noticed she had a message.

She plugged her earbuds into the phone so she would be the only one to hear the message and hit play. When she heard Paige's frantic voice telling her she was a target, all doubt of her assistant's loyalty was erased. She glanced behind her to make sure she wasn't being followed.

Vanessa fought the urge to call Paige right then to get an update. She knew all too well that panicking now was the worst thing she could do. Undoubtedly, whoever was targeting her had planned to pick her up at the airport. Now that she was clear, she could use her training to go underground and stay there until she knew where the danger was coming from.

After checking in under Lina's name at the hotel, she made her way to her room, approving of the cab driver's taste. The room was large and airy, a king-sized bed taking up the far side of the room.

She immediately crossed to the bed and pulled the covers down, sitting on it long enough to make it look like it had been slept in. She then used the bathroom and turned on the shower briefly. Wadding up a bath towel, she draped it over the side of the tub.

Satisfied that the bathroom now looked well used, she opened her purse and took out what looked to be a pen but was really a webcam. She positioned it so the camera was aimed at the door.

After roaming the room for another minute and repositioning various items to make it look like someone was staying there, she opened the closet door and found a drawstring bag used for laundry service.

Vanessa put her suitcase on the luggage stand inside the closet, turned the laundry bag inside out to hide the hotel logo, and then proceeded to change her clothes and pack the rest of her things into the drawstring bag.

She tucked her soiled clothes and everything she had been wearing in the airport into the dresser drawers, stringing them out so it looked like there was more in the drawers than there really was.

Retrieving her phone from her pocket, she downloaded and encrypted the two photos she had taken earlier, one of the female custodian and the other of the man who had claimed to be her contact.

She forwarded both photos to Warren with a single-word message: Compromised. Though she wished she could trust Warren to help her figure out what she should do next, she knew he would have to work within the framework of CIA operational policy. Vanessa didn't feel she had that luxury at the moment.

She had hesitated to take Paige so fully into her confidence yesterday, but faced with her husband's disappearance, she had felt she needed to keep all her resources available to her. Trusting Paige allowed her to do that.

She knew Paige wouldn't have the ability to decrypt the photos, but she forwarded them to her as well, along with a different message: Make the call.

She did a thorough search of her purse to make sure no tracking devices had been planted on it. Satisfied she was signal free, she slid her purse onto her shoulder, picked up the laundry bag filled with her things, and walked out the door, making sure to put out the Do Not Disturb sign.

Leaving through a side exit, she strolled down the sidewalk and headed for the nearby shopping district.

CHAPTER 21

"Hello?" A man's voice with a measure of audible concern came through the line.

"Hi, um, Vanessa told me to call you if I couldn't get ahold of her. She isn't answering my calls."

"Who is this?" he demanded.

"My name is Paige. I'm Vanessa's assistant."

"Okay, Paige. Here's what I need you to do. First you're going to go to the drugstore and get a passport photo taken, and then you're going to buy a pay-as-you-go cell phone."

"All right," Paige said, not sure why in the world she would need a new passport photo. She already had a passport. "Then what?"

"Then you're going to bring them both to me at this address." He rattled off an address in Virginia Beach. "Also, how old are you?"

"Twenty-four. Why?"

"Meet me at that address in thirty minutes."

"Okay, I'll see you then." Paige hung up and headed for the door, wondering if maybe she was about to get more excitement in her life than she had intended.

***

"How can you go shopping at a time like this?" Damian asked Paige. He had been impressed so far that she seemed like such a logical, down-to-earth person. Yet now, in the middle of a crisis, she wanted to go to the store.

"I won't be gone long. I promise."

"It's not a matter of how long you'll be gone. What if Vanessa tries to call in and you're in the middle of the grocery store?"

Her eyebrows lifted. "Then I'll look like every other person who gets a phone call they feel they can't ignore."

"You know what I mean. You can hardly talk about classified information in the middle of the checkout line."

"I've always thought that was quite rude, you know. Talking to someone else when you should be interacting with the cashier."

"Paige." Damian let out her name in an exasperated breath.

"I'll be right back. Trust me."

"Whatever. If you feel you have to go when we should be figuring out a way to save our bosses' lives, then go right ahead."

Paige put her hand on his arm and waited for him to look at her. "Trust me," she repeated.

Damian was a little surprised to find that amidst the stress they were currently under, Paige had found some sense of calm.

He didn't think she understood how frustrating she was being right now. He wanted her to stay here, to help him figure out how to reach Vanessa and find his team. Part of his conscious mind also recognized that he didn't want to let her out of his sight, afraid for some irrational reason that she too might disappear and cause what little security he had left in his new life to unravel.

Realizing she was going to do what she wanted despite what he said, he waved a hand in surrender. "Go do what you need to do, but don't be long, okay?"

"I won't be. I'll see you in a little while."

Damian watched her go and forced himself to turn his attention back to the map on the wall. He looked at the target area, trying not to think that his team might be lying dead in some ravine somewhere or being tortured for information.

He shook those thoughts out of his mind. *Positive thinking.*

If stranding the Saint Squad truly was a decoy to draw Vanessa out into the open, then it was time he figured out where his team could be.

He knew much of the search area well. Besides spending the first thirteen years of his life in Venezuela, he had been back to visit at least once a year until he had joined the navy. During his year working in international banking, he had traveled there often.

Grabbing a notepad and pen, he redefined his search parameters and started making a list. He was going to find them. And he wasn't going to stop until he did.

* * *

Andrea stormed into the room and threw her purse down on the couch. "She got away."

"How?"

"I don't know what you were thinking, sending some random government type as a backup plan, but I found him passed out in his car, and Vanessa Johnson was nowhere in sight."

"How did she get past you?" Terrance asked.

"We were in a crowded airport with hundreds of people around," she said, stating the obvious.

"Did you see her?"

"Yeah, I saw her," Andrea confirmed.

"Then she probably saw you."

"Don't take that smug tone with me. What are we going to do now?"

"Find her," Terrance said. "We know which hotel she was registered in."

"She wasn't there."

"Then I suggest you start looking for her. She didn't have transportation. Start with the rental car companies and taxi services. We know she didn't walk away from the airport. You, Luis, or Pablo would have seen her."

"This plan of yours had better work," Andrea said irritably. "The money Morenta paid me for setting up the Saint Squad is almost gone."

"It's going to work," he said confidently. "Of course, that's assuming Morenta doesn't find out what you're up to. If he does, you won't have to worry about the Americans anymore. You'll be too dead to worry about anything."

"Trust me. Only the three of us know what's really going on," Andrea assured him. "Morenta is pleased with the new trade routes we've set up, and he's happy knowing he's sent a message to the Americans by killing those SEALs. He'll never know I accessed his files and found Ramir's money."

"I thought Rodrigo was suspicious," he said, referring to Morenta's righthand man.

"If he didn't trust me, he would have told Morenta by now," Andrea said, although her confidence wavered.

"Are you sure you can trust this silent partner of yours?"

"Absolutely. We just have to find Vanessa Johnson and do our part. When we're done, we won't have to deal with Rodrigo or Morenta anymore, and we'll never have money problems again."

* * *

Vanessa carried several shopping bags through one of the shopping districts in Maracaibo, her new purse hanging from her shoulder. Even though she hadn't seen any visible sign of a tracking device on her other one, she didn't want to take the chance that the man at the airport had put some kind of marking spray on it.

She knew her purse would be one of the best ways to track her since she would obviously change her clothes at some point in the next day. A purse, however, was something most women rarely went without. Her old purse was now tucked safely beneath the table of the restaurant where she had stopped and indulged in her favorite drink from the region, a frozen papaya concoction.

After making a few additional clothing purchases, she had transferred the clothes she'd brought with her into the shopping bags and hid the laundry bag in the bottom of one. She now made her way down the street, away from the hotel she had checked into and toward several tall buildings she believed were also hotels. When she passed the first one, she did a quick threat analysis and decided it didn't have enough exits if she ended up on an upper floor. The second one she approached belonged to a well-known American chain, and the one across the street looked a bit sketchy, with several twenty-something-year-old men loitering near the doorway.

She kept going, finally finding one she felt comfortable with. Not sure who might have access to her various aliases, Vanessa approached the desk, pulled a wad of Bolivars out of her pocket, and paid for two nights in cash.

As soon as she was checked in, she headed for the little café off the lobby rather than going to her room. She selected a table that had a clear view of the door and set her bags down in the chair beside her. She took her time looking over the menu, though she already knew she wanted arepas con queso.

When the cheese-filled corncakes arrived, she ate slowly, lingering over her meal. After more than an hour, she paid her bill and headed for the elevators.

Her room was basic, with two double beds on one side and a television perched on a wide dresser. Vanessa bolted her door closed and retrieved a sensor alarm from her purse. She attached it so that any movement of the door would set it off. Then she crossed to the window.

Though she knew many of the rooms at this hotel had a view of Lake Maracaibo, she considered herself fortunate that hers overlooked the street below. From the sixth floor, she was close enough to see the street clearly but high enough to have a decent view of the surrounding businesses.

Resigned to having to wait until Warren or Paige could decrypt and identify the photos she'd sent, she pulled the chair out from under the desk and set it by the window. She retrieved her tablet out of her purse and pulled up the app that would allow her to watch the video feed from the hidden camera she'd planted in her first hotel room.

Perching the tablet beside the window, she shifted in her chair to get comfortable so she could people watch.

* * *

Seth saw the jet's contrail long before he heard it. They had cleared the evergreens a couple miles back and were now hiking steadily uphill through a narrow clearing. "What do you think? It looks like a passenger plane to me."

"I agree," Brent said, slowing his steps as he looked upward. "We're in a good spot right now to keep it in sight and double-check our heading." He turned to the rest of the squad. "Everyone take a break. Get some rest while you can."

"Brent, do you care if I forage around here to see if I can find something for us to eat?" Jay asked. "It's been awhile since lunch, and it would be nice to have something besides pineapple."

"Go ahead."

"Thanks."

"I'll keep an eye on the plane," Seth offered.

"Sounds good." Brent settled down on the ground and leaned up against a thick palm a few feet from where Quinn had already stretched out and was using his pack for a pillow.

A colorful bird resembling a parrot fluttered its wings above them. It quieted for a few minutes, just long enough for both Quinn and Brent to fall asleep. Then it started squawking as though annoyed that they had invaded its territory.

They both ignored it for several minutes, the bird continuing to express its frustrations. But then Quinn opened one eye. "I swear, if that bird doesn't shut up, I'm going to shoot it."

"Save your ammo," Tristan said and stood up to chase the bird away. He picked up a stick and swung it at the bird, only to have it squawk louder.

"That worked well," Quinn said. He pulled his sidearm free. "If I shoot it, we can eat it for dinner tonight."

"It's not big enough for dinner. For you, it probably isn't even big enough for a snack. Besides, I don't want to make a fire," Brent responded with his eyes still closed.

Jay walked into the clearing with an armful of fruit and gave Seth a dopey grin. "Are they really battling a bird right now?"

"Yeah, and they're losing."

"Shut up, Seth," Quinn said without heat, shifting to get comfortable once more.

"Well, I have some bananas if anyone wants one." Jay set several bunches on the ground. He picked a banana up, peeled it, and took a huge bite. Then he made a face and spat out the fruit he had just tasted. "Gross. That is not a banana."

Quinn pushed himself up on one elbow and looked at the fruit. "No, it's a plantain, and it isn't ripe. You'll want to cook it so it doesn't taste so bitter."

"I don't have time to cook it." Jay spat on the ground to try to get the taste out of his mouth.

"Besides, Brent doesn't want us to build a fire, right, Brent?" Seth added.

"That's right."

Jay looked down at his wasted labor and scowled. "Maybe we should send Quinn out looking for food next time."

The bird squawked again, and Quinn eyed it. "If I fix dinner, we're going to need a fire."

CHAPTER 22

PAIGE PULLED UP IN FRONT of the self-storage warehouse. The man she had spoken to on the phone had given her this address and what she thought was an apartment number. Could it have been the number for a locker?

She climbed out of her car and headed for the office only to find it locked. She looked around, seeing no one. Then she looked at her watch and saw she was right on time. The whirr of a motor sounded, and she turned to see the automatic gate beside her swing open. For a moment, she felt like she was in the middle of some sort of spy movie. Then she remembered. She was, sort of. Only it wasn't fiction. It was real.

Her heartbeat picked up as she moved forward and walked through the gate. She was several yards inside when she jumped at the sound of it closing behind her. Now locked in, she had no choice but to keep going. She looked at the numbers posted outside the lockers and found the one she was looking for six units down.

"I gather you're new at this."

Paige's hand went to her chest, and she whirled around to see a man in his late twenties standing behind her. "You startled me."

"You startle easily." He didn't introduce himself but opened the door that led inside. "Did you bring the stuff?"

"Yes." Paige opened her bag and retrieved the passport photos. "But I don't understand . . ."

"And the phone?"

Paige reached back into her bag and handed over the unopened phone as well.

He took it out of her hand and headed inside the unit. She stood outside, not sure what to do.

"Are you coming in, or are you going to stand outside and freeze?"

Paige reminded herself that she didn't even know this man's name. Then another consideration overshadowed her doubts. Vanessa trusted him.

She walked into the storage unit to find it was outfitted like a workshop. A workbench stretched along the wall to her right, and various tools hung from racks on the walls.

He was already standing at the bench, affixing her passport photo to a passport that read Jessica Archibald. Paige stepped forward. "Is that a phony passport?"

"Hand me that over there." He pointed to a thin sheet that looked like clear plastic.

Paige did as she was asked and watched as the man laminated her photo in place. "Why are you making me a fake passport?"

"Because Vanessa thinks you're going to need it."

"Did you talk to her?"

"Nope."

"I'm confused."

"So it seems." He laid the passport aside and shifted his attention to the phone. He took it out of the package and pulled off the back cover to expose the battery compartment.

When the man picked up a soldering iron, Paige asked, "What are you doing?"

"Disabling the GPS." He remained concentrated on his task.

Paige tried to figure out why in the world Vanessa had sent her here to this man and what she was expected to do next. Since he clearly wasn't going to talk to her until he was good and ready, all she could do was stand and watch him while he worked.

Fifteen minutes later, he opened a drawer in his workbench and pulled out a thick manila envelope. He slid the new passport inside it. Then he turned on the phone.

"Where's the phone Vanessa gave you to contact her with?"

"How did you know . . . ?"

"I know Vanessa." He held out his hand until she passed the phone to him.

"She sent me a couple of files, but they're encrypted, and I haven't been able to figure out how to retrieve them."

"I can take care of that." He plugged a cord into her phone and connected it to a laptop at the end of his workspace. As soon as he downloaded the files and started a decryption program, he retrieved Vanessa's current cell phone number and programmed it into the new phone. When that task was complete, he sent Vanessa a text message that included nothing more than a five-digit code.

"What's that?"

"That's the proof for Vanessa that this is the phone I set up for you. You'll use this one now instead of the other one." He took the back off of the phone Vanessa had given her and took the battery out.

"Wait. I need that phone. It's how I'm supposed to communicate with the deputy director of operations."

"Did Vanessa tell you to call Warren?"

Paige noticed this man's casual use of the DDO's first name. "Not exactly."

He retrieved her old phone, stuck the battery in, and turned it on. Then he sent a text message to Warren. This time, the message was a single letter: *G*.

As he proceeded to disassemble the phone again, Paige asked, "Will he know what that means?"

"Yeah."

"What *does* it mean?"

"It means you're getting your resources from me now and he won't want to know about it."

"You and Vanessa aren't planning on doing anything illegal, are you?"

"Not illegal. Just under the radar." When he saw the confusion on Paige's face, the guy relented and expanded on his answer. "Warren has people he has to answer to. This is one of those times he may be better off not knowing what's going on."

He took the battery out again and dropped both the phone and the battery into a plastic bag and then slid it into the bulging manila envelope. After closing the clasp, he handed the packet over to Paige.

"Exactly what is all this?"

"Your passport, some surveillance and audio tools, a jamming device, and a few other toys," he said. "As soon as Vanessa calls you, she'll let you know what to do."

"Thanks," Paige said, though she was still confused. She took a step toward the door before turning back to face him. "I'm sorry. I didn't catch your name."

"They call me Ghost."

"Ghost?"

He nodded toward the door. "You'd better get going. If I know Vanessa, you need to pack. I have a feeling you'll be taking a trip very shortly."

Paige hadn't gotten any indication from her conversation with Vanessa that she would be traveling anytime soon, but she didn't feel like she knew enough to dispute Ghost's observation. Instead, she said, "Thanks for giving me a safe way to talk to her."

"Don't call her unless you don't hear from her in the next twenty-four hours. Let her call you."

"Why?"

"Because you don't know if she's still trying to establish a safe zone. She may need to stay dark a bit longer." He must have mistaken Paige's sense of uncertainty for a lack of understanding because he expounded on his answer. "You know, off the grid, not using electronics?"

"Right." Paige started toward the door once more. Then she remembered the encrypted files. "What about the files Vanessa sent me?"

"I'll forward them to your phone as soon as I'm done decrypting them. It could take an hour or two." He opened a cooler tucked along the wall beside the door. "There's one more thing you forgot."

"What's that?"

He pulled out a bag from a local deli. "Lunch."

"Why are you giving me lunch?" Paige asked.

"Because you're going to tell the people at the office that you stopped by the deli to pick up lunch. That's why it took you so long."

"Wow. You think of everything."

"That's my job."

Paige offered him a smile. "You do it well."

"Let's hope I do it well enough."

* * *

Paige walked into Damian's office to find him prowling around the room. His focus seemed to be torn between the map on the wall and the doorway she had just entered. She saw relief on his face. "What took you so long?"

"I thought I'd stop and pick up some lunch." Paige set a plastic bag down on her desk. "You haven't eaten yet, have you?"

"No, not yet." He crossed to her. "Sorry, I didn't mean to jump on you like that, but I was worried about you."

Touched by his obvious concern, she reached out and squeezed his hand. "That's okay. I should have called to let you know I was running later than I expected."

"This is really nice of you. What did you get?"

Since she didn't know the answer, she started pulling out sandwiches, lining all four of them up on her desk. "See for yourself."

"Why did you get so many?"

"I thought Kel might want one too, and I wasn't sure what everyone would like." She motioned for him to choose one. "Do you want me to go see if Kel is in his office?"

"That's all right. I can call him." Damian picked up his phone and dialed the commander's office. When he hung up, he told Paige, "He'll be right over."

True to his word, Kel walked in a minute later. "So what did you bring me?"

"Take your pick," Paige offered.

As soon as they all had their lunch, Kel sat down in Quinn's chair. "Have you guys had any more luck with tracking down Morenta or getting ahold of Vanessa?"

Realizing she couldn't hold back such important information from Kel, she said, "I got a text message from Vanessa a little while ago. She sent me two files that I'm having decrypted."

Relief filled Kel's voice. "Then she's all right?"

"So far." Paige slid one of the sandwiches closer to her but didn't unwrap it. "I'll feel better when I can hear her voice on the phone."

"Have you tried calling her again?" Kel asked.

"No. I'm supposed to wait for her to call me."

"Says who?" Damian asked before Kel had a chance to.

"It's just how it works. Something about making sure she can't be traced by any electronic signatures."

"She should be using a clean phone, but I guess that makes sense." Kel sounded hesitant but didn't press Paige for more information.

Paige's cell phone vibrated in her pocket. She reached for it and then remembered. It was her other cell phone, the one Ghost had given her. She pulled it free of her purse and opened the e-mail that had been sent to it.

"I just got the files Vanessa sent. They were photos." Paige read through the decrypted message Vanessa had sent with the pictures. "She said the woman was dressed as a custodian, but she was pretty sure she was following her. The man approached her as she was leaving the airport and said he was her contact, but he called her by her real name."

"Can you pull up the pictures?"

"Sure." She opened the first one, which was of a man passed out in a car. "Any idea who he is?"

"Never seen him before," Kel said. "What about the other one?"

"No way." Paige breathed the words under her breath when she looked at the photo.

"What?"

"I know who this woman is." Paige looked up at the two men watching her expectantly. "But I was told she was dead."

"Dead?" Damian repeated.

"I was counseling someone who was struggling with her death. He was convinced she was alive. He was right."

"Who is she?"

"Andrea Kemper. She was an undercover CIA operative in Colombia, in Morenta's organization. She reportedly went overboard while sailing and was presumed to have drowned at sea."

"How close were they to shore?"

"I'm not exactly sure, but it was far enough out that she couldn't have swum ashore safely."

"Then she must have had some help to disappear like that. What's her nationality?"

"She's from the U.S. There weren't any significant international ties for her other than the ones the CIA created."

"Maybe she decided to join forces with Morenta for real."

"Maybe," Paige said uncertainly. "When I noticed her name in a report on Morenta earlier, I thought maybe she'd gotten in over her head and faked her own death to protect her family."

"Sounds like you may need to do another psych profile," Kel said.

"I guess so." Paige looked up at the wall, which was now nearly covered with sticky notes. Damian pointed to the empty stretch of wall near his desk. "Use that one. I'll get you some more sticky notes."

"Thanks."

"Let's send these photos to NCIS and see if they can get a hit on the man," Kel said.

"I'd rather keep this in the CIA's realm. With a dead helicopter pilot and the Saint Squad missing, we can't be sure if there are still leaks within the navy."

"Okay, have it your way, but we need it quickly," Kel insisted.

"I'll forward them right now and see what I can get from CIA headquarters."

"Keep me posted." Kel picked up the remainder of his sandwich. "I want an update in two hours."

"I guess we'd better get started."

Half an hour was all it took for the CIA to get the information Paige had requested. She looked over the computer files and the analysis that accompanied the identities of the two individuals.

"What do they say?" Damian asked.

Paige skimmed through the first file. "Alex Brown is currently an employee at one of the field offices. He's administrative, so he hasn't had any field training."

"Any idea who he might be working with?"

"I don't think he was working with anyone but us. He said he got a message to go pick up Vanessa Johnson at the airport, and when he tried to, she attacked him and locked him in his car."

"I would have thought Vanessa would use an alias when she travels."

"She was using an alias. That's probably what tipped her off," Paige said. "I don't know why someone would send this guy to pick her up, though, if the woman was there to try to get to her."

"I have no idea. What about the woman?"

"This is interesting. Take a look." Paige pointed to her computer screen, inviting Damian to read over her shoulder. "The agency confirmed that this is Andrea Kemper."

"Do they have any idea why she might have faked her own death?"

"They have analysts looking into it, but it will probably be at least a few hours before we hear anything."

"I don't know if I can take much more of this, just sitting around waiting for people to figure out what to do," Damian said.

"Have you had any luck figuring out where your team might be?"

Damian looked back at the map and stared at it as though willing it to give him the answers. "I might have an idea."

"Well?" Paige asked.

"I need to do a little more research, but I'll let you know when I get it figured out."

CHAPTER 23

It was time for action, and after a day and a half of analysis, Damian was ready to move. He had scoured the various possibilities in the search area, eliminating them one by one. Finally, he had a destination in mind, even though he still wasn't sure about the specifics.

If the Saint Squad really had been stranded rather than captured, he could think of only one place remote enough that they wouldn't have been able to find a mode of either transportation or communication by now—Canaima National Park.

Granted, the area was huge and rugged, but it was also impossible to get in and out without air support, and it was largely uninhabited. Even if they ran across any indigenous people, they likely would not be able to communicate with them or get help from them because they lived so simply.

Damian didn't know how to find their exact location, but one thing was certain: he wasn't doing them any good sitting in an office.

Leaving Paige to her files and sticky notes, he headed down the hall to Kel's office and knocked on the open door.

"Come on in," Kel said, looking up from a mountain of papers on his desk. "What have you got?"

"My best guess is that the pilot dropped them in Canaima National Park." He went on to describe the isolated, rugged area.

"The question is how do we find them? From what you're saying, that's still a lot of area to cover." Kel drummed his fingers on his desk. "And that's assuming they weren't really captured . . ."

The unspoken words *or killed* hung in the air. Damian wasn't going to entertain such thoughts. If they were dead, there was nothing he could do, but if they were alive, he had to do everything he could to find them.

"Assuming they are okay, I have to think our search radius is shrinking. There are hotels by Lake Canaima and a small airstrip where a jet plane can land when bringing people in and out of the area. I think the squad would try to head there."

"That makes sense."

"Kel, I want to go in and try to find them."

"Damian, it's too dangerous. I can't send you in there, especially not alone."

"He won't be alone." Paige's voice sounded from the doorway.

"Excuse me?" Kel rose at her entrance.

"He won't be alone. He'll be taking his new girlfriend home to meet his grandparents."

"Excuse me?" Kel repeated. "I can't send you two into an unstable area, especially not knowing what we're facing. We need more information."

"That's why we need to go," Paige said. "I speak Spanish but not well enough to do this alone. Someone has to go to Venezuela and get Vanessa and the Saint Squad safely out of there."

"No offense, Paige, but it makes more sense to send in someone from the local field office to get her home. You aren't exactly trained for this."

"Normally, I would be the first to suggest having someone with more experience make contact, but we can't be sure who we can trust. The man who tried to pick her up from the airport might be telling the truth, or he could be working with Morenta. We don't know who else is involved or why they're trying to get to Vanessa in the first place."

"I have people under my command who I trust. If I do let Damian go into Venezuela, I'd feel more comfortable sending him in with another SEAL, someone who has language skills," Kel countered.

"But none of your SEALs will be able to recognize Andrea Kemper, and they won't have access to CIA intel."

"We have Andrea Kemper's personnel photo."

"She's a master of disguise. That photo isn't going to do you any good."

"What makes you think you would recognize her, then?" Kel asked.

"I spent three months counseling her father. He was proud of her abilities and often brought in photos of her in various disguises. I've seen dozens of photos of her, and I know her background through her father," Paige said. "I'm your best shot at finding her."

"She's right," Damian said. "If Vanessa really is the target, we need to get her out of the country without Andrea Kemper getting to her first."

"And we need to figure out if Andrea is working with anyone. Even if we get everyone home safely, there's no guarantee someone won't try to go after the Saint Squad again to get to Vanessa," Paige said.

"I don't know how I'm going to get approval for this." Kel shook his head. "Especially in a way that we can keep it under wraps."

"Maybe all you need to do is approve Damian's request for leave," Paige suggested.

"I don't know—"

"I'll have my leave slip on your desk in ten minutes," Damian said before Kel could finish his sentence.

Kel fell silent for a moment. "Okay, here's the deal. I'm going to have one of the other squads fly out to the USS *Harry S. Truman* to be on standby for when we make contact with the rest of the Saint Squad. If you two really want to do this, I want you to focus on getting Vanessa out of there."

Even though Damian would have preferred to go straight to Canaima, he found himself agreeing. After all, once he got Vanessa and Paige safely on a plane home, he could search for his squad himself.

"How soon do we leave?" Damian asked Paige.

"If we catch the red eye to Miami tonight, we can be in Maracaibo by noon tomorrow."

"Paige, can you get me the flight information you were looking at so I can book the tickets?" Kel asked.

"I'll go get it right now." Paige started for the door.

"Thanks," Kel said. "When you get back, we'll go over some basic procedures and come up with a plan."

As soon as she left, Damian asked, "Is it okay if I call to let my family know we're coming, or should I just show up unannounced?"

"Actually, I'm going to make a hotel reservation."

"Why? I have a lot of family who would let us stay with them."

"I understand that, but the main reason Brent decided to leave you behind on this mission was because he was worried your family connections might complicate things." Kel motioned to his computer. "For now, let's make sure you and Paige have everything you need for a successful mission. As soon as I finish briefing you guys, you'll both need to go pack."

"Yes, sir." Relief, anticipation, and trepidation pulsed through Damian. He was going on his first mission. And he was going without his team.

* * *

Paige rolled four shirts together to keep them from wrinkling and put them in her suitcase. She had no idea how long she would be gone, but she remembered one pointer Vanessa had given when Paige had sat in on her class: learn to pack lightly.

Terrified at the thought of being noticed in a foreign airport, she concentrated on making sure everything she needed could fit into her carry-on.

As soon as her suitcase was packed, she started loading her backpack. She slid her laptop and charger inside. She then retrieved the envelope Ghost had given her and dumped the contents on her bed.

Her eyes widened when she saw a bundle of currency, a mixture of U.S. bills, Mexican pesos, Venezuelan bolivars, and Colombian pesos. She grabbed it, flipping through the U.S. bills to see there were several thousand dollars.

What in the world had she been thinking when she had suggested she go with Damian to Venezuela? The fact that she could identify Andrea Kemper hardly made her qualified to work undercover. Even if she did find Andrea, would she know what to do? With more cash in her hand than she had ever seen in one place before, she couldn't help but wonder if she was getting in over her head.

Setting the money back on her bed, she began sorting through the other items. A ballpoint pen, a hardback book, a power converter, her new passport, a credit card, and several other random items that seemed to have common uses. Tucked beneath the book, she found a folded piece of paper and slid it free.

The heading read "Travel Clean." Eager to learn anything she could before going overseas, she sat down on the edge of her bed and began reading. The first section outlined basic travel procedures, including making sure she left all identification behind. Kel had given her that direction when he had briefed Damian and her earlier.

Next was an inventory list with basic specs. The hardback book wasn't really a book at all. Paige lifted it to find that it had been hollowed out and was to be used to hide the currency. The identity on the credit card matched her fake passport and could be used when cash wasn't feasible. Other items were actually surveillance equipment and things she might need while traveling.

Paige cleaned out her wallet, securing her own identification and credit cards in the small safe she kept in her closet. She then took the other items and packed them in her bag so they looked like they truly were everyday items.

She was debating whether to take her personal cell with her when the other phone rang. She answered it to find Vanessa on the other end.

"Vanessa. Are you okay? I've been worried sick about you."

"I'm fine, at least for now," Vanessa said, though she sounded distracted. "Did you see Ghost?"

"Yeah, and he decrypted those photos."

"Do you know who they are yet?" Vanessa asked.

"One of them is one of our operatives, Andrea Kemper. She was undercover with Morenta but supposedly died at sea six months ago."

"What about the guy who tried to pick me up at the airport?"

"He works in the local field office out there. It's possible he was just a decoy or a pawn who was unwittingly helping out Andrea," Paige told her. "The station chief questioned him, and he still has no clue why you didn't go with him."

"Have you heard anything from my husband or his squad?"

"No, nothing," Paige said. "Damian thinks they might have been dropped off deliberately in a place called Canaima. I guess it's a rugged area only accessible by air."

"Why did you send me that message that you think I'm the target?"

"We think someone was deliberately trying to draw you out in the open by going after Seth's squad. Apparently, that day we met them at the restaurant, someone had sabotaged the rappelling tower. We think they were hoping someone would die so they could find you at the funeral."

"I knew they were keeping something from me. Any idea why someone wants me?"

"I was hoping you would know."

Vanessa fell silent. "Let me know if you find anything else out. I'll call you in a day or two."

"Okay, but—" Paige didn't get the chance to tell Vanessa she was coming to help. The phone went dead. She tried calling her back only to have the call go straight to the generic voice mail.

Paige's other phone buzzed when a text message came through. She picked it up and saw a message from Damian, offering to give her a ride to the airport.

Remembering the way Ghost had disabled the disposable cell phone's GPS, she responded to Damian's text and then set her phone on her dresser. Better safe than sorry.

CHAPTER 24

Damian knocked on Paige's apartment door, a suitcase in one hand and a pizza in the other. The curtains in the window beside the door shifted when Paige looked out, and then the door swung open. "What are you doing here? We don't have to leave for the airport for another three hours."

"I brought dinner. I hope you haven't already eaten."

"No, actually. I just finished packing." She stepped aside to let him in.

Damian led the way into the kitchen, calling over his shoulder, "I wasn't sure what you liked, so I just got cheese."

"That's great, actually." Paige retrieved two paper plates from her cabinet.

"What is your favorite kind of pizza?" Damian asked, eager for any conversation that wasn't about their mission.

"Pineapple."

"Just pineapple?"

She opened the box and pulled out a slice. "I know. Everyone always thinks I'm weird."

"Well, yeah. Most people at least add ham or Canadian bacon to their pineapple pizza."

"But I don't really like ham or Canadian bacon."

Damian chuckled. He took a slice for himself and settled into a chair in her kitchen. They chatted comfortably over dinner, both of them choosing to stay on safe topics that didn't have anything to do with the task they were about to undertake. It wasn't until the leftover pizza was passed along to the next-door neighbor that the topic turned professional.

"Did Kel arrange for a car to take us to the airport?" Paige asked.

"Yeah. A taxi is going to pick us up here at nine thirty. You don't care if I leave my truck parked here while we're gone, do you?"

"No, that's fine," Paige said.

Damian glanced down at his watch. They had almost two more hours until they needed to leave and he struggled against the abundance of nervous energy that had built up inside him throughout the day. Hoping for a distraction, he asked, "Did you have any other plans for tonight?"

"Just unpacking boxes . . . or pacing around my apartment, pretending I'm not nervous."

"Any chance I might be able to distract you while we're waiting?" Damian asked.

She looked a little wary. "Maybe. What did you have in mind?"

"Come with me to the range. I can teach you how to shoot and show you guns aren't as bad as you might think."

Paige instantly took a step away from him. "I can't."

Damian saw the absolute terror on her face, and he found a sudden sense of clarity. Paige didn't just dislike guns; something in her past was causing her to truly fear them. He studied her for a moment, searching for the right words to put her at ease once more. Then he realized maybe he should take the direct approach he had seen her take so often.

"What happened?" he asked. "Why do guns scare you so much?"

She kept her eyes on his, and he could almost see the internal debate going on in her mind. He stepped forward, closing the distance between them. Then he took her hand in his. "Just tell me. I said last night I wanted to get to know you better. Let's start here."

Still, she wavered, and he found himself analyzing what he knew of her. "Does this have anything to do with why you left nursing?"

"No, it has more to do with how I got into nursing in the first place."

Taking her response as a positive cue, he tugged on her hand and led her into the living room so they could sit together on the couch. She settled down beside him and still seemed to hesitate.

"Talk to me," Damian said, shifting to face her. "What can it hurt?"

* * *

What can it hurt? Paige repeated Damian's question in her mind. Just the thought of that day her sophomore year of high school caused her stomach to clench and made her yearn to go back and erase the images. Yet, she also knew that if she kept hiding from her past, she would never truly be free of it.

So many times she had encouraged others to face their fears, but she often struggled to take her own advice. Not once since leaving high school had she trusted anyone with her past. But knowing she had to try, she let the memories come. "There was a shooting at my next-door neighbor's house when I was in high school," she began, not sure how much she could reveal or even how much Damian really wanted to hear.

"What happened?"

"My friend Ellie came over, her arm bleeding. I found out later that her older brother had cut her with his hunting knife when she ran outside."

Damian didn't ask for more details. He waited patiently, holding her hand in a silent gesture of support.

"We called 9-1-1 and went to her house. We were right outside the door when we heard gunshots."

"Who was shot?"

"My friend's brother. Russell, Ellie's older brother, had cornered their mother in the kitchen. She had cuts on her arm, apparently from when she tried to fight him off. When he wouldn't back off, she grabbed the gun over the stove and shot him."

"Did he survive?"

"Yeah. His mom shot him in the leg, and she managed to get around him once he fell to the floor. Unfortunately, her first shot went wide. She didn't see her twelve-year-old son come around the corner. He was killed instantly by the stray bullet."

"That's awful. Do you have any idea what caused the older brother to go after his mom like that?"

"He had drugs in his system. He had some sort of paranoid delusion and was convinced his mom was going to kill him in his sleep. He decided to kill her before she could get to him."

Damian rubbed his thumb over the back of her hand. "That sounds really traumatic, but I would have thought you'd be just as afraid of knives as you are of guns."

"I was, actually. It's taken me a long time to get to where I don't feel like I have to lock up my kitchen knives."

"Did you know the older brother well?"

"He was my sister's boyfriend."

"What?" Damian's eyes widened.

"Well, ex-boyfriend, really. When she found out he was getting into drugs, she broke up with him. When she heard what happened, she really struggled with guilt, convinced it was her fault for not telling his mother what was going on."

Paige gathered her thoughts before continuing. "Ellie and her family had a lot of post-traumatic stress. So did my sister and I, but my struggles didn't seem that bad compared to what they went through. I spent the next couple years watching both of them go in and out of the mental hospital while they learned to cope."

"Are they okay now?"

"My sister is doing great. It took a little while, but she eventually came to grips with what happened and that it wasn't her fault."

"And your friend's family?"

"They're . . . still struggling."

"That's too bad." Damian looked at her intently. He stretched his arm out along the back of the couch, his fingers toying with her hair and sending an unexpected ripple of comfort through her. "And what about you?"

"What about me?"

"It sounds like you spent an awful lot of your high school years trying to take care of everyone else in addition to dealing with the memories of what happened. That had to have an impact on you."

"Mostly I learned how to look for cues. Ellie tried to commit suicide a couple of times during our senior year, and I never knew when my sister was going to act like herself or when she was going to pick fights because she didn't want to deal with life." Paige's shoulders lifted. "And I developed an irrational fear of guns."

"Did you ever see a counselor to get help for yourself?"

"I went to a counselor right after it happened. Logically I know what I need to do to overcome my fear, but it's hard to face something you don't necessarily see that often."

"Until you met me," Damian said, his voice low. "Do you think you can ever get over your fear of guns?"

"Maybe. I am trying."

He shifted beside her, his eyes locked on hers, his fingers trailing lightly against the back of her neck. "You're pretty amazing, you know that?"

She shook her head, as much in answer to his question as to clear the shiver working through her.

"You know," Damian continued. "You did refer to yourself as my girlfriend earlier today."

Her cheeks flushed with embarrassment. "That was just a cover story."

"It doesn't need to be." He drew her close, pausing when their lips were just a breath apart.

She didn't have any reason to be nervous, she reminded herself. He would be like the other men she had dated in the past, someone to spend a week or two with until they both decided to part as friends. Yet when she thought of how much she had already come to trust Damian, she found herself hoping this would last.

Never before had she found someone she could confide in so completely, someone she always looked forward to being with. His lips pressed against hers in a tender kiss, and she felt herself melting against him.

Her hand came up to rest on his arm, and she could feel the strength there. She sensed the bridled energy humming through him, and yet he kept the kiss light and easy, his hands gentle as he held her close.

When he pulled back, she saw confusion in his eyes, and she wasn't sure what to say. She was saved from needing to say anything when Damian's cell phone rang.

"Sorry," Damian said, shifting away from her so he could retrieve his phone from his pocket. He looked down at the screen. "It's Kel."

He answered it, and his forehead wrinkled in confusion as he listened to Kel for several minutes. "Okay, if you think that's necessary." He paused for another moment. "Yes, sir."

"What was that all about?" Paige asked after he hung up.

"He said he was going to text me a phone number to call to check in with him when we get to Venezuela. He doesn't want to take the chance that I'll be connected back to him."

"That makes sense."

"Maybe we should consider getting you one of those prepaid phones for the same reason. I know you and Vanessa have talked on your phone."

"Actually, I already have one. I'm leaving my regular phone here." She wasn't sure how much she was allowed to tell him. Then she took a leap of faith and decided to trust him completely. After all, she needed him to trust her. "Vanessa had someone alter one so the GPS signal can't be traced. I also have an alias to travel under."

"What's the alias?"

"Jessica Archibald."

"Does that mean I have to call you Jessica?" Damian asked.

"In public, I guess you do."

"This is going to be weird."

"Of course, that's assuming anyone would even be paying attention," Paige said. "Honestly, I still haven't quite gotten used to the idea of traveling to another country tomorrow, much less being undercover."

"When you decided to switch careers, you definitely went to the extreme."

"Trust me. It wasn't intentional."

CHAPTER 25

VANESSA WATCHED THE DARK STREET below, the activity picking up as people came and went to the restaurants throughout the dinner hour.

She had gone down to the hotel restaurant and ordered her meal to go so she wouldn't be away from her surveillance for long. She had a policy against ordering room service. Too many potential problems with strangers coming into her room.

Her ruse of changing hotel rooms appeared to have worked, and her attention was now primarily on the video feed coming from her first hotel room. She was a little surprised no one had shown up looking for her yet, and a seed of hope sprouted that perhaps no one was really after her.

That hope bloomed for another fifteen minutes. Then it was squashed. A motion sensor sounded, followed by a shadow crossing in front of the camera.

Vanessa fiddled with the resolution, adjusting it so the image cleared despite the darkness of the room. She was a bit disappointed to see it was the same woman she had spotted in the airport, the woman who, according to Paige, had faked her own death. Vanessa had hoped to see someone else, someone who could help her figure out why she was being targeted.

The woman checked the room and then set about planting her own surveillance equipment. Vanessa's eyes widened when she picked up the pen camera Vanessa had planted, replacing it with an identical device. The picture went black when the woman slipped it into her bag. Vanessa hoped she didn't realize what she had picked up, but a few minutes later, the feed came back for a split second before the unit was disabled and the picture was replaced with static.

"Great," Vanessa said out loud. "Now what do I do?"

Remembering her conversation with Paige, Vanessa activated an encryption program on her tablet so her web history couldn't be traced. Then she did a search for Canaima. She read through the description of the national park that was home to the longest waterfall in the world. The lack of accessibility and ruggedness of the terrain gave Vanessa a glimmer of hope.

If Damian was right, it really was possible her husband and his squad were stranded. That idea was so much better than the alternative. Still, she couldn't quite fight the negative thoughts that crept into her mind. No matter how many times she went over the possibilities, she struggled against one glaring fact: her husband was a whiz with communication equipment, yet no one had heard from anyone in his squad since they'd left the ship.

Regardless of the hope she felt in Damian's analysis, she couldn't just sit and wait for her husband to magically appear. She needed information, and the only way to get it was to continue living the identity of Lina Ramir and taking her chances with Morenta.

* * *

Seth stirred from his spot on the jungle floor, his senses suddenly alert. The sounds of the night had changed. Silence stretched out before him, the rustling of small animals nearby no longer evident. A couple of birds squawked a warning, feathers ruffling anxiously.

Seth opened his eyes and saw Tristan keeping watch a short distance away. The gun in his hand indicated he had noticed the change too.

Moving slowly and silently, Seth reached for the sidearm buried beneath the palm leaves he had used to cushion his head. His fingers gripping the gun, he sat up and looked around.

Nothing was visible in the darkness, nor did he hear anything but the looming silence.

But that alone told him what they were dealing with, or at least narrowed down the possibilities. A predator loomed out there, but this time, it wasn't the human variety. Humans made noise, and Seth couldn't detect any scent that people so often carried with them. No, this was a different kind of predator.

The camp was dark on purpose, a precaution to protect them from the people who had tried to kill them. Seth decided a change in plan was in order.

Drop Zone

Tristan was standing now, his own gun drawn. With his teammate to back him up, Seth stood as well, retrieving a pack of matches from his vest.

He struck one now, picking up a palm leaf to provide fuel to the flame. Holding it out, he circled slowly. When he held it out to his right, he didn't see anything, but to his left, he caught a glimpse of two eyes illuminated less than five yards away.

* * *

Seth aimed his gun in the direction of the animal staring at him. He thrust the flaming palm leaf toward it, now able to make out a vague outline of the creature, some sort of cat.

"What is it?" Tristan asked, the other squad members now stirring.

"Not sure. A panther or puma, maybe." The heat from the flames licked near Seth's hand, and he leaned down to pick up another palm leaf. He used his foot to clear a space on the ground and dropped the flaming leaf, quickly picking up another and setting it on fire.

The crackling of the fire masked the movement of the sleek cat, and when Seth looked into the darkness again, it was no longer visible. "I've lost it."

Brent moved to the center of their campsite clearing. "Quinn, help me make a fire pit. Jay, climb up that tree and cut down some more palm leaves for us to burn."

"Always up a tree," Jay said, moving cautiously to the tree closest to him, which was on the opposite side of the clearing from where Seth had spotted the animal. He tugged on some gloves and checked his knife before starting his climb.

"Anyone hear anything?" Quinn asked.

"It's hard to with all the racket you're making," Seth said, again swinging the palm leaf in a circle in search of the threat.

He thought he heard a rustle of leaves a short distance away but couldn't distinguish it from the movement behind him. Jay cut two palm leaves and threw them down to Quinn, who placed them in the area he and Brent had cleared. Brent leaned down to light it, and Seth heard another faint sound a short distance away.

Seth lifted his hand to silence the team. Brent and Quinn froze, Brent squatting beside the fire circle and Quinn holding another palm leaf in his hand. Jay also stopped what he was doing, now watching from his spot seven feet up the tree.

At the edge of the clearing, Tristan remained upright, his gun still at the ready. Several seconds stretched out in silence. Then a series of rapid movements accompanied by a growl broke through the stillness.

"Tristan, watch out!" Jay shouted.

A blur of muscle and fur bounded straight for Tristan from behind, giving him no chance to turn and aim. Instead, he reacted by swinging his arm as he spun. He cried out, the panther's claws gouging his arm. A fraction of a second later, Tristan's gun struck the animal's skull, knocking it back, staggering.

With Tristan now between him and the panther, Seth picked up a rock and sent it flying. Startled by the projectile and stunned by the blow to the head, the cat retreated a step.

Brent set the palm fronds ablaze, frightening the animal further. With one last look at Tristan, it shook its head and bounded back into the darkness.

"How bad is it?" Seth asked, dropping the palm leaf he held and rushing forward. He could see blood seeping through Tristan's shirt, the fabric shredded by the animal's claws.

"We're about to find out." With Seth's help, Tristan tore away the fabric. Blood pooled in the four claw marks, making it difficult to see how deep they were.

Quinn pressed a thick gauze pad against the wound to stop the flow of blood. Tristan fisted his hand and then flexed his fingers. "I can move everything okay. I think he just got flesh."

"It still looks deep enough to need stitches," Seth said.

"Great. Who wants to do the honors?"

"I'll do it." Quinn offered, his med kit already in his hand. "But since we have a fire, how about we have Jay dig out some of those plantains. He can roast them for an early breakfast."

"It's two in the morning."

"So?" Quinn looked up expectantly. "I'm about to work up an appetite. And Tristan needs to keep up his strength."

"Why not," Brent said. "Jay, find some sticks. It looks like we're going to have a banana roast."

"They're plantains," Quinn corrected him automatically.

"Whatever."

CHAPTER 26

Damian made his way down the aisle of the plane as he returned to his seat. He hated sitting in the passenger section of a plane, finding he much preferred being in the pilot's seat since learning how to fly during his extensive training with the navy. He had gotten up to stretch his legs a few minutes before, certain that they must be getting close to their destination. The fasten seat belt sign came on when he was three rows back.

He reached his seat to find Paige dozing and was grateful Kel had managed to upgrade them to business class. Just the advantage of not having someone sitting beside them was worth whatever the upgrade had cost.

The moment he sat down, Paige shifted in her seat, her head sliding down until it rested on his shoulder. He stared down at her, something inside of him softening.

He thought of their time together the night before, of the kiss they had shared, of the nightmare she had suffered as a teenager. Her story and her obvious struggle in sharing it touched him. Not only had she lived through a frightening event, but she didn't seem to recognize that her instinct had been to help those around her, even when she was struggling herself.

He worried a bit about her abhorrence of guns, especially since the Saint Squad routinely wore sidearms. Then he caught himself. He barely knew Paige, and here he was trying to figure out if his profession would be a deal breaker in their relationship.

He looked past her to see the clouds out the window. Trying to take his mind off the woman beside him, he considered his possible courses of action when they arrived in Maracaibo.

His first instinct was to go straight to Canaima, but he fought against that, knowing how long the odds were that he would stumble across his squad in such a vast area of wilderness. He could do it, given enough time and a helicopter, but with the civil unrest in the country of his birth, he doubted he could secure both without alerting the government that something was amiss.

He certainly couldn't go after Morenta alone with only Paige as his backup. No, he would have to be more creative in searching for information and the trail that would lead to his squad.

He felt the plane start its final descent and saw where water gave way to land. Paige stirred beside him again, and her eyes fluttered open. She straightened in her seat, and when she looked up at him, he saw insecurity reflected on her face.

Hoping to calm them both, he reached for her hand. "Everything will be fine," he said in Spanish, aware that she could speak a limited amount of the language.

Paige's response was a subtle nod of her head and a squeeze of his hand. This was foreign territory for her, but as she looked up at him with those chocolate brown eyes, he realized this was foreign territory for him as well.

* * *

Paige stood silently beside Damian as he checked them into their hotel, curiosity eating at her. Kel had made their travel arrangements, but she had assumed they were going to stay with Damian's family to keep with their cover story.

Instead, Damian had instructed their taxi driver to bring them here to a hotel overlooking Lake Maracaibo.

He spoke rapidly in Spanish. She could pick out words here and there, but not enough to really know what was going on.

The clerk slid two hotel keys across the counter to Damian. After thanking the man, Damian turned, handed one key to Paige, and put his hand on her back to guide her to the elevators.

Paige held back her urge to question Damian about why they were here as they followed an older couple into the open elevator car.

Though it took great effort, she waited until Damian unlocked a hotel room and motioned her inside before she asked, "Why are we staying here?"

"I don't want to take any chances. Kel told me the reason my squad left me behind was because of my family," Damian said. "Besides, if a Colombian drug lord really is behind my squad's disappearance, I don't want to take a chance that my presence might put anyone in danger."

"I guess that makes sense." Paige stood awkwardly by the door and held up her room key. "What's my room number?"

"Actually, we're both staying in here."

Her eyebrows went up. "Excuse me?"

"Don't worry, it's a suite." Damian walked her farther into the room, where a table and four chairs occupied one corner. A couch stretched along the wall beside the window, and a television sat on a dresser across from it. He motioned to a door to the right. "You can take the bedroom."

"Can I ask why we're sharing a room?"

"Security." Damian dropped his bag beside the table and crossed the room. Standing to the side of the window, he peered outside.

"Security?" Paige repeated. "Security for whom?"

"Both of us." He shifted to face her. "If we're in the same room, we know any knock on the door is a potential threat."

"Or we could look through the peephole to see who's on the other side."

The intensity that came into Damian's eyes surprised her. "If Morenta really is behind all this, he and his men are just as likely to shoot through the door as they are to wait for one of us to open it."

Paige felt her face pale, the gravity of what they were trying to do suddenly weighing on her. "I'd better try to call Vanessa." She dialed the number and was concerned when it rang once and then went to a generic voice-mail account. "She isn't answering."

"Did she say where we should meet her when we got here?"

"I never got the chance to tell her we were coming. I only talked to her for a minute last night, but she ended the call suddenly, and when I tried calling her back, her phone had been turned off."

"Do you think her phone is off now?" Damian asked.

"That's my guess."

"Do you know where she's staying?"

"No. She didn't tell me."

"I'll check in with Kel," Damian said, retrieving his own phone.

He made his call, but he did more listening than talking, so Paige couldn't make out what they were discussing. A couple minutes later, he hung up, and she asked, "Is everything okay?"

"Yeah. One of the leads he uncovered gave me an idea of how we might track down Morenta," Damian said.

"What about Vanessa?"

"She wouldn't want us to sit around all day and wait for a phone call," Damian said. "Is there anything you need to put in the hotel safe before we go?"

"You want me to come with you?" Paige asked.

"I may need your help to blend in." Damian located the safe in the closet and opened it. "Don't worry. You won't be in any danger. If I find out what I need to, I can have a cab bring you back here."

Paige took out the various items Ghost had given her. "Should I bring any of this with me?"

He looked through the toys, as Ghost called them. He picked up a small spray bottle that looked like it contained body spray. "Is this a marking spray?"

"Yeah."

"We might be able to use that." He slipped it into his jacket pocket. "Go ahead and lock everything else in the safe except for the bolivars. We may need the cash to secure some weapons."

Paige swallowed but did as he suggested. She separated out the money and handed him a stack of bills, then locked everything else in the safe.

Damian separated the bills further, stuffing some into his front pocket and putting more in his wallet. "Come on. Let's go."

Paige followed him out the door, once again wondering how in the world she had ended up here.

CHAPTER 27

Paige looked up and down the street, shops and restaurants lining the busy section of town. A cab had dropped them off half a block away, and Paige guessed they were only about five miles from their hotel. "Why are we here?"

"Remember how Kel said they think Morenta is trying to open drug routes using the oil industry?" Damian kept his voice low as he guided her forward.

"Yeah." She matched her pace to his, the scent of grilled meat and baked bread making her mouth water.

"My squad was sent in to try to find the flow of drugs out of Venezuela."

"And?"

"We're going to look in the other direction. We'll follow the flow of payment going back to Colombia."

"How are we going to do that?" She lowered her voice to a whisper. "I'm sure the CIA is tracking money transfers."

"We aren't looking for money transfers. We're looking for diamonds."

"Why diamonds?"

"Diamonds are hard currency the Venezuelan government can't readily seize. Not to mention they're small enough to easily pay off people along their new drug routes."

"And exactly how do you plan to trace these diamond payments?"

"We're going to follow the courier. When I called to check in, Kel told me they had a tip about a particular jewelry store, and there was a mention of tonight."

"Damian, you aren't making any sense. Even if you can identify the diamond couriers, how in the world would you know which one to follow?"

"Remember how I told you I worked in the oil industry and then in banking?"

"Yeah."

"Part of my job was to process payments in and out of Maracaibo. I know pretty much every diamond courier in the city. We're looking for one I don't know."

"It could take days to find the right person," Paige said.

"I don't think so. Banks only do diamond exchanges on Tuesdays and Fridays. Today's the first one available since my squad disappeared."

"You think someone might make a payment for capturing them?"

"Or dropping them off where they couldn't be found. Come on. I think it's time we get something to eat." Damian took her hand and led her toward an outdoor café. Along the edge of the café, Paige could see a huge fireplace where meat was being grilled on spits.

Damian greeted the hostess in Spanish, and a moment later, he pulled out a chair for Paige at one of the tables nearest the sidewalk.

"Thanks." Paige took her seat, and Damian sat in the chair beside her.

The hostess handed them each a menu, and Paige looked inside, though she needed Damian's help making an order. "Any suggestions?" she asked.

"Do you trust me?" Damian asked in response.

"Sure, I guess."

He took her menu from her and handed it to their waitress when she approached. He proceeded to speak rapidly in Spanish, apparently giving the woman their orders.

As soon as the waitress left them, Paige asked, "What did you order?"

"Don't worry. You'll like it."

He couldn't have been more right. The arepitas smelled almost as good as they tasted, the white cornmeal mixture forming something that looked like a flattened hush puppy. Their main dish consisted of grilled beef and chicken.

"This is wonderful."

"Glad you like it." They lingered over their meal and were debating whether to order dessert when Paige felt Damian's attention shift away from her.

She leaned forward and spoke softly. "Is something wrong?"

"I think I found our courier."

Remembering the training Vanessa had drilled into her students, Paige fought the urge to look around. "Where?"

"To your ten o'clock. The guy heading into the jewelry store."

Paige let her eyes wander just enough to glance in the direction Damian was indicating. Three people stood near the store: a woman in her early twenties, a man wearing grubby clothes and looking like he was probably in need of a roof for the night, and a well-dressed man in his forties.

"The man in the suit?" Paige whispered.

"No, the other one." Damian took her hand in his.

"That can't be someone carrying diamonds. He looks like he's homeless."

"Exactly. What better way to make sure no one tries to steal what you're carrying than to look like you don't have anything to steal?" The confidence in Damian's words left little room for doubt.

Damian lifted Paige's hand and pressed a lingering kiss to the back of it. Warmth seeped through her from the old-fashioned gesture, and she barely registered his words when he said, "I think we're about to become engaged."

He stood and pulled some bills from his wallet, dropping them on the table.

"I'm sorry. What did you just say?"

Reaching for her hand again, he helped her up, slipped his arm around her, and leaned down to whisper in her ear. "Promise me you'll play along."

"Okay," she said, doubts rushing through her.

Damian guided her out onto the sidewalk, and Paige reminded herself that he wouldn't take her anywhere too dangerous. Surely she could make it through this and help Damian get closer to locating the people they had been sent here to find.

* * *

Damian watched the diamond courier enter the jewelry store. He knew the procedures well and suspected he would only have one shot at tagging him with the marking spray.

Damian's original plan had been to simply follow the man, but couriers were always on the lookout for someone who might be trying to rob them. When Paige had shown him her tools, he had adjusted his plans.

He hated involving her, but he couldn't think of a better way of occupying and distracting the store employees than to buy an engagement ring.

"What exactly do you want me to do?" Paige asked.

"Be very indecisive about what ring you want. Ask lots of questions of whoever is helping us."

"My Spanish isn't very good."

"Even better." Damian kept her hand in his. "I just need everyone's attention to be on you, not me."

Paige swallowed. "I'll do what I can."

"You'll be fine," Damian assured her. He opened the door and did a quick assessment.

A single store clerk, a woman in her forties, stood at the counter. A door to the side of the store appeared to lead to a work area for the jewelry maker, and Damian could hear voices coming from inside.

"May I help you?" the clerk asked.

"Yes," Damian spoke, knowing Paige would only understand a portion of what was being said. "We are looking for an engagement ring."

"Congratulations," the woman said, beaming at them both.

"Thank you." Damian motioned to Paige. "She doesn't speak much Spanish, but do you think you can help her find something she likes?"

"Of course." The woman motioned for them to sit at a nearby counter, and she reached for a key ring to unlock the display featuring diamond rings.

Damian deliberately didn't sit, taking up position behind Paige. He couldn't hear more than an occasional word or phrase from the other room, but it was enough for him to be sure the man was indeed a courier.

Determined to play the doting fiancé, Damian put his hand on Paige's back, commenting on her selections as she went from one ring to another. She slid one onto her finger, a round-cut diamond surrounded by diamond chips. Though the stone wasn't terribly large, Damian approved of the elegance of the setting and the clean lines.

"What do you think of this one?" Paige asked.

He very nearly approved of her choice before he remembered the real reason they were here. "It's a possibility," Damian said instead, suggesting she look at a few more.

Paige asked one question after another, using hand signals to communicate and sometimes relying on Damian to translate. He was starting to worry they would exhaust the supply of rings before the meeting in the other room broke up when finally the door opened. A well-dressed man in his late forties emerged with the courier.

Damian reached out and motioned to the ring Paige had set aside. "I think you should go with that one." He nudged it forward to the store clerk. "We'll take this one. How much?"

She gave him a price, one that was within his ability to pay cash.

Damian dug some bills out of his front pocket, the vial of marking spray coming with it and falling onto the floor.

The courier was nearing him, and Damian deliberately dropped some bills so he would have an excuse to stay squatted down longer. He picked up the spray bottle first, holding it in his right hand while he took his time gathering bills with his left.

When the courier walked past him, he pressed the top of the small sprayer, aiming it at the man's leg. Gathering the last of the bills, he stood and placed the bills on the table.

"Sorry about that." Damian counted out the bills and laid them on the counter.

The woman gave him his change and handed him the ring rather than giving it to Paige. Belatedly, Damian realized she expected him to give it to Paige himself.

With a nervous smile, he pulled the ring out of the box and reached for Paige's left hand. He slipped the ring on her finger and leaned forward to press his lips to hers, as much for his benefit as for show. "Perfect."

Clearly delighted with being part of their engagement, the store clerk gushed over them with another stream of congratulations.

Damian had hoped to get out of the store in time to see which direction the courier had gone in case the marking spray hadn't worked, but by the time they made it outside, the shabbily dressed man was nowhere in sight.

Keeping in character as a newly engaged man, Damian slid his arm around Paige and started down the sidewalk.

"Now what?" Paige whispered.

"Now I call Kel. He'll call in our tech guys to see where our courier goes."

He lifted his hand to hail a cab. "By the way, you were great in there."

"Thanks." She smiled. "You were pretty amazing yourself."

CHAPTER 28

Paige rubbed her thumb against the band of the ring on her finger. She felt like she was living in an alternate universe. First she was sharing a hotel suite with a man, a situation that came dangerously close to violating her personal moral decision to avoid such a thing, and now she had an engagement ring on her finger, put there by a man she wasn't engaged to. Very strange.

They walked into the hotel suite, Damian quickly checking it out to make sure they were really alone before he made his call to Kel. Paige took the opportunity to call Vanessa once more only to find that her phone was still off.

She could hear Damian talking to Kel and had the forethought to give him the specs for the tracking spray so the navy would have the ability to access the technology. As soon as Damian hung up the phone, she slid the ring off her finger. "Where's the ring box? We should probably lock this up in the safe."

"Keep it on." Damian crossed to her, taking the ring and sliding it back onto her finger. "It's safer on your finger than it would be locked up here."

"It feels strange wearing an engagement ring and not being engaged," Paige admitted.

"Not any stranger than when I put it on your finger." Damian slipped a hand behind her back and drew her closer. "I did realize something tonight though."

"What's that?"

"We share the same taste in rings. The one you picked out is very classy." He leaned down until his lips were a whisper from hers. "Just like you."

Without thought, Paige leaned into him until their lips met. She thought she knew what to expect, but this kiss was different. An onslaught of emotions tangled inside her, his lips pressing lightly against hers and then persuading her to take the kiss deeper.

She lifted her hand to his chest, his heart beating wildly against it. Her own heart pounded out an erratic rhythm, her thoughts racing.

Damian had seemed unsure of himself when his squad had left him behind, but today she'd seen a level of confidence she hadn't noticed before. She also sensed a strong commitment to protect others and wondered if she was imagining things to think she mattered more than most.

Already, she had shared more of herself with him than with anyone else. Not even her family truly understood what had driven her to go into nursing or why she'd had to leave it.

Remembering where they were, alone in a hotel suite, she drew back, lingering over one last kiss.

"Maybe I should get my own room," she said, her voice hoarse. "I think it might be more dangerous for me to be in here with you than out there facing Morenta."

He gave her a wicked smile. "You could be right." With a chuckle, he loosened his hold on her, leaving his hand resting casually on her hip. "I think I'd rather you take your chances with me though."

"I'm sure you would."

"Don't worry. I'll be good. I promise." But he didn't resist stealing another quick kiss before leading her to the table. "Kel should call back soon to let us know what's happening with the courier."

"Now explain to me how the diamond payments work. I'm confused."

"It's hard to be sure until we know where the courier goes next, and we can't be sure where he started." Damian sat across from her. "It's possible the jeweler is holding diamonds for someone, kind of like a bank, only for diamonds instead of money. The jeweler could also be a broker, where he receives diamonds and then sends a payment to a third party."

"So one person sends the diamonds to him, and then he pays someone else?"

"Exactly. It's extremely difficult to trace funds that way, especially if the jeweler does a lot of business."

"That shop didn't look very big."

"No, but that doesn't mean he isn't heavily involved in wholesale," Damian said. His phone rang, and he answered it.

As soon as he hung up, he said, "Or there's a third option."

"Which is?"

"Kel said the courier went from the jewelry store to a bank, Banco Central de Venezuela. He probably exchanged diamonds for cash and took the money there to deposit or transfer it to an account."

"So you think Morenta sent diamonds to Maracaibo with this courier, had him exchange them for cash, and then had him deposit the cash into someone's account?" Paige asked.

"Exactly. If our intel is correct, the money was deposited into an account belonging to one of the oil companies or one of their employees as a payoff for helping smuggle drugs."

"This is making my head spin."

"Me too. I think I prefer it when someone just tells me what my objective is and gives me directions on how they want me to do it."

"I'm sure the rest of your squad would have preferred that too."

"Yeah," Damian agreed. "I don't know what I'll do if we don't find Vanessa before Morenta does."

"I'm worried too." Paige reached across the table and took Damian's hand. "But we are going to find her."

"I hope you're right."

* * *

"You've got to be kidding me." Quinn was the first to express what they were all thinking. The cliff in front of them dropped at least eighty feet, and the face of it was worn smooth by constant wind and rain.

Seth looked out in the distance and could see the river snaking through the relatively flat terrain below. It had taken them three days to get this far, circling flat-topped mountains, struggling through the thick evergreens that gave way to an even thicker jungle area. The flatlands below would be a piece of cake compared to what they had already traversed, assuming they could reach them.

Tristan stepped beside him. "I think when we prayed this morning, we should have been more specific when we asked for guidance in finding our way out of here."

"You could always pray that the Lord will move the mountain," Brent suggested.

"With the way our luck's running, He would move the mountain for us, but we'd end up in the middle of an earthquake."

"How much rope do we have?" Brent asked.

"Not that much. Fifty feet maybe."

Seth moved along the edge and studied the drop. He couldn't explain the sense of urgency that had been growing inside him for the past two days. It wasn't that someone had tried to kill them. This certainly wasn't the first time he and his squad had seen battle. It was something else, something that made him feel like if they didn't escape this place soon, his life would never be the same.

He was a good twenty yards from the rest of the squad when he found what he was looking for.

"Over here," he called out to them.

"What did you find?" Brent asked, closing the distance between them.

"Look over there, about forty feet down. There's an outcropping wide enough for us to stand on. We can rappel down to there and try to climb the rest of the way."

"Handholds are few and far between," Brent said. "And we don't have the right equipment with us to anchor ourselves to the cliff face."

"Do you have a better idea?" Seth asked.

Brent looked down the terrain in both directions. "Not really."

"I'll go first. If I get down there and see it isn't possible, I can use the rope to climb back up."

"Maybe we should see if there's another way down," Jay suggested.

"We can walk for days, and we're just going to end up back here," Quinn countered. "Mountains like this one are the reason people have to fly into Canaima instead of drive."

Seth watched his friend and commanding officer consider his suggestion and found himself wondering if he too felt the same drive to press on. "I can do it, Brent."

"I guess we don't have much choice. We have no idea why someone wanted us dead, and I'm not going to rest easy until we have answers." Brent gave instructions to the rest of the squad, and they all went about securing rope and preparing what few safety precautions they could.

Seth tugged on his gloves, set his feet on the edge of the cliff, and prepared for his descent. As soon as he saw that his teammates were ready to guide him down, he stepped off the edge.

* * *

Rodrigo stood at the edge of the inner courtyard of Morenta's villa and waited to be acknowledged. Morenta sat on a stone bench a short distance away, apparently enjoying the solitude and beauty of the various trees and flowers planted within.

"Is there a problem?" Morenta called out, his gaze still on some nearby miniature palms.

"I hope not, but I did find a discrepancy I wanted to discuss with you if you have a moment."

"What is it?"

"Six months ago we suspected someone accessed some of your financial records, but we couldn't identify who it was. We thought it must have been someone accidentally getting into the wrong file since no one ever tried to access any of the accounts."

"And?"

"The accounts were viewed again a few weeks ago. It showed up on the monthly security logs."

"Who?"

"Andrea Kemper."

"The spy." Morenta's voice hardened. "Do you know what she was looking at?"

"Yes. The money transferred to Ramir. I don't know why she would care about that particular account. Those funds are frozen. We tried ourselves to recover them."

"Maybe she found a way to unfreeze the account."

"The only way to do that would be to get to Ramir."

"Or his niece. You said she was released from prison recently. Maybe those Navy SEALs know how to get to Lina. Are you sure the SEALs were killed?"

"The helicopter pilot confirmed five men were in the clearing when they opened fire."

"Check to make sure," Morenta ordered. "And I want you to go yourself. I don't want secondhand information."

"I'll leave right away."

"And, Rodrigo?"

"Yes?"

"If Andrea Kemper double-crossed me, I don't want just her punished. Make sure you take care of everyone involved. We need to set an example."

"Yes, sir."

CHAPTER 29

Her forty-eight hours were up. Vanessa had prayed she would find some evidence of Morenta in Venezuela or a clue as to how her husband had disappeared. Damian's idea that the squad had been dropped off in Canaima was the best theory so far, but it didn't explain why.

According to his logic, the sabotage on base and their current disappearance were related, both designed to draw her out. But why?

She looked out her window for a moment before closing the curtains and calling Warren.

"What have you got?" Warren asked the moment he picked up.

"A whole lot of nothing." She explained what had happened in her first hotel room and the loss of her surveillance device. "All I really know is that Andrea Kemper is the person looking for me. What do you have on her? Any idea of a motive?"

"None. Her dad is agency and has been on overseas assignments most of her life. She joined up out of college, spent a few years at headquarters, and then transferred overseas. She's been in Colombia for two years and was supposed to be infiltrating Morenta's organization."

"How deep was she able to go?"

"Not very. According to her reports, she never got past the ground floor of his organization. Intel reports are consistent with her story. We aren't even sure she's ever had personal contact with Morenta."

"Any red flags on her psych test or poly?"

"Nothing of significance. The polygrapher noted that she didn't have a strong response when she was told to deliberately lie, but some people are like that."

"Yeah, but that also means if she was lying, she might not trigger a concern."

"Exactly." Warren went on to tell her about Terrance Gunning, the man they believed might be involved in the pilot's murder. "Since he disappeared, it's possible he's in on this with her. According to Andrea's father, Gunning dated Andrea for a couple years while she was working at headquarters. The dad didn't particularly like the guy and thought they broke up when she moved to Colombia."

"Maybe they're still together," Vanessa said. "I think we may have to push them to reveal their hand."

"How are we going to find out what they're really up to?"

"We may have to give them what they want," Vanessa said.

"What they want is you," Warren reminded her.

"Yes, but there has to be a reason, and until we figure out for sure who 'they' are, we're at a standstill."

"I think we need to give the navy another day to find your husband," Warren said, altering his original plans.

"Warren, we both know that won't stop this. Even if we find him, the perpetrators are still going to go after him or his squad until they draw me out."

"That may be true, but I'd feel better if you took some time to think this through. If you're going to lay a trap, do it right."

"All I know so far is that I'm the bait." Vanessa pulled back the curtain slightly, staring out the window.

"I have our analysts looking for connections between Morenta and Terrance Gunning. We're also hoping Andrea's father can shed some more light on why his daughter might have faked her own death."

Fighting back her impatience, Vanessa relented. "Okay, I'll give you your day. After that, I'm going to do whatever it takes to find Seth and his squad."

"Understood," Warren said. "Stay safe. I'll talk to you tomorrow."

Vanessa hung up and paced along the window. She looked out onto the street again, restless. Feeling the need for some fresh air, she secured her room and grabbed her purse.

Even though she was convinced no one had tracked her to her current location, as soon as she stepped outside, her eyes swept the area in search of anything suspicious.

She didn't see any familiar faces, but she continued to look for unusual behavior as she started down the path that led along Lake Maracaibo.

For a moment, she let herself relax and appreciate the view—water rippling along the shore, sunlight streaming through the clouds. Though she didn't often eat breakfast, she started toward several restaurants down the street, her eyes continually scanning her surroundings.

She turned to look in the window of a waterfront shop and caught a glimpse of someone behind her slowing his steps. Though she fought to hide her increased awareness, her mind was already skipping ahead to where she might be able to slip out of sight and how she could check to see if the man was following her.

She took her time looking in the window front and then started forward again. At the next business, a lakefront restaurant, she paused again, glancing across the sidewalk to the lake so she could improve her range of vision. Sure enough, the same man was still a short distance behind her, and once again, he slowed his steps to match hers.

Vanessa let out a sigh in an effort to calm her racing heart. What was she thinking when she decided to come to Venezuela alone? She needed backup, and at the moment, she had no idea whom she could trust.

* * *

Paige woke to the scent of warm corn tortillas and melted cheese. She climbed out of bed and picked up her cell phone, trying once again to call Vanessa. Her stomach clenched when it went straight to voice mail again. Were they too late? Had Morenta already found her? Or had Andrea?

Paige pulled on a pair of jeans and a sweatshirt and headed into the living area. Damian sat at the table, a fork in one hand and a newspaper at his elbow. An untouched plate of something wonderful sat on the table across from him.

"Is this for me?"

"Yeah. I went downstairs and got us some breakfast a little while ago. I figured you needed some more sleep."

"Thanks. What is it?"

"Cachapas con queso. It's like a corn pancake with melted cheese inside."

Paige picked up her fork and took a bite. The warm cheese oozed into her mouth, the delightful sweet-corn taste complementing it beautifully. "Mmmm. This is good."

"Glad you like it." He pushed the newspaper aside. "Were you able to get ahold of Vanessa?"

"No. I'm really getting worried."

"I know." Damian motioned to Paige's breakfast. "Go ahead and take your time eating. I'm going to get us some transportation, and then I want to check a couple things out."

"Where are you going to get transportation?"

"I have a few ideas. I used to live here, remember?" Damian reached for the door and said over his shoulder, "I should be back in about an hour. Don't open the door to anyone. I can use my key to get back in."

Paige wanted to ask more questions, but she sat silently and watched him go. She went into her room and retrieved several of the items Ghost had given her. Using her notes, she figured out how to set up the mini-camera disguised as a pen and send the feed to her phone. She played with the position of it for a few minutes, finally situating it on the dresser so it was aimed at the door.

Setting her phone down, she crossed to the window and stood to the side like she had seen Damian do earlier. Her eyes focused on the view of the lake first. Then she looked down at the various pedestrians walking four stories below her.

She saw Vanessa immediately, but it took a moment for her mind to catch up with the image in front of her. The woman she was trying to find was only half a block away.

Paige looked at her watch. Damian had only been gone a few minutes, and he had told her to stay in the room. Surely that didn't include a situation like this one.

Paige knew she might be able to contact Vanessa again through her cell phone, but after failing so many times before, she wondered if she should take advantage of her current good fortune.

Vanessa stopped to look in a store window, and Paige was amazed at how casual she looked. Had she not known firsthand that Vanessa worked for the CIA, she would have sworn she was just like anyone else walking along the sidewalk.

Vanessa glanced up at a restaurant sign, still looking very much like someone more interested in the local businesses than in finding a drug lord.

Then the man a short distance behind Vanessa caught Paige's attention. The moment Vanessa stopped, he did too. He tried to look casual but wasn't nearly as successful as Vanessa. Paige watched intently, now realizing she couldn't wait for Damian. She had to warn Vanessa.

She grabbed her purse and hotel room key and rushed out of the room. The elevator seemed to take forever, even though it was only a few seconds.

When she emerged outside, Vanessa was nearly upon her. Not knowing what else to do, Paige hurried forward as though she was running late.

The moment she reached the sidewalk, she looked over her shoulder as though she wasn't paying attention and plowed right into Vanessa.

She deliberately let the contents of her purse spill out onto the concrete and pasted an annoyed expression on her face. "Hey! Watch where you're going!" Paige said to Vanessa, making her voice loud enough to draw the attention of several people close by.

"Siento," Vanessa said in return, leaning down to help Paige pick up the contents of her purse.

"A man is following you. Blue T-shirt, standing next to the restaurant a half block down."

"I want you to ask for directions. Ask someone else first and ask in English. Then go ask the man following me." Vanessa handed back Paige's wallet, but on top of it was a patch the size of a small pea. "See if you can plant this on him."

"What about you?"

"After you plant it, just keep walking," Vanessa whispered back. "I'll call you as soon as I'm clear."

Paige scooped up a handful of pens that had scattered.

"You can do this," Vanessa said, straightening. She offered another apology for the benefit of anyone close by before continuing down the sidewalk.

Now left alone, Paige forced herself to move forward. She spoke to the person closest to her, a woman holding a small child on her hip. "Excuse me. Do you speak English?"

The woman shook her head. "No, no hablo ingles."

Paige turned to the man in the blue shirt and saw immediately that he was going to try to avoid her. Afraid of being too obvious, she pulled out her cell phone and looked down at the blank screen as though trying to retrieve information. She waited for the man to get a step past her. With the miniature patch in her hand, she hurried after him.

"Excuse me," Paige called after him, putting her hand on his shoulder, presumably to get his attention. "Do you know where the closest pharmacy is?"

He turned and scowled, quickly pulling free of her. His answer was short and hard. "No."

"Well, thanks anyway." Paige followed up on her act by asking yet another person for help. Out of the corner of her eye, she glanced in the direction Vanessa had headed, pleased to see she wasn't anywhere in sight.

* * *

Seth didn't look at anything but the side of the cliff, his focus entirely on his task. Without a proper harness, his progression down the side of the rock face was slow and tedious. He was also highly aware that his rope ended more than thirty feet from the ground below. He made it the first twenty feet and found enough of an outcropping to use as a foothold and provide a spot for a short rest. His back and shoulders could already feel the strain of trying to climb down hand over hand instead of rappelling.

"How are you doing?" Brent called down to him.

"Okay." He thought of when he had free-climbed down the rappelling tower to help Jay and Damian, remembering the observation by his teammates that his wife would not have been pleased. He couldn't imagine she would be happy with him right now, but she could hardly blame him for trying to find a way home to her.

At least she was safely working in Virginia right now. Since she didn't have access to what his mission entailed, she wouldn't know their mission had been compromised, nor would she have any reason to worry.

He had so looked forward to the possibility of returning home with the knowledge that Morenta was in custody, that yet another threat against Vanessa's previous alias could no longer harm her.

Seth continued his steady climb, walking down the side of the cliff as his hands worked the rope. He was nearly to the ledge when an unsettling thought came into his mind.

Amy. She was supposed to receive a communication from them when they made their landing zone. That was three-and-a-half days ago, and Amy wasn't known for her patience.

Undoubtedly the navy was looking for them by now since they hadn't made their rendezvous point, but he couldn't keep from wondering if Amy or someone else in the navy might try to enlist Vanessa's help. After all, she was the only person within the U.S. government besides him to ever see Morenta in person and live to tell about it.

Seth's foot knocked some pebbles loose, and he heard them ricocheting off the side of the rock as they skittered down to the ground below.

Focus, he reminded himself. Whether Vanessa knew enough to worry or not, he wasn't going to do anyone any good if he ended up as part of the scenery below.

"Shift a couple feet to your left," Tristan called down to him.

Seth did as he was told, and a minute later, his foot connected with the small ledge. He shifted, planting his foot more firmly on it, testing his weight to make sure the outcropping was solid.

Drop Zone

Cautiously, he moved along the ledge, ensuring that it was indeed safe. Then he knelt and studied the mountain below him. As Brent had suspected, handholds were few and far between. He plotted a course in his mind, calculating the distance between the possible hand- and footholds and comparing that with his reach.

The first few feet offered little to hold on to, but if he used the rope for that part . . . He looked up and shouted. "I think I can make it."

"I'm sending Jay down first. He can help guide you."

Seth accepted Brent's direction even though his sense of urgency continued to increase.

With Seth helping to guide him, Jay's climb down to the ledge went smoothly. As soon as he took position beside Seth, Jay too studied their objective.

"I don't know, Seth," Jay said hesitantly. "The reach looks pretty long on some of those."

"I want to try." He outlined his strategy, using his hand to point to the various possibilities. "Talk me through it."

Seth took hold of the rope and pulled it up until he was holding the end. Then he tied a thick knot in the end so he could identify it. He let it fall free again, gripping a section to help lower himself the first several feet.

"Okay." Jay shifted his position to gain a clearer perspective. "Your first target is about six or seven feet down on your right side."

The climb was grueling. Only five feet after he released the rope, he had to use the full extent of his reach to bridge the gap between two of the footholds. In that moment, he realized he had a choice to make. He and Jay were the tallest on the squad, with Brent about an inch shorter. If he could barely make it, there was no way Quinn could complete the climb with the six-inch difference in height.

If he continued down, he would do so alone. If he climbed back up, he and Jay could return to the rest of the squad to find another alternative. Something pressed him to continue forward, his mind already formulating ways to extract his team from this wilderness.

CHAPTER 30

Damian parked his grandfather's old clunker in the hotel parking lot. The pickup truck wasn't much to look at, but it would blend in where they needed to go, and it was so old there wouldn't be any concern about anyone trying to track the GPS.

He locked it and hurried through the lobby to the stairwell. He didn't have the patience to wait for the elevator, eager to see Paige again and make sure she was still doing okay in his absence.

He jogged up the four flights of stairs and made his way to his room. He knocked as he opened the door to make sure Paige had some warning before he walked in.

"I'm back."

He took several steps in before he realized he was talking to himself. The silence and stillness of the room sent alarms screaming through his head, and he quickly checked the empty hotel room.

Muttering under his breath, he dashed back out into the hall and headed to the stairwell. He was all the way to the lobby before he realized he had no idea where he should look.

He searched the lobby area and hotel restaurant without success. Quickening his pace, he checked the business center and workout room and circled back to the lobby again. Everywhere he looked, he could see people going about their lives as though they didn't have a care in the world, yet his world felt like it was tipping dangerously out of control.

Becoming more frantic by the minute, he pushed his way outside. He looked up and down the street, seeing no sign of Paige. Continuing his search, he passed through the parking lot and then reached the wide strip of sidewalk that spanned the area between the lake and the many businesses overlooking it.

He still didn't see her. He stepped into the flow of pedestrian traffic so he could see farther and found himself swept along with the many people in his path. He walked as quickly as he could without bringing attention to himself, constantly searching. After walking nearly a mile, he turned around and headed back to the hotel.

Where could she be? Was it possible she had wandered off and gotten lost? Or worse, could whoever was after Vanessa have found Paige? His thoughts pulled his emotions into a downward spiral, and he struggled to consider what to do next. He was nearly back to the hotel when he caught a glimpse of Paige's blonde hair.

Relief poured through him. She was walking his direction but apparently hadn't noticed him yet. For a moment, he just stared. Her dark eyes were currently hidden behind sunglasses, the breeze sending her hair dancing.

The way she moved, she seemed so self-assured, yet he had seen glimpses of those private struggles that made up her inner core. He couldn't say why he felt so drawn to her after such a short time, and he realized he wasn't happy about getting to know her under these circumstances. It was time to find the people they'd come for and get her back to the States, where they could explore their growing feelings without worrying about their safety.

Paige's eyes swept over the crowd, and finally, she saw him. He thought he saw a hint of apology on her face. Perhaps she already knew him well enough to anticipate the lecture that was already formulating in his mind.

She started toward him but was jostled by a man in a blue shirt when she was a mere ten feet away. Protective instincts shot through him when he saw the man take Paige by the arm.

"Where is she?" the man asked in English. "I know you helped her."

"Hey!" Damian darted forward. In the amount of time it took him to close the distance between them, the man released Paige and sprinted away in the opposite direction.

"Go inside," Damian urged Paige as he took up pursuit.

The man weaved in and out of the pedestrian traffic, and Damian struggled not to knock anyone over. His target didn't appear to care about such things, pushing into a couple and sending the woman sprawling.

The distance between them narrowed, and Damian was certain he would overtake him in another block. Suddenly, the man darted into an alleyway and an engine revved.

Damian continued his pursuit but went only a half dozen steps before he saw the taillights of a motorcycle disappearing around the far corner of the building.

* * *

Seth's fingers were raw and cramped by the time his feet touched the ground. He rolled his shoulders to loosen his tense muscles, and he looked up at Jay.

"I'll have Tristan come this far before I climb down," Jay shouted down to him.

Seth shook his head, exaggerating the movement to make sure Jay understood. "The rest of them won't make it. The reach is too far."

Seth waited for Jay to relay the information up to Brent. He could hear most of the conversation between Brent and Jay, but Jay repeated it anyway.

"Brent said they'll try to find another way down."

"Negative. It will take too long," Seth said. "I'll keep going and secure a helicopter to come pick all of you up."

Jay related the information. This time, Jay didn't have to repeat Brent's words. "Jay, go with him. Code three."

"Yes, sir." Jay turned back to look down at Seth. "It's your turn to guide me. I'm coming with you."

Seth took the news with conflicting emotions. He still felt an urgency to get to Vanessa, and waiting for Jay would take at least another half hour. On the other hand, securing a helicopter to retrieve the rest of the squad would undoubtedly be a lot easier if he had help.

Knowing there was no arguing with Brent once his mind was made up, Seth stepped away from the rock face, where he would have a better view. He then began calling out instructions while he silently prayed Jay would make it down safely and quickly.

* * *

Paige waited by the lobby door, not sure if she should hope Damian did catch the guy who had been following Vanessa or if she should hope he'd gotten away. She thought she had been so clever, taking the time to find the closest pharmacy and fumbling through making a purchase so her request for directions would be believable.

Obviously, the man following Vanessa had seen through her guise.

The door opened, and Vanessa strolled in as though she didn't have a care in the world. With her suitcase rolling behind her, she looked like anyone else about to check in to the hotel.

Reaching into her pocket, Paige retrieved her hotel room keycard. She crossed the lobby to the check-in desk, deliberately brushing past Vanessa so she could slip the keycard into her hand.

"Excuse me," Paige said loud enough for Vanessa to hear. "I'm afraid I left my key in my room. Could I get another one? It's room 412."

Behind her, Vanessa continued through the lobby and headed straight for the elevator while Paige went about answering questions so she could get another key. The hotel clerk slid a new key to her, and she thanked him, turning to head for the elevators. The door opened, and she saw Damian walk inside, clearly annoyed. His annoyance hiked up another notch when he saw Paige standing in the lobby.

Trying to look casual, Paige met him by the elevator and attempted a smile. He looked at her stonily, taking her by the arm and ushering her into the empty elevator car.

"What were you doing out of our room?" he demanded as soon as the doors slid closed. "I told you to stay inside."

"I saw Vanessa."

"Where? When?"

"A few minutes after you left. I knew you wouldn't be back in time to help me make contact with her, and I noticed someone following her, so I went outside to help."

He looked at her with something that resembled a combination fury and frustration. "You did *what*? We have no idea who might be after her!"

"I know." Paige took an automatic step back. "I gather you didn't catch the guy."

"No. He had a motorcycle stashed a few blocks up. Do you know who he was?"

"Not a clue."

"I need to find Vanessa." The doors slid open on their floor, and Damian walked with her to their room. "Please stay here until I get back." He unlocked the door and held it open long enough for him to add, "I mean it."

"Damian, you don't have to find Vanessa."

"Of course I do." He lowered his voice to a whisper. "I need to make sure she's safe before I go look for my squad."

"I know, but—"

"Stay here," Damian demanded again. He nudged her inside and prepared to close the door.

"Damian, wait." Realizing Damian was too focused on his objective to listen, Paige reached out and grabbed his hand and held it firmly. "I have to show you something before you go."

"Fine." Damian huffed out the word and let her pull him inside. "What is so important—"

Vanessa stepped into view, slicing through Damian's question and silencing him.

"Maybe we should sit down and compare notes," Vanessa suggested. "It's time we pool our resources so we can find my husband and the rest of your squad."

Damian gave a solid nod, and his voice filled with resolve. "I completely agree."

* * *

"Are we really going to just sit here and wait for them to come back?" Tristan asked.

"That's exactly what we're going to do, but I think we can do a bit more than just sit around," Brent said.

"What did you have in mind?"

"See those vines over there?" Brent motioned to some vines twining their way up a nearby tree. "We're going to harvest some of those and see if we can make our own rope."

"So we can climb down too?"

"If it comes to that. I agree with Seth that it will take them two days to make it to the airport. If we don't see any sign of them in three, we may have to improvise."

"I think we should improvise now," Quinn suggested.

"You can start improvising by finding us some dinner," Brent said. "Anything besides pineapple."

* * *

Damian listened to Vanessa describe how she had spent the past two days trying to track down the people following her while attempting to remain unnoticed. He updated her on the events that had brought Paige and him here, including his theory of where the Saint Squad was currently.

"How can you be so sure the Saint Squad is in Canaima?"

"I'm not sure. It just makes the most sense to me." Damian could see Vanessa's uncertainty, which sent off a cascade of doubt in his own mind. "I looked at the radius of where the helicopter most likely would have landed, and Canaima was right at the edge of it. Every other place was somewhere where they could have made it to a town or village to send out a message."

"Unless they really were captured."

Damian tensed. "I prefer my scenario to that one."

"I do too." Vanessa swallowed and seemed to choke back her emotions. "The truth is, if they are in the wilderness somewhere, they're fine. It's the hostage situation we need to worry about."

"What do you propose we do?"

Vanessa retrieved her tablet and opened an app. "Paige helped me plant a tracking device on the guy who was following me. I suggest we turn the tables and see if he'll lead us to your squad."

Damian looked over at Paige, instantly thinking of all the things that could have gone wrong when she went out to meet Vanessa. Her eyes met his, and he could see her awareness of the risks she had taken. Wisely, he decided not to remind her of them.

Damian edged closer so he could see the tracking program on the screen. "Where is he now?"

"It looks like it's on the east side of town," Vanessa said.

"That's where a lot of warehouses are located."

"We need to find out if the squad is really there." Paige picked up her purse.

"You stay here while I check it out," Damian said.

"Damian, I appreciate that you want me to stay where it's safe, but I'm the one who recognizes Andrea Kemper," Paige reminded him. "I can't do that from a hotel room."

"I understand that, but we also don't want to walk into a hostile environment. You aren't trained for that. I am," Damian said. "Besides, I know the area, and it will be easier for me to blend in."

Before Paige could respond, Vanessa held out an arm and looked at her dark skin. "I think I'm more likely to blend in." She looked pointedly at his hair. "May I remind you that you're blond? You might be from here, but you don't look like it."

She made a good point, but he had a better one. "That may be, but I'm not the person Morenta or whoever is trying to lure out into the open. You are. I can't stand by and watch you walk into a trap."

He could see Vanessa waver. "Fine, but I'm coming with you. I can be your backup."

"You need to stay here where it's safe."

"That's not going to happen."

Damian recognized the determination in her eyes. "Fine, but you're staying in the truck."

"What about me?" Paige asked, still clutching her purse.

"You definitely stand out as a foreigner too." Vanessa set her tablet on the table. "I want you to stay here and keep an eye on the signal. If there's any movement, call me."

Paige clasped her hands together, her fingers linking nervously. Damian put his hand on her arm and spoke with confidence. "We'll be back soon." Turning back to Vanessa, he said, "Let's get going. I want to make sure our worst-case scenario doesn't get any worse."

"I agree completely."

CHAPTER 31

"It doesn't look like anyone's here," Vanessa said quietly from the passenger seat. The old truck rumbled to a stop.

"Call Paige and see if the signal has moved."

Vanessa did so, confirming that they were still in the right place. She reached for the door handle. "Come on. There's only one way to find out if they're here."

"You said you were going to wait in the car."

"No, *you* said I was going to wait in the car." Vanessa climbed out and prepared to head off Damian's objections. "I'll wait here until you make your first sweep."

"I'm starting to see why all the guys are scared of you."

"You have no idea," Vanessa said, the hint of humor briefly overshadowing the deep-seated fear of what they might find inside.

Vanessa watched Damian circle the building to make sure they were really alone. She studied the structure for points of access but saw only the door in front of her. It was exactly the type of place someone might use to hold others captive.

When Damian approached the door, Vanessa moved forward, glancing around to make sure they were still alone. Damian shone a light around the doorframe, obviously looking for any sign of tampering.

"Is it clean?" Vanessa asked.

"It looks good, but maybe you should stand back just in case."

"Why?"

"This is my first time doing this for real. I'm supposed to be here to protect you, not get you killed."

Vanessa reached out her hand and took the light from him. Quickly, she examined the doorframe before handing the light back to him. "This isn't my first time, and it looks good."

"Humor me anyway," Damian insisted.

Vanessa let out a long-suffering sigh, but she did as he asked. She couldn't help but notice Damian's protectiveness, a trait she had seen often in Seth. She also found herself wondering if Paige and Damian could see the parallels in their relationship and her own with Seth.

Her focus snapped back to the present when Damian cautiously opened the door. As soon as he stepped inside without any incident, Vanessa hurried forward.

The room was dim, the only light coming from the open doorway. Damian flashed his light around the room, stopping when it illuminated something along the far wall. Vanessa recognized the form as a lifeless body at the same time he did.

"Oh no." She breathed the words out in a whisper, praying it wasn't Seth or any other Saint Squad member.

Damian worked his way around the room, making sure there weren't any other surprises, but Vanessa couldn't wait. She rushed forward, lowering to her knees the moment she reached him—she assumed it was a male from the person's obvious height.

"Flash the light over here," she urged Damian.

He complied, approaching where she knelt with the beam of light cutting through the darkness. When the light reached the man's face, Vanessa looked up at Damian with relief and surprise.

"He's the man who was following me." Vanessa reached down and checked his neck in search of a pulse. The feel of his cool skin told her there wouldn't be one. "He's dead."

"What do you think? Did his own people kill him, or was it the Saint Squad?"

Vanessa reached a hand out for the light, and Damian handed it over. "He took a bullet to the back of the head. That wasn't our guys."

"I didn't see any sign of the guys being held here. I don't like this. It feels like a trap." Damian motioned to the door. "We need to get out of here."

"Just a minute." Vanessa searched through the man's pockets. She didn't find a cell phone or wallet, but she did find a folded-up piece of paper tucked away in his jacket pocket. "All right. Let's go."

She handed the flashlight back to Damian and followed him across the room, both of them deliberately staying to the side of the door in case someone really had lured them here. Damian held up a hand when he reached the door, signaling for Vanessa to stop.

In the distance, she heard what had alerted him. The sound of an approaching engine.

"We need to make a run for it," Vanessa urged.

Damian poked his head out, quickly checking the area. Then he turned to her. "Follow me."

Sprinting forward, he headed for the truck, and Vanessa did what she could to catch up, skidding to a stop next to the passenger side door Damian already had open for her. "Get down," he urged.

She dove inside and shut the door so she wasn't visible.

The engine drew closer, and she could only imagine it had turned the corner to the alleyway where they were parked. She felt rather than saw Damian climb into the bed of the truck, presumably to stay out of sight.

Vanessa struggled to keep her breathing regular and quiet. So many emotions bolted through her. The terror that the man in the warehouse was Seth hadn't completely subsided, and now she was faced with the heart-pounding fear that whoever was looking for her might be a few yards away.

She squeezed her eyes shut, willing back the tears that threatened. Seth had to be okay. She repeated the words in her mind, desperate to find some sense of peace.

The car came to a stop, and she heard a door open and slam shut. Though it pained her to do so, she fought the urge to look. She thought about trying to slip a surveillance device onto the dashboard, and she reached into her bag to follow through, but before she could activate one, a car door slammed again, and the engine roared back to life.

Tire rubber squealed against the pavement, and a moment later, Damian opened the driver's side door.

"Any chance you got a look at them?"

"Yeah. It was only one guy, but I doubt he's worth going after," Damian said.

"What makes you say that?"

"He's just a local hire."

"How can you be so sure?"

"He was a cop, but he didn't sound the alarm when he went inside the building and found a dead body." Damian slid the key into the ignition. "Makes me think he already knew about it. Most likely, he's the one who killed that guy."

"This whole situation is getting more confusing by the minute."

"You're telling me." Damian started the engine. "Any idea of what we should do next?"

"Maybe." Vanessa held up the paper she had retrieved out of the dead man's pocket.

"What is it?"

She unfolded it to find a piece of letterhead from a local bank. On it was a date and time beneath the word *exchange*. "Take a look. What do you think is being exchanged?"

"Diamonds." Damian tapped a finger on the letterhead before putting the car in gear. "That's the same bank where Paige and I followed a diamond courier."

"What diamond courier?"

"We got a tip that Morenta was using diamonds to pay off his contact with one of the oil companies. We were able to tag the courier."

"Any idea where he is now?"

"Here. You can use my phone to call Kel and check." Damian handed his phone over to her.

Vanessa hit the talk button and waited for the call to connect. Kel didn't offer a greeting. Instead, he demanded, "Did you find her yet?"

"They found me," Vanessa said, feeling a little guilty now for not letting Damian contact him sooner.

"I've been worried sick about you."

"Sorry. Someone was waiting for me at the airport, so I had to drop off the grid."

"How are you on supplies and cash?"

"Not great, but I can manage."

"I think you should stay at the hotel with Damian and Paige. It's safe, and it's already paid for."

"I may do that." Getting back to the point of her call, she asked, "Can you tell me where the courier has been since he left the bank?"

"He took a flight into Cali, Colombia, this morning," Kel told her. "He's at Morenta's compound there right now."

"Then we do know Morenta has been operating here in Venezuela."

"We do, but we don't have any confirmation of whether he's there or still in Colombia," Kel said. "We're using satellite imagery to search for the squad. We thought maybe they were dropped off in Colombia rather than Venezuela. There's a part of the country that was within the helicopter's range."

"I assume you haven't found anything."

"No. Nothing."

Vanessa told him about the man who had been following her. "We didn't find any identification, but we think there's going to be another payment at the bank three days from now at nine o'clock."

"Where did you get that from?"

"A paper from the guy's pocket."

"Any chance you can get some backup from your agency? I'd like to give Damian a chance to follow up on his theory of where his squad ended up."

"I can call Warren when we get back to the hotel."

"Great. Tell Damian and Paige to pack. They're going on a trip tomorrow."

"Why Paige too?"

"Because Damian is going to need her with him to secure a helicopter."

"I'm confused."

"Just trust me on this one. And do me a favor and get me your phone number. This phone is a disposable and can't be traced."

"I'll text you from my phone when I get back to the hotel."

"Stay safe."

"I will. Thanks, Kel." Vanessa hung up the phone and handed it back to Damian. "Kel said for you and Paige to pack your bags. You're going to Canaima."

CHAPTER 32

Finally, Damian thought as he boarded the plane to Canaima.

He and Paige had barely made their flight out of Maracaibo to Caracas because of an accident during morning rush hour. In fact, they probably would have missed it if he hadn't relented and let Vanessa drive them.

He hadn't expected Seth's wife to be such a speed demon. At least no cop had dared to try to catch up with her as she had weaved her way through traffic to drop them off.

Damian didn't think he would have been able to take sitting around and waiting for the next flight out, a flight that would have missed their connection, the only flight going into Canaima today.

He prayed his instincts were right about this. What if he couldn't find them? What if they really were in Colombia being tortured while he went sightseeing with his girlfriend?

Not that Paige was officially his girlfriend, but they were heading that direction. He took Paige's suitcase from her and stored it in the overhead bin. The sparkle of the diamond on her hand caught his eye, and he experienced an odd flutter in his stomach. He liked the look of the ring on her finger, but even more, he liked knowing he had been the person to put it there.

Paige slid into the window seat, and he lowered himself into the one beside her, his hand automatically reaching for hers. Lowering her voice, she asked, "Is everything okay?"

"So far, so good." He glanced around to see the midsized plane was nearly full. "Just a little worried about what could happen if I'm guessing wrong."

"Everyone has to make educated guesses sometimes. Kel obviously trusts you, or we wouldn't be on this plane right now."

"I suppose you're right."

She squeezed his hand. "I know I'm right."

* * *

The succulent scent of roasting chicken wafted through the air, giving Seth and Jay their first sign of civilization since arriving in Venezuela. They kept to the trees, making their way silently forward as they hiked along the river.

Following the scent, they came upon a clearing where several men were tending to a fire. A half dozen spits, each six feet long, balanced against each other and formed what looked like a teepee frame. Each one was laden with whole chickens.

Seth's mouth watered. From the smell, he guessed the food was ready to be served, but the quantity didn't match the number of people in the clearing.

Jay nudged him and nodded toward the water. Coming around the bend of the river, three longboats were moving forward, each one carrying six to eight people, an onboard motor at the back of each propelling the boats against the current.

From their dress and the number and variety of hats the occupants wore, Seth quickly concluded they had stumbled upon a tourist group.

The men in the clearing must have seen the tourists approaching as well. One began setting out plates and eating utensils, and the others started carving meat and dishing it onto large platters.

Ignoring his grumbling stomach and his growing impatience, Seth waited silently while the longboats were beached and their occupants disembarked. As soon as the locals began serving the food, Seth motioned to Jay, and they used the sound of the new arrivals to skirt along the edge of the clearing toward the riverbank.

He planned to give the tourists a wide berth, but when he noticed three more longboats beached around a small bend, he changed his mind. Jay shifted his path as well, both men taking care to remain hidden as they made their way to the water's edge.

With the thick trees making them invisible to the group, the two men quickly slid one of the boats into the water and climbed in.

Jay picked up an oar and used it to push off from the bank, and Seth tried to determine a destination. Unable to see any other signs of civilization, he opted to head the same direction the longboats had come from. Besides being the likely starting point for the tourists, it also had the added advantage of being out of sight of the feast going on a short distance away.

Using the natural rhythm and current of the river to carry them forward, Seth and Jay used the oars to steer but otherwise were able to conserve their strength. Over an hour passed before they saw the first sign that they were on the right path. Seth spotted two more longboats upriver, undoubtedly another local tour.

Thought it pained him to have to wait longer, Seth motioned to Jay, and the two men rowed to the side of the river, where they could take cover in the shadows of the trees.

"Seth, look over there," Jay said, keeping his voice down even though they appeared to be alone.

Seth looked up to where Jay was pointing and saw a white streak through the sky. As they waited for the longboats to continue slowly in the opposite direction, a passenger airplane slowly came into view and began its descent. Projecting its path forward, Seth estimated it would land less than five miles away.

"I think we found our next stop," Seth said. Another boat came into view, and he motioned to the tall grass and nearby trees. "I think we may have to go the rest of the way on foot. We'll be too easy to spot if we stay on the water."

"It would be faster if we stay on the water. We could wait until dark."

"It's too risky. We have no idea what's ahead of us." Seth continued to watch the airplane in the distance, using his compass to mark its heading. Another tourist group came into view. "We may have to wait until dark to move regardless. The trees aren't thick enough through here to hide our movement, and we don't want to lose track of the river."

"I doubt these tourists will stay on the water much past dinnertime." Seth motioned to two boats in the distance. "I think we should wait for a few hours, and then we can start up again."

"In that case, what's for lunch?"

* * *

Vanessa made the call to Warren. He answered on the first ring. "Finally! I was starting to wonder about you. Is everything okay?"

"I'm fine," she assured him.

"What's the latest?"

"Damian and Paige are heading to Canaima. Damian is convinced that's where the Saint Squad was dropped off."

"I thought they were taken captive."

"I'm still working that angle," Vanessa said, trying not to consider the possible implications. "With Paige and Damian gone, though, I wanted to see if you can find me some backup here in Maracaibo." She proceeded to bring him up-to-date on everything that had happened since they'd last spoken, including the diamond courier and the suspected upcoming exchange at the bank.

"You've been busy. Let me check with Maryanne and see who I have available to help you." The line went silent for a moment, presumably because he put her on hold as he conferred with his secretary and checked his sources. After a couple minutes, he came back on the line. "Antonio is in town. Give me the details and the hotel you're staying in. I'll have him come to you."

"I'm not giving out my address over the phone, not even to you."

"How can he contact you?"

"I'm going to check out the bank this afternoon, get the lay of the land. Have him meet me at the restaurant two doors down. I'll have a table under the Spanish version of your oldest son's name."

"What time?" Warren asked.

"Four o'clock."

"I'll get the message to him," Warren said. "Be careful."

"Always."

* * *

Paige watched Angel Falls out the window, fascinated. The water seemed to be a small trickle at the top, barely visible, with the white cascade of the falls becoming more evident as it drew closer to the ground. When it disappeared from her view, she shifted to look at Damian. "That's something I never thought I would see."

"Pretty amazing, huh?"

"It is. Have you been here before?"

"A couple times. The last time was when my family brought me here after I graduated from high school. I doubt it's changed much though."

"Why's that?"

"With the political unrest and the lack of access to the area, most businesses wouldn't want to invest here even if the government would allow it."

When they touched down, Paige was surprised to see that the airport consisted of little more than a boarding ramp and a primitive wooden structure with a thatched roof. The sun was already hanging low in the sky when they deplaned and collected their luggage. "Do you think we'll be able to go on that helicopter tour today?"

"Unfortunately, no. But before we leave the airport, I'll make sure we have a reservation for tomorrow." Damian looked down at her hand and lowered his voice. "Speaking of which, I need to steal your ring back until tomorrow."

"Okay." Paige slipped it off her finger. "Why?"

"Just a hunch I might need it to make sure we're the only passengers." Damian saw the tourism counter a short distance away. "Stay here with the luggage. I'll be right back."

Paige watched him walk across the airport structure in a dozen strides. He spoke to the man behind the counter of what appeared to be a helicopter tour company. She had seen only a single helicopter outside, but maybe there were others out giving tours at the moment.

Damian motioned to her and leaned closer to the man conspiratorially. Both men looked at her briefly before the conversation continued. She saw Damian slip several bills to the man before they shook hands. The man said something else to Damian, something that brought a smile to his face.

When Damian returned to Paige's side, she asked, "What was that all about?"

"He approves of my taste in women."

"Is that so?"

"Absolutely." Damian leaned down and gave her a quick kiss.

Her cheeks flushed at the unexpected display of affection.

"Come on. Let's go find our ride." He led her back outside, each of them pulling their carry-on luggage behind them. An airport shuttle was waiting right beside the door. Damian took both of their bags and loaded them into the back, helping other passengers until the driver indicated it was time to leave.

They rode in silence, Paige afraid to say anything on the crowded minibus. She was surprised at how quickly they arrived at their destination, guessing the drive was only a mile or two at most. The resort was a series of huts, all with thatched roofs and looking very much like they belonged to a primitive village.

Several passengers jostled for position as people headed for the large hut overlooking a beautiful lake area.

"I thought Canaima was on a river," Paige said.

"Lake Canaima is fed by the El Carrao River." Damian motioned to the line of people at the reception desk. "Let's go get something to eat first and wait for the lines to die down."

"That sounds good." Paige followed him to the other side of the hut, where a restaurant was located, warmth spreading through her when he took her hand.

Wicker chairs and bamboo place mats offset the cream-colored tablecloths, and only a handful of tables were occupied. They were shown to a table overlooking the water, two waterfalls flowing into the deep blue.

Damian tucked their luggage beneath the far side of the table and sat across from her.

"It's beautiful here," Paige said, wishing they truly were here simply as tourists. She turned her gaze back to Damian to see him staring at her. "What are you thinking?"

A waiter interrupted before he could answer, and Paige was surprised when Damian ordered for both of them. As soon as they were alone once more, he said, "Sorry, I didn't want to wait too long to eat. I'm a little anxious to get checked in so I can take a look around."

"That's okay." Paige kept her voice low. "Is there anything we can do tonight?"

"As soon as we drop our luggage off in our room, we'll take a walk so I can get my bearings. Other than that, I'm not sure there's much we can do until tomorrow."

"I guess you'll have to pretend to enjoy yourself for a while."

"I won't have to pretend," Damian replied. "I just can't figure out how to stop feeling guilty that I'm sitting here with you while my team is out there doing who knows what."

"They're probably sitting around drinking coconut milk and trying to figure out how they're going to harass you when they get back."

A smile pushed back the worry in his eyes. "You seem to already understand them better than I do."

"I don't know about that, but they all do seem to have a pretty healthy sense of humor."

"I think you're right."

* * *

"I am so bored." Quinn threw a coconut up in the air and caught it.

"You're breaking my heart," Tristan retorted.

"If you're so bored, why don't you go collect some fuel for our fire tonight?" Brent suggested.

"I'm not *that* bored."

"Go find some fuel anyway." Brent's tone shifted from a mild suggestion to an order.

Quinn accepted the direction good-naturedly. "Come on, Tristan. You can help me."

"Hey, I'm injured."

"A couple of scratches and you call that an injury?" Quinn asked. He didn't wait for an answer before heading into the brush.

"You know he's not going to last much longer just waiting here," Tristan said as soon as Quinn's footsteps had faded.

"I know." Patience had never been Quinn's strong suit. Brent looked out at the horizon. "How's your arm doing?"

"Better."

"Better, as in it's starting to heal, or better as in you can climb down a cliff?"

"Both."

Brent considered his answer. "We'll give them until noon tomorrow. If we don't see any sign of them by then, we'll start after them."

"Do you think those vines will hold us?"

"They'd better." Brent motioned to the tree above them. "But we'll test them in the morning just to make sure."

* * *

"I know Quinn said the terrain was rough, but this is getting ridiculous," Jay said.

Seth stood beside him, staring at yet another steep drop, this one situated between two thirty-foot waterfalls. He looked at the water flowing on either side of them. It appeared when they had ditched their longboat, they had inadvertently come ashore between two tributaries of the same river. They were trapped by the rapids on either side, but if they could reach the lagoon below, they could skirt around to the village. If necessary, they could swim across.

"At least it's not as bad as the last one."

"The last one we had rope, and we still had to leave half the squad behind," Jay reminded him.

Seth couldn't argue with that.

"And," Jay added, "we didn't have to worry about an audience."

Less than a mile away, they could see the thatched roofs of a community of huts clustered by the lagoon. A number of people were currently taking advantage of the wide beach and peaceful setting.

Seth studied the cliff face, pleased that this one had a decent number of hand- and footholds. He considered their dilemma. They couldn't climb at night, or they wouldn't be able to see to get down. If they tried during the day, they would most definitely be noticed, and he hesitated to be in a position of drawing attention to themselves. "I think our best bet is to wait until sunset. The shadows will hide us, but we'll still have enough light to see. The airport looks like it's only a mile or two past the village. We can make it there easily tonight."

Jay pointed to some nearby trees. "We should be able to hide out there and get some rest while we wait."

"And eat some more pineapple?"

Jay rolled his eyes. "And eat some more pineapple."

CHAPTER 33

Vanessa stood across the street from the restaurant. She was early. She was always early.

The restaurant had barely opened for dinner when she approached the host and made her reservation for four o'clock. At the same time, she had pressed a small audio device to the underside of a wooden podium just inside the door.

She had no intention of sitting exposed at a restaurant. She would wait for Antonio to come to her. Then she would show up after she was sure neither of them had brought any unwanted company.

From her position, a shadowed alley between two buildings across the street from the restaurant, she had the added advantage of being able to observe the comings and goings at the bank. Damian had told her how to spot a diamond courier, but after an hour had ticked by, she hadn't spotted anyone who fit the profile.

The courier Damian and Paige had tagged with the marking spray was who they expected to see tomorrow, but their sensors showed he was still in Colombia. If she did see a courier tonight, it would be someone else, someone they hadn't seen before.

Business continued at the bank and the restaurant as usual. The earpiece Vanessa wore gave her access to the people entering and leaving the restaurant, but so far, no one had asked for Guillermo, the name Vanessa and Warren had agreed on. Four o'clock came and went, Vanessa growing apprehensive as the minutes ticked by.

One of the rules she often tried to drill into her students' heads was the importance of being on time for a meet. She also emphasized that when someone wasn't on time, the likelihood of intelligence being compromised grew exponentially. Ignoring her own advice, she lingered thirty minutes longer, hoping Antonio really was just running late or perhaps had gotten caught in traffic.

When it became apparent that her contact wasn't coming, Vanessa finally stepped out of her hiding place. She strolled casually down the sidewalk past one business and entered the next one, a bakery she had scouted when she'd first arrived. She went through the motions of buying a baguette.

After making her purchase, instead of heading back out the front door, she walked to the back of the shop as though she was going to use the restroom. Just past the restroom doors, she reached the back door of the bakery, turned the knob, and stepped outside.

Now in another alleyway, she used the buildings on either side to conceal her as she traveled a full block before entering the underground garage of another building, this one a hotel, where she had parked Damian's truck.

Though she knew she should wait until she got back to the hotel room to call Warren, she pulled out her phone and dialed. "Your guy wasn't there."

"I don't understand. I confirmed with him right after we spoke. He had the address and the time. Are you sure you didn't miss him?"

"Positive. I was two hours early, and I waited another half hour past the meet time."

"I'm sorry, Vanessa. I'll check to see what happened. We can try for another meet tonight."

"Tonight's not good," Vanessa said, feeling like she would be pushing her luck to try for a first-time meeting after dark. "I'll get back with you."

She didn't wait for Warren's response. She hung up the phone, turned it off, and slid the key into the ignition. The truck roared to life, and Vanessa pulled out of the parking garage. Using her own brand of CIA protocol, she circled away from the bank and drove in a different direction than her final destination.

She made sure she wasn't being followed and finally stopped to eat dinner. She took her time over her meal, waiting until it was dark before making her way back to the truck and circling through the city once more, this time toward the hotel.

* * *

"You aren't going to believe this," Terrance said as he walked into the room.

Andrea looked up from the stack of real estate listings that currently littered the kitchen table. "You'd better not tell me Vanessa Johnson is dead."

"No, but she disappeared again."

"Did she show up at the bank?"

"I caught a glimpse of her heading into a bakery across the street," he said. "Are you sure your friend at CIA is giving you good information?"

"The information is good. You just aren't using it very well."

"She didn't see me there. She'll be back in a couple days. Obviously, she thinks the clue we left her is credible, or she wouldn't have shown up today."

"I hope we don't end up regretting killing Pablo," Andrea said.

"He had become a liability, and you know it," Terrance insisted. "Vanessa could identify him, and we couldn't take the chance that he would be picked up and talk."

"I thought you just didn't want to pay him the extra money he was asking for."

"That too. Paying off that cop to kill him was a whole lot cheaper than what Pablo was asking for," Terrance said. "Besides, it could prove helpful to have someone on the police force helping us look for Vanessa."

"This is getting ridiculous. We should have had her days ago."

"We'll get her." He tapped his finger on the real estate listing closest to him. "You just concentrate on how you're going to spend all of this money once we do."

* * *

"Is this all for us?" Paige stood in the center of the large living room, a half dozen wide chairs arranged with several occasion tables to make a nice conversation area. Three doors spanned the wall across from the entrance, a shared bathroom situated between the two bedrooms.

She pulled her suitcase to the room on the left to find two full-sized beds as well as a hammock hanging from the wall to her right and a pillar located a few feet from the end of the beds. Leaving her suitcase inside the door, she turned back to Damian. "Seriously. Is this all for us?"

"It is." Damian put his suitcase in the other bedroom. "I'm not sure if this was all they had available when Kel booked our room or if he's being optimistic about us finding the rest of the guys."

"Let's assume it's the latter."

"I want to take a walk around. Do you mind coming with me?"

"Not at all." Paige followed him outside, raking her fingers through her hair when the wind picked up and sent it dancing around her face. They walked in silence past a large thatched building that appeared to house standard guest rooms, each one equipped with a hammock hanging from the pillars on either side of a small patio.

She could have guessed he would head straight for the water. After passing by the resort restaurant, he took a path through some tall palms and led her out to the beach. In the distance, the sun was dropping on the horizon, shadows playing over the water.

Seeing they were alone, Paige asked, "Any idea how you're going to find them?"

"Not really. At this point, it's pretty much a matter of luck and prayer." Damian slipped his arm around her waist. "The earliest I could reserve the helicopter tomorrow was eleven. Assuming the helicopter is fully fueled, that will give us at least a couple hours of search time. The challenge will be convincing them they want to be found."

"You think they'll try to stay out of sight?"

"I would," he said. "They're in a country they have no business being in, and they wouldn't have any idea who is flying above them."

"You make it sound impossible."

"Not impossible, but challenging, to be sure." Damian squinted his eyes, staring out at the waterfalls. "It can't be."

"What?"

"I think I may have just found them."

"What are you talking about? Where?" Paige followed his gaze, but all she saw was the shimmer of the sun on the water and the white of the rapids coming over the falls.

He drew her closer to his side and leaned down as though telling her a secret. "Look at the falls on the right. Between them—can you see it?"

She leaned her head against his shoulder so it wouldn't look like she was staring. For a full minute, she didn't see anything but what she expected to see. Then she caught a glimpse of movement. "Is that someone climbing down the cliff?"

Excitedly, he gave her a quick squeeze. "I can't think of anyone else who would do that in this particular spot. Tourists would be with guided tours and wouldn't be able to reach the cliffs between the falls. The locals would know better than to get trapped between the sections of river."

Paige continued to watch, but she didn't see anyone besides the one figure approaching the bottom of the cliff. "I only see one person."

"I saw two when I first spotted them. The rest of them must already be at the bottom."

The last man disappeared into the shadows. "I can't see anyone now."

"They're either behind the waterfall, or they're in the lake." Damian kept searching the water, and Paige could feel his need for action.

"Now what?" she asked when he continued to stare intently.

"No matter how they decide to get there, I have a pretty good idea of where they're going."

"The airport?" Paige asked.

"It's the only way out of here." Damian slid his arm off her shoulders and reached for her hand. "Come on. Let's get you back to the room, and then I'm going to go track them down."

"Is there anything I can do to help?" she asked when they stepped aside.

"For now, I just want you to stay inside and out of sight."

"Do you want me to call Kel or Vanessa?"

"There's no cell service here. Besides, I don't want to say we found them until I'm sure." Damian walked her inside. "Please don't go anywhere. It will look odd if you're outside alone, and I don't want anyone wondering where I am."

"I'll be waiting."

"This might take a while. You might want to try to get some sleep. I have a feeling it'll take them at least an hour or two to make it to the airport."

"Just be careful."

"I will." Damian leaned down and gave her a quick kiss. Then Paige found herself in the middle of a beautiful hotel suite completely alone.

CHAPTER 34

The words of Damian's various instructors paraded through his mind as he lay in wait. Even though he was sure his teammates would come here to the airport, assuming that really was them he'd seen on the cliffs, searching for five men who were trained to stay invisible wasn't going to be easy.

A total of five aircraft were currently on the ground: a four-passenger Cessna, two medium-sized passenger planes, and two helicopters. The planes were parked at the far end of the runway; the helicopters were off to one side of the airport, over two hundred yards away. That area was huge when considering who he was searching for.

Forcing himself to be logical, he discounted the Cessna as being inadequate for their needs. He wavered between the other options. The passenger planes were large enough to carry them all out of here, but so was the larger of the two helicopters.

"What would I do?" Damian asked himself. He couldn't cover the entire airport by himself, and he knew his best chance of finding his squad was to wait for them at their destination, so he headed for the largest helicopter, the same one he had chartered for tomorrow. While the planes had enough space to carry them home, they also needed a runway to land. The versatility of the helicopter made it the better choice.

Keeping to the trees near the airport, he made his way to the helicopters. Each step was painfully slow as he checked for underbrush and anything that would make a sound before putting his foot down. He knew his squad would be doing the same thing, but they were more experienced and undoubtedly faster.

A man emerged from a structure nearby. His easy gait and lack of awareness of his surroundings told Damian he was some sort of employee.

Cautious, Damian stopped. Realizing a single person wouldn't deter his teammates, he willed his rapid heartbeat to slow.

He continued to skirt along the edge of the trees. The man did a cursory check of the helicopters before heading across the field for the village. With any luck, he was closing up shop.

Damian didn't see any other signs of life at the airport. If he remembered correctly, airplanes didn't fly in and out of Canaima at night, partly because of the remoteness of the airport and partly because tourists wanted the chance to see the falls when they flew overhead.

The man continued forward, disappearing down a path at the edge of the airport building.

As soon as the footsteps faded, the airport fell silent until a second man walked outside. Damian identified him as a security guard making his regular rounds.

The man was clearly bored. His hands were shoved deep in his pockets, and his head was down as though his entire focus was on the ground three feet in front of him. Occasionally, he slowed long enough to kick a pebble in his path.

A light drizzle began, the splatter of raindrops providing some background noise.

Damian watched the man make his loop down the runway, stopping to check on each of the airplanes before swinging by the helicopter pad and then heading back to the airport's main building.

He went inside, presumably to take a break and get out of the rain. Damian crept forward, his eyes scanning the area for any sign of his team. He had to be able to pick out at least one.

He studied the helicopter in front of him, trying to determine what they would do. With the security guard nearby, they wouldn't want to open the door for fear that the cockpit light would draw attention.

Disabling that light would be the first order of business, at least for him. Locating the panel where they would have to access the electrical system of the aircraft, Damian lowered himself beneath the helicopter, lying on the ground beside the runner.

When the security guard made his next pass, he had to remind himself to keep his breathing slow and easy. Thirty minutes ticked by excruciatingly slowly.

The security guard disappeared inside again. As soon as the door clicked closed, he heard it—the faint crunch of a palm frond, barely audible.

Damian stayed where he was, his eyes still scanning. Several more minutes ticked by before he finally saw what he was looking for. A pair of U.S. Navy–issued boots approaching his position.

He wasn't sure he had ever seen Seth more surprised than when he leaned down to access the helicopter panel and found Damian lying in wait.

"It's Damian," he said quietly.

"How did you find us?" Seth asked, stunned.

"I guessed."

"That was one heck of a guess!"

"I have this helicopter chartered for tomorrow, and I have a room at the village." Damian slid out from under the helicopter. He could just make out someone at the edge of the trees twenty yards away. From his height and build, Damian identified him as Jay.

"Where's everyone else?"

"Still out there." The airport door opened. Seth fell silent but signaled for Damian to follow him, and they both headed for cover.

Damian fought the urge to hurry. As soon as they reached cover, Damian started to head for the village, but Jay stopped him. He pointed to a spot a short distance away where he could just make out several large gas containers. "What should we do with these?"

"Are those filled with fuel?"

"Yeah. It's never a good idea to commandeer a vehicle without making sure it's ready to go first." Jay held up a long coil of rope. "Or a way to accomplish our objective."

"Camouflage all of that beneath some of those palm leaves. We'll need it all tomorrow," Seth told him. The men quickly hid their supplies. Seth motioned for Damian to take the lead as they headed through the strip of jungle between the airport and the resort. Keeping to the shadows, they made their way forward, determined to stay unheard and unseen.

* * *

Paige couldn't sleep. She sat in one of the cushioned wicker chairs, her elbows on her knees, her hands steepled in prayer, praying Damian would come back safely.

She heard the doorknob rattle and sat up straight. The latch opened and relief poured through her when Damian walked through the door followed by Seth and Jay.

Both men were covered with dirt and grime, and it was obvious from the pungent smell they carried that they hadn't had a real shower in days.

"I can't believe you found them."

"That makes two of us," Seth said with a sense of wonder.

Jay closed the door behind them.

"Where is everyone else? Are they okay?" Paige asked.

"If you consider being stranded on a mountain fine, then, yeah, they're great," Seth said.

Damian motioned to the chairs. "Why don't we sit down and talk."

"First, I need food," Jay insisted.

"I'll go get you something," Paige offered. She could see Damian hesitating. "I'll be fine. I'll just say we want a romantic dinner in our room."

"That's a great idea, but I'll go. You can fill them in as well as I can. Probably better." Damian headed for the door. "I'll be back in a few minutes."

Paige sat back down and motioned for them to make themselves comfortable.

Seth took the seat across from her and looked around the room. "Where's Vanessa? Is she here with you? Is she okay?"

"She's fine. She's in Maracaibo right now. She was following what we believe is a diamond payment from the drug cartel to someone working in one of the big oil companies."

"Why is she in the field?"

"Amy told her you were missing, and then the CIA's deputy director of operations asked her to go back undercover. We think someone was using you as bait to draw her out," Paige said. "We still don't understand why, but we're pretty sure we know who. We've been able to trace one diamond payment back to Morenta. It looks like he's the one who set you up."

Seth rubbed both hands over his face. "He would certainly have the resources to do it."

"Vanessa found a clue that indicates another diamond exchange is supposed to happen day after tomorrow. That's why she stayed behind in Maracaibo. She thought she might be able to use the courier to find you."

"When is the exchange supposed to happen?"

"Nine in the morning," Paige said. "So what exactly happened with you guys?"

"First tell me what you know about Vanessa while we wait for Damian," Seth insisted.

Paige filled him in on how someone had been waiting for Vanessa when she arrived in Maracaibo and how she'd been followed ever since. "I wish I could figure out a motivation for why they're trying to get to Vanessa," Paige said. "It seems so extreme to hijack an entire squad of navy SEALs and then murder their pilot."

"What?" Seth straightened, his entire body suddenly alert. "What happened to the pilot?"

"Amy told us the doctor estimates the pilot was killed about half an hour after he returned to the ship."

"Any idea of who did it?"

"A couple people left the ship before the pilot's body was discovered. We don't have any direct evidence connecting him, but one of the people who took that transport hasn't been seen since."

"Who is he?"

"Terrance Gunning. He's a civilian contractor."

"Any leads off him?"

"Not that I know of."

Paige continued to bring him up to date, relaying the events of when Vanessa had been followed near her hotel and how that man had also been killed.

Jay spoke up for the first time. "It sounds like somebody is using local hires to do their dirty work and then tying up loose ends before they can get traced back to him."

"I have to think Gunning is one of the people behind this since he hasn't shown up dead," Seth said.

Paige nodded. "We also think Andrea Kemper may be involved. She was CIA until she faked her own death several months ago. She was undercover as a low-level employee for Morenta. She also used to date Gunning."

"Any idea why she would fake her own death?"

"None. Again, it comes back to motive. We need to know what is driving these people. What is so important that they'll go to such extremes and even kill to get to Vanessa?"

"I wish I knew," Seth said.

They speculated until Damian arrived a few minutes later with food and a couple bags from the gift shop.

"I picked up some clothes for you guys. No offense, but you could both use a shower."

"Jay, you can go first," Seth offered.

"Really?" Jay stood up, not giving Seth a chance to change his mind. He took the clothes Damian offered and headed for the bathroom.

Turning his attention back to Damian, Seth said, "Explain to me what the plan is with the helicopter."

Damian motioned to Paige. "I slipped some extra money to the guy at the reservation desk to say the flight was full. I told him I wanted privacy when I proposed to my girlfriend over Angel Falls."

Seth looked from Paige to Damian. "Well, that was quick."

"Don't start." Damian shook his head.

"I have the coordinates for where we left the rest of the guys. I want you, Jay, and Paige to go pick them up."

"Shouldn't we call Kel and have him send a helicopter in to get them?" Paige asked.

"After someone tried to kill us the other day, I don't think a night extraction is going to work, especially since they don't have any comm gear," Seth explained. "They'll need to see us coming, and a navy chopper can't come here in broad daylight."

"That's true, but why do you want the rest of us to get them? Where are you going to be?" Damian asked.

"I'm going to be a tourist flying back to Maracaibo."

"Why don't you just wait and come with the rest of us?"

"I don't want to wait that long. I have to make sure Vanessa is okay, and I don't like the idea of her staking out that diamond exchange alone."

"She said she was going to call Warren and get some backup."

"No offense to the CIA, but I'll feel a lot more comfortable knowing I'm the one backing her up."

"I suppose I can understand that," Paige said.

"There may be one glitch in your plan. You're assuming there's a flight out tomorrow."

"We've been using the flights in and out to guide us here. It looks like a flight arrives every day about noon and then leaves around two." Seth looked at Damian hopefully. "Any chance you have extra cash? Ideally, I can buy my ticket before you guys leave tomorrow and make sure there really is a flight."

"I have cash." Paige stood up and disappeared into her room. She returned a moment later with the remaining currency Ghost had given her and laid it out on the table. "Take what you need."

Seth counted out enough bills to pay for his ticket a couple times over. "Thanks, Paige. I'll make sure I get you a receipt."

"Do you want me to write down where Vanessa is staying?"

"No," Seth and Damian said in unison.

When she looked at them, confused, Damian explained. "We don't want anything in writing that someone might be able to use to find her."

Damian then gave Seth the location of the hotel and her room number.

"Do you want her phone number too?" Paige asked.

"I don't have a phone to call her with," Seth said, sitting up straighter. "Do you have a way to call her now?"

"She's been keeping her phone off most of the time, and unfortunately, there's no cell phone service here, and we don't have a satellite phone," Paige said.

"Here. You can use my cell phone to access the hotel's Internet." Damian handed his phone to Seth.

"That's a good idea. I can send her a message in case she does turn on her phone. Otherwise, I'll catch up with her tomorrow."

"What do you want us to do after we retrieve the rest of the squad?" Damian asked while Seth attempted to access the Internet.

"Meet me in Maracaibo."

"In a stolen helicopter?"

"Good point. You may have to be creative on this one." Seth paused long enough to type in a short message to Vanessa. After he sent it, he looked up at Damian. "We can sneak in again tonight to make sure it's fully fueled. With the extra fuel we have hidden, that would ensure you could make it all the way without stopping."

"Actually, I already took care of that. I told the guy I wanted to be able to stay up as long as possible in case I lost my nerve and needed extra time."

"Good thinking."

"I do what I can," Damian said. "We will probably have to set down somewhere, though, and wait until nightfall to travel. Otherwise, it's too likely the wrong people will notice us."

Jay emerged a few minutes later looking like a new person. "It's all yours, Seth." He looked from one bedroom door to the other. "Which bunk is mine?"

"Paige is in that room over there, so I guess you guys are bunking with me."

Jay walked in, immediately flopping onto the nearest bed. Seth looked inside as well and gave Damian a cocky look. "I hope you like hammocks."

"What? I was here first."

"Yeah, but I outrank you."

Damian sighed. "That you do."

CHAPTER 35

"Are you sure about this? Can't we just pay off the pilot?" Paige asked.

"We have to be sure he won't have a chance to go blabbing to somebody," Jay insisted. "Seth's flight doesn't leave until after we're supposed to leave for our tour."

"Paige, you can handle this." Damian's words of confidence gave her the push she needed. She also couldn't deny the feeling of comfort she had felt come over her when Seth had offered a prayer before they all left their room. Amazingly enough, that feeling had remained with her.

She drew a deep breath. "Wish me luck."

"You won't need luck." Damian gave her a cocky grin. "But good luck anyway."

Paige rolled her eyes and felt some of her nerves fade. She found it interesting how protective Damian could be, but when the situation called for it, he could put that aside and give her the courage and support she needed.

She followed the path to where the helicopters were parked, a pilot leaning over an open panel as he went about his preflight check.

"Excuse me," Paige said. "Do you speak English?"

"Sí, señorita. Un poco." He paused as though realizing he had just responded in the wrong language. He held up his thumb and forefinger, holding them slightly apart. "A little."

"My boyfriend said I should meet him here."

"Ah. Sí, sí." He nodded understanding.

"Have you seen him?"

He looked confused now, like he was trying to decipher her words. He motioned her to the side, indicating for her to wait a short distance from the helicopter.

She pretended not to understand. "Are you sure you don't know where my boyfriend is? He was supposed to be here already."

Again, he motioned her to the side. When she ignored him a second time, he took her by the arm and guided her to a waiting area.

Paige nodded, pretending she just now understood. As soon as the man turned around, Damian appeared a short distance away and started heading toward them. He called out and lifted a hand in greeting.

The man turned, his focus now on Damian, and Jay rushed at him from behind. The helicopter hid them from view from anyone who might be standing at the airport, but the blow to the back of his head, followed by the administration of a sedative sent him to the ground.

Damian continued forward like he hadn't noticed anything unusual.

"What are we going to do with him?" Paige asked as soon as Damian had reached her.

"We're taking him with us."

"What? Why?"

"If we leave him here, there's too great a chance someone will find him or he'll raise the alarm when he wakes up. The sedative will only keep him out for an hour or so."

"How can we bring him with us?" Paige asked as Jay and Damian loaded him into one of the backseats. "This helicopter is only intended for six people."

"Don't worry. We have a plan." Damian buckled the man in and secured his hands while Jay checked out the helicopter. As soon as he completed his preflight check, the two men retrieved something from the woods. Paige thought they were just gathering their belongings, which they had stashed before she had approached the pilot, but her eyebrows lifted when she saw they were loading gas cans as well as their luggage.

"Is that the extra gas you guys were talking about?"

"Yeah. We can't make it all the way to Maracaibo without refueling. Those will save us from having to stop at some airport and explain why we're flying a helicopter that doesn't belong to us." Damian waved Paige toward the seat beside the unconscious pilot. "Grab a seat and strap in."

Paige did as she was told. Damian closed her door and stepped out to talk to Jay. After a quick discussion, Jay climbed into the pilot seat, and Damian took the seat beside him.

Jay handed a coil of rope to Paige. "Can you tie three knots at the end of this? Each knot needs to be about a foot apart."

"Sure."

Jay shifted his attention back to Damian. "What's the time?"

"Two minutes until eleven."

"Get on the radio and clear us with the tower."

Damian put on the headset and flipped the switch to activate the radio. He spoke in Spanish, and Paige noticed the way he disguised his voice, presumably to make him sound more like their pilot.

Jay started the engine, and within a few minutes, they were lifting off the ground.

Paige's stomach leapt into her throat as they lifted off. The noise from the engine was much louder than she'd expected, making communication difficult, if not impossible.

Jay started toward Angel Falls, the direction everyone on the ground would expect them to go. Once they were clear of the immediate area, he veered off to the east.

After twenty minutes or so, Jay hovered over a wide grassy area not far from the river's edge. She could see the two men in front of her pointing and discussing something between themselves. They apparently came to an agreement when Damian nodded and Jay took the helicopter down to the ground.

Paige looked around, searching for the other members of the Saint Squad. No one was in sight.

As soon as they touched down, Damian climbed out and unbuckled the pilot from his seat. To her surprise, he pulled him out of the helicopter and settled him in the shade of a small tree. After he untied the man's hands, Damian ran back to the helicopter and took his seat once more.

"You're just going to leave him there?" Paige asked, leaning forward and raising her voice to be heard.

"He'll be fine. He can follow the river to get back to the village. It just may take him a day or two."

"Shouldn't we leave him some food or something?"

Jay shook his head. "There's plenty of fruit around. How do you think Seth and I managed to make it without any rations? Personally, I hope I never see another pineapple again."

The moment Damian strapped himself back in, Jay lifted off, called out some coordinates, and headed toward the flat-topped mountains in the distance.

Not sure what to think of her first helicopter ride, Paige tried to settle back and enjoy the view.

* * *

Rodrigo walked through the clearing, leaning down to pick up a piece of camouflage fabric. Palm fronts blanketed the area where the Navy SEALs had supposedly been standing, and several coconuts lay split open by automatic weapons fire.

Decoys. The men sent to kill the SEALs had shot decoys.

Now he had to face the unsettling question of how the intended targets had known to create the illusion that they had been killed. Did Andrea Kemper use them as a way to gain Morenta's trust and ultimately a way to access his financial records, or were these men really that lucky?

Regardless of the answer, he knew what he had to do. The Saint Squad had to be found. And then they had to die.

* * *

"Something must have happened to them," Tristan said.

"Maybe they found another cliff they couldn't scale," Brent suggested.

"Are we going to go?" Tristan asked. He lifted a section of the vine rope. For days they had braided long sections together, being careful to intermingle where one began and another one ended so they could extend the length.

"It's time we do something," Quinn insisted. "I can't sit here any longer."

Brent turned and eyed Quinn. "Has anyone ever told you that you need to learn some patience?"

"Sure. My wife, my mom, my sisters, Tristan."

"Have you ever thought about listening to them?"

Quinn considered the question, then shook his head. "No, not really."

"All right, Quinn. Are you volunteering to go first?" Brent asked.

"Definitely. I'm the shortest of everyone. If I can make it down, you guys should have it easy."

"Provided those stitches hold," Brent said, motioning to Tristan's arm.

"He's fine," Quinn insisted.

"He's right. I'll be fine."

"All right." Brent secured one end of the vine rope to a tree. "Put on that harness you made. We'll have you use both ropes as far as they'll go. That way if the vine one doesn't hold, you've still got something to hang on to."

Quinn did as Brent suggested and tugged on both ropes to test their strength.

Brent watched him back to the edge of the cliff and waited for him to give the final go-ahead. His own impatience mirroring Quinn's, Brent fought his doubts and nodded his approval. "We'll talk you down to that ledge."

"I've got this," Quinn insisted. He tugged one more time on the rope Jay and Seth had used three days earlier, then took his first step off the edge, his weight falling backward as he started his slow and steady descent.

Brent watched him reach the narrow outcropping, where Quinn took advantage of the opportunity to rest.

Now was the time for the test. Rather than rappelling, Quinn would have to use the ropes as a safety harness and begin free-climbing down the cliff. He made the first few feet without any trouble, though Brent could see the way he had to grope and search to find the hand- and footholds since he had no one to guide him from below.

"If you don't think you can make it without help, I can come down to the ledge."

"I'm okay so far." Quinn came to the end of the rope, and Brent sensed his reluctance when he let go of it and was forced to rely entirely on the braided vines.

He felt his own muscles tensing as he watched Quinn shift from one side of the narrow ledge to the other in search of more handholds. When he reached the section Seth had warned them about, the vine supporting a good part of his weight, Brent saw Quinn's foot slip on the rock just below him. The surface was smooth as glass and slick with last night's rain.

"Reach six inches to your left. I see a break in the rock." Brent continued to help guide him the best he could from above. Adrenaline pumped through him as Quinn reached the point where he would have to trust the rope rather than rely on himself to free-climb.

Quinn's foot slipped, and Brent saw the first sign of another problem. The rope Quinn had trusted had been rubbing up against the protruding ledge, and the vines had cut away and were fraying badly. "Hold on, Quinn! The vines are fraying."

Brent cursed himself for letting Quinn go first. He should have led the way and made sure it was safe for the rest of his men. Quinn fought to regain his previous position, gripping the narrow grooves tighter.

The vines continued to fray, Quinn struggling for a solid hold. Brent saw his dilemma and struggled for the right answer. Quinn could either trust the rope to hold his weight despite the weakening integrity or cling to the rock, knowing he had nowhere to go. With so few hand- and footholds, Brent doubted he would be able to get back up by himself.

Determined to find a third option, Brent grabbed the rope. "I'm going down to help him climb back up. Tristan, guide me to him."

He hadn't yet taken that first step when he heard the low rumble of an aircraft. Brent identified it as a helicopter without looking, and a new sense of uneasiness came over him. What had he been thinking? He should have trusted Seth. Or more precisely, he shouldn't have let any of his men trust the wrong rope.

Images of bullets spraying from the helicopter several nights ago drove home how vulnerable they all were at the moment, especially Quinn.

Tristan grabbed his assault rifle and handed another one to Brent. They all knew they were outmatched if this helicopter was loaded with armed men.

Clearly aware of the possible threat, Quinn struggled to climb back up. He tried to find purchase with his right foot without success. A second attempt caused his other foot to slip, his arms and fingers tensing as he hung on for dear life.

The helicopter drew closer, the downdraft from the rotors making it even more challenging to hold on as it circled above them.

Torn between wanting to climb down to help Quinn and facing the new threat, Brent lifted his weapon and took aim. If someone started shooting, he wasn't going to be able to help Quinn if he was hanging on to a rope too.

He saw the helicopter circle three times before coming to hover over them. A rope dropped, dangling out the open door of the helicopter above, three knots tied at the bottom. Code three. It was a signal from his teammates. They had come to take them home.

Brent signaled for the helicopter to come closer, and he reached for the rope. As soon as he had it firmly in his grip, he tied the rope around him and used hand signals to communicate his intent. He waited for the weightless sensation to come over him when the helicopter lifted up again, this time with him dangling from the rope below.

His teammates lowered him until he was even with Quinn. Brent shouted to Quinn over the noise of the rotors, but he wasn't sure he could be heard. As soon as he was close enough, he hooked his hand under Quinn's arm.

Knowing his grip was the only thing standing between Quinn and a thirty-five-foot drop, Brent tried to position himself so Quinn could also grab the rope.

The helicopter lifted them both until they were over the clearing at the top of the cliff. Their feet touched the ground, and they both collapsed onto it.

Brent looked up again, expecting to see Seth or Jay in the open door. When he saw Damian's face, he wondered if perhaps his impression to leave the new kid behind wasn't so much for his protection as it was for theirs.

Chapter 36

Andrea looked at the screen on her phone, instantly alarmed when she saw the number was blocked. She answered it, her concern heightening when she heard the familiar irritated voice on the other end of the line.

"We have a problem. The Saint Squad is flying out of Canaima today."

"How did they manage that? They were dropped off where there's no access, and Morenta said his men killed them all."

"Obviously they survived, and there was better access than you thought. This whole plan isn't going to work if Vanessa Johnson knows her husband is safe."

"Then we'll have to change his circumstances," she said.

The voice turned harsh. "See that you do."

* * *

Seth didn't like this. He didn't like the complete absence of intelligence, the lack of knowledge about the motivation behind whatever was at work against Vanessa. He needed to put the pieces of the puzzle together, to understand them so he could keep his wife safe. He also worried that he had yet to receive a response to the e-mail he'd sent last night.

The breakdown in communication they had experienced was beyond frustrating, not only the sabotaged comm gear his squad had received but also his inability to talk to Vanessa. Whoever had dumped them in Canaima had done their research. Without a satellite phone, the only means of communication was through the outdated Internet service or the hotel phone systems. Not only were the phones not secure, but they also weren't private.

The one positive about Canaima was the complete lack of security at the small rural airport. Since air travel was the only way into the park, the airport didn't worry about checking identifications of those flying out.

Since he had been able to purchase his travel all the way through to Maracaibo, he was also able to bypass security in the Caracas airport. Surveillance cameras had been easy enough to avoid when he had moved from one gate to another. Hopefully he could remain unnoticed now that he had arrived at his destination.

His height alone typically caused people to take notice of him, but he tried to stick with the crowds.

He deliberately stayed to the far side of the hall when he exited by the security checkpoint. He had given his assault rifle to Damian in Canaima, but he had kept his sidearm with him, unwilling to travel unarmed, especially knowing he wouldn't have to go through a full security check.

Staying close to the wall, he took the time to circle to the far exit so he could hail a taxi. He saw a policeman wander in the same direction he was heading, and Seth decided it was a great time to check his shoelaces.

He leaned down, retying the left one, his eyes still tracking the cop. When he stood, the person who had been behind him bumped into him.

"Siento," Seth mumbled, using some of his limited Spanish to try to blend in.

"I'm sure you are," a man responded in English.

Seth turned halfway around, but that was as far as he got before he felt a sharp pinch in his arm. The room went dark, and his muscles went lax as he dropped to the floor.

* * *

The courier hadn't moved from Morenta's villa in Cali. That fact alone unsettled Vanessa. Why would Morenta need more than one courier? If there really was going to be an exchange today, the courier would have been on a plane hours ago.

Also, why hadn't her backup ever shown up? The question rattled through her head, and an uncomfortable possibility wound its way into her brain. For years, she had trusted Warren above all others within the agency. He had been the one to send her undercover in Akil Ramir's organization. He had ultimately been the person to send the Saint Squad in after her when her handler had suffered a heart attack.

Now she questioned why she was here and how information only he had been privy to seemed to keep falling into the wrong hands. Of all people, Warren would know the only thing that could possibly bring her back into the field was a threat against her husband.

With his position in the agency, he would have access to military personnel. He could easily have facilitated the rappelling "accident" and the wrong coordinates for dropping off her husband's squad. But why?

She needed to leave for the bank in a matter of minutes, but she couldn't shake the feeling that something wasn't as it seemed. Warren had given her a second opportunity to meet her backup, and again, the guy hadn't shown. She supposed it was possible that it was her contact who was messing up rather than Warren, but she found herself afraid to trust anyone in the CIA right now.

Needing someone to brainstorm with, she turned her phone on with the intent of calling Kel. She saw the indicator that she'd received a message and opened it. Gratitude and relief flooded through her. Seth was safe. She let it sink in for a minute before she dialed the phone and called Kel to pass along the news.

She then confided in him her suspicions.

"Don't go to the bank, Vanessa," Kel insisted. "The only intel you have is unreliable, and you can't be sure it isn't a trap. Wait until the squad catches up with you. We can always track the courier and set something up when we have adequate personnel in place."

"I hate to let this possibility go, but I think you're right. I don't like this whole situation. If Warren is involved, he would have to know I would be suspicious by now."

"I agree. Wait for Seth to come to you. When we know everyone is safe, we'll figure out a plan of attack," Kel promised. "In the meantime, I'll have Amy coordinate with the squad of SEALs I have on standby aboard the *Truman*. They'll figure out how to get you all out of Venezuela."

"I would appreciate that. I'm sure all of us are ready to go home."

* * *

Jay landed the borrowed helicopter near Lake Maracaibo, several miles away from the city. Eager to clear the area so they wouldn't draw attention to themselves, the Saint Squad and Paige hiked two miles in silence before Damian suggested another mode of transportation. "Brent, how would you feel about me calling my uncle for a ride?"

"I don't know about involving your family, especially at seven in the morning," Brent said.

"We can trust my uncle," Damian said. Unlike his uncle who drank himself to death, this particular uncle had always demonstrated a well of integrity and faith. He lowered his voice and added, "Paige can't keep up this pace much longer, and we can't leave her behind."

"I don't want anyone to know where we're staying."

"I'll have him drop us off somewhere else, and we can take taxis from there," Damian suggested.

"Okay," Brent relented. "Make your call."

Damian called his uncle, giving a brief explanation of why he hadn't let him know he was in town and then asking him to meet him a short distance away. Fifteen minutes later, he and Paige slid into the cab and the rest of the squad climbed into the bed of his truck.

"Uncle Fernando, this is my girlfriend," Damian said in Spanish, not giving her name so he wouldn't have to choose between her real name and the alias she was currently traveling under. "Thanks so much for picking us up. We had some engine trouble a ways back."

"Anything for family." He looked speculatively at Paige. "Your girlfriend. She doesn't speak Spanish?"

"Not much."

"You'll teach her," Fernando said confidently. "Now, who are these men in the back of my truck, and where am I taking you?"

Damian saw his uncle's uneasy glance over his shoulder. "Don't worry. They're friends." He gave Fernando the name of a hotel on the way to his uncle's home. After his uncle dropped them off, Damian promised to visit him later and said his good-byes. When he turned to Brent, he said, "I think we should split up. We'll be harder to find that way."

Brent nodded in agreement. "Quinn, you and Tristan stick together. I'll go with Damian and Paige. Switch cabs a couple times to make sure none of us are being followed."

"Where's our final destination?" Quinn asked.

Damian rattled off the address. "Whoever gets there first can hang out in the restaurant downstairs. There's a bar area in sight of the front entrance. Then we can all meet upstairs on the fourth floor."

"See you there." Quinn and Tristan started down the street, waiting until they were a block away before Quinn raised a hand to hail a cab. As soon as they were safely on their way, Brent flagged down another taxi.

Paige slid into the middle of the backseat, with Damian on her left and Brent on her right. A moment later, the taxi was headed toward the hotel.

* * *

"What do you mean Seth isn't here?" Damian asked. When they had abandoned their helicopter, he had thought their biggest challenge of the day would be to make it back to the hotel without being followed. Now they were standing in the hotel suite with Vanessa only to find Seth hadn't arrived yet. He sensed Vanessa's concern but couldn't bring himself to hide his own worry. "He should have been here last night."

Vanessa's face paled, but her voice was rigid. "Why wasn't he with you?"

"He was worried we wouldn't get back before you were supposed to go to the bank. He wanted to stop you or at least make sure he was here to back you up in case you didn't get his e-mail."

"Maybe his flight was canceled or delayed," Vanessa said hopefully.

"It's possible. He would have had to connect through Caracas."

"I'll check," Tristan offered. A few seconds passed. His voice was edgy when he gave them the news. "His flight was late, but he still should have been here seven or eight hours ago."

Brent put a hand on Vanessa's shoulder, but he looked at Tristan. "See if there's any way to tap into the surveillance video for the Caracas and Maracaibo airports."

"Maybe he was being followed and didn't want to take a chance of leading anyone back here," Vanessa said.

For the next two hours, they utilized their various resources to search for Seth. Damian tried to help Quinn and Tristan access the surveillance video feed, and Brent contacted Amy and Kel to have them join in the search.

Tristan was the first to access the videos. All of them split up the possibilities, no one finding any sign of Seth.

"Maybe he didn't get out of Canaima. He could have gotten detained," Brent said.

"He didn't have identification on him," Tristan said.

"And he kept his sidearm with him," Jay added. "Either of those things would have flagged him if the airport had more security than he expected."

Hours crept by. The tension in the room continued to rise, the chatter between them limited to direct questions and answers. Paige quietly left to get everyone food at lunchtime and again when it was time for dinner.

Vanessa barely managed to eat anything, worry consuming her. When the proximity alarm sounded on her tablet, she automatically silenced it.

The only surveillance equipment she had activated since arriving had been stolen from her first hotel room.

The alarm sounded a second time, and she nearly turned it off again. Then her thoughts caught up with reality. The hidden camera hadn't been destroyed. It had been turned off.

Quickly, she picked up her tablet again and accessed the surveillance program.

Her breath backed up in her lungs, her chest tightening painfully as she stared at the image on the screen. She blinked hard against the tears that threatened.

Paige was the first to notice the extreme change in her expression. "Vanessa, what's wrong?"

She couldn't speak, could barely breathe. She held up the tablet to show an image to the rest of the group. Blindfolded, with his hands bound in front of him, her husband lay in a heap on a concrete floor.

CHAPTER 37

Seth kept his breathing deep and steady, not stirring as he woke. He could feel the drugs still in his system, the pounding in his head, and the sluggishness in his mind.

Unsure of whether he was being watched or not, he remained motionless as he fought against the fuzziness in his brain, his senses waking.

His eyes still closed, he began analyzing his surroundings. The texture of cold concrete against his face, the scent of meat and spices, the sound of a man's voice followed by silence. A nylon cord bound his wrists together, but thankfully they were tied in front of him instead of behind his back.

A minute passed, and he heard another voice, this time a woman's. "This had better work."

"It will. Trust me," the man responded. "If Vanessa was able to figure out the exchange at the bank was a trap, she'll figure out where we want her to go now."

"Let's hope she falls for the same trick her husband did. It won't be as easy with her because she'll be looking for us."

"She'll be looking for you. She doesn't know what I look like."

"You think she doesn't," the woman said warily. "The real question is whether she'll cooperate once we get to her."

"To keep her husband alive, she'll do whatever we ask," he insisted. "There had better be as much money in Ramir's accounts as you think there is."

"More than fifty million," she said confidently. "More than enough for us to disappear if we want to."

"Or we can make sure no one is left behind who can identify us."

"That would work too." The sound of a chair scraping against concrete sounded. "Are the explosives set?"

"Yeah. The charge will go off if anyone tries to get through the door . . . or if you press the magic button on the detonator."

"Excellent. In that case, make sure he can't get out of here. It's time to go."

"He's tied up, the room has no windows, and the door is wired with explosives that can only be disarmed from outside. He's not going anywhere," the man promised. "If you really want, we can leave Luis here to watch him."

"Are you sure you don't want him to come with us?" she asked. "We can't be sure if she will have help with her."

"The girl with her is just a paper pusher. As for the new Navy SEAL, we don't need him, so we shoot to kill."

"Just make sure you don't take out Johnson, at least not until we have what we want from her." The woman lowered her voice. "Does Luis have any idea what we're really after?"

"Not a clue. He's happy to take our money and do whatever we ask."

"In that case, lock the door and let's see if your plan will work."

* * *

"There isn't any sign of him on the airport security cameras," Quinn said, concern evident in his voice.

"Seth would avoid the cameras," Brent said. "There's no way to be sure when or where he was captured."

"Regardless of when he was captured, I'm sure he's here in Maracaibo," Vanessa said, clearly fighting to keep her voice calm.

"How do you know that?" Brent asked.

"The camera feed. This particular device only has a range of five miles."

"That's still a lot of area."

"Not really." Damian pointed to Vanessa's tablet. "Pull that feed up again."

Vanessa complied, clearly struggling against the images on the screen as she replayed the recording of the earlier transmission.

"We're pretty much in the center of the tourist district," Damian said.

"So?"

"Look at where he's at. The floor is concrete, and the lighting looks fluorescent."

"It looks like a basement to me," Jay put in.

"Exactly," Damian agreed. "Most of the buildings in this area have underground parking, and basements in general aren't common. Not to mention that half of our search area is in Lake Maracaibo. Clearly, he's not there."

"I'll do a building search for this part of town," Quinn said, accessing the Internet on the laptop Paige had lent him.

Damian stared at the image of Seth, desperately searching for anything that would help him narrow the search further.

Paige stood beside him, apparently content to watch the activity around her. She put a hand on his back, and Damian felt her silent support.

"I don't see anything nearby that matches this," Damian said, frustrated as he conducted his own search on his phone.

"What about a laundry room or an unfinished storage room in one of the hotels?" Brent asked.

"Wait. I think I found something." Quinn shifted so he could show the computer screen to everyone else. "There's an office building a couple miles away. According to the specs, it has a basement. The parking garage for the building is next door."

"Any other possibilities?" Brent asked.

"Not that I can find. Damian's right. Most of the buildings through here are hotels with underground parking or businesses that don't have basements."

Damian felt a sense of pride at Quinn's words. Maybe he was finally going to make a difference here. Maybe he could find his place.

"I hate to say it, but this feels like a trap," Paige said, interrupting his thoughts. "Assuming Andrea Kemper is behind this, she would know the range of the camera and be aware that Vanessa has been trained as an operative. Anyone with that training knows the camera feed can only go five miles."

"Paige is right. We have to think they're going to be waiting for us," Vanessa said. At Damian's confused look, she added, "Andrea had a reason for sending us an image we could identify so quickly. She wants me there."

"Maybe you should stay here, then," Damian said.

"No, I'm coming. You may have to use me as bait."

"Are you kidding? Seth would kill us if we did that," Quinn said.

"Not if he's dead. I'm not going to let anything else happen to him," Vanessa said. "I'm coming. Besides, she's expecting me. Not all of you."

Brent didn't dispute her claim, taking charge as Quinn pulled up more information about the surrounding buildings and they began formulating a plan. Damian found himself in the middle of the discussion, his knowledge of the city proving useful.

"We need transportation," Brent said finally. "We can't be sure of Seth's condition or if he will be able to walk, much less run."

"We can use my grandfather's truck," Damian offered. "It's parked downstairs."

"Great. We'll have you drop us all off near the building. Then you can park and join us."

"I'll have to go a few blocks away to park unless you want me to use the building's parking garage."

"No, park somewhere else. I don't want to take the chance that they might have surveillance in the garage."

"What about me?" Paige asked.

"I want you to stay here," Damian insisted before Brent could answer.

"You can handle communications for us," Brent added before she could object. "We're limited on phones, and we don't have any of our usual gear. If we get into any trouble, we'll call you."

"What exactly would you want me to do if you *do* have trouble?"

"If you can't figure out a solution, call Kel. Actually, you can call Kel now and let him know what's going on," Brent said before turning his attention to everyone else. "Let's roll."

Damian saw the concern on Paige's face. He lowered his voice and spoke to Brent. "Vanessa has my keys. She can show you where my truck is parked. I'll be down in a minute."

Brent looked from Damian to Paige, apparently understanding there was more going on here than Paige's feeling abandoned. "Don't take long."

Damian nodded. He waited until everyone else had left the room and dug the diamond ring out of his pocket. "Maybe you should hang on to this again."

She reached out automatically to take it, but Damian captured her left hand and slipped the ring into place. He slid his hand around her waist and lowered his lips to hers.

I missed this. Why such a thought would go through his mind at a time like this was beyond him. It had been barely more than a day since they had stood on the beach of Lake Canaima together, since he had last held her in his arms. How could she so quickly become so central to everything he wanted?

Reminding himself his squad was waiting for him, he broke the kiss and took her hand. "Everything is going to be fine."

"Be careful," Paige whispered.

"I will." He squeezed her hand and forced himself to turn away and leave her behind.

CHAPTER 38

Vanessa knew it was a risk, but it was a risk worth taking if it would bring her husband back to her. Besides, if these people wanted her dead, they wouldn't have gone to such great lengths to lure her here. Assuming that theory was correct.

Her thoughts continued to fester as she considered Warren, who was so well respected within the intelligence community, whom she had trusted with her life on numerous occasions before. Everything over the past few days pointed to him. So many pieces of information were leaked, most of them ones only he knew.

It's all circumstantial, she reminded herself. If Warren really was behind this, she needed proof. And she needed a motive.

"Ready?" Brent asked.

"I'm ready," Vanessa confirmed.

"Tristan and Quinn should already be in position on the far side of the building," Brent said. "Jay will cover this side, and I'll watch your back."

"What about Damian?" Jay asked.

Vanessa didn't wait for Brent to respond. "I don't want to wait."

"I understand, but let's give him a couple minutes," Brent said. "As soon as Damian gets back from parking the truck, we can have him watch this entrance so Jay can give us extra backup."

"I'll keep watch for him." Jay took a step back so he was deeper in the shadows of the building next door, where he had a better view of the road.

Not happy with Brent's decision, Vanessa looked down at her watch. "Five minutes. After that, I'm going in with or without you."

"I understand," Brent said quietly. "But we both know there's no way I'm going to watch you go in there alone."

* * *

Seth waited until he heard a door close in the distance before he opened his eyes and surveyed his surroundings. The room was completely bare, the walls and floor made of concrete. A single lightbulb shone overhead, a string dangling down to turn it on and off.

As he'd already heard, the only access to the outside world was through a single door. The hinges were on the inside, but on closer study, he could see the wires attached to whatever explosive device they had rigged to the door.

With the proper tools, he might be able to disarm it, but not without some way of seeing what it looked like.

He knew the likelihood of someone finding him here was slim, but Seth couldn't take the chance that one of his teammates might miss the signs. Though it wasn't an easy feat with his hands tied together, he dug through his pockets, searching for anything hard.

A one-piece bolivar became his first choice, but when he tried to tap it against the concrete floor, the sound barely carried. Putting two coins together wasn't much better.

He took off his shoe and tried that, again with dismal results. His belt buckle became the next possibility. This time, when he struck the metal against the concrete, it sounded clearly.

Though someone would have to be close to hear it, he decided it was worth a try. He settled himself down against the wall beside the door and began tapping out a steady rhythm of Morse code: Door rigged.

* * *

Damian weaved through the traffic, wishing he were already back with his squad. He hated knowing Vanessa was putting herself at such risk, and he didn't doubt Quinn's assessment that Seth wasn't going to be happy about it. He considered how he would feel if it was Paige risking herself for him. That thought alone made him press down harder on the gas pedal.

The parking spaces along the street were already occupied, and he tried to think of the closest alternative. Since a fire had burned several buildings in this section of town a few years ago, many of the businesses had changed. The light in front of him turned yellow. He hesitated only a moment before he ignored the possible consequences and punched through it as it blinked to red. Feeling only a little guilty, Damian continued his search.

He noticed a restaurant down a side street with a parking garage beside it. *That's new*, he thought to himself. He turned toward it just as flashing lights appeared in his rearview mirror.

"Great," he muttered. He pulled off to the side of the road opposite the garage he had been heading toward. He stared at his intended destination and was struck by a moment of clarity. If a parking garage had been constructed here, it was possible that some of the new buildings through here could have basements. With the government corruption over the past several years, it was also likely that some of the building specs hadn't been updated after the fire.

Damian quickly grabbed his cell phone and called Paige.

"Is everything okay?"

"A cop just pulled me over, but I need a quick favor." He gave her the cross streets of his location. "See if you can find anything on updated specs on the buildings here after a fire a few years ago. There might be basements in some of them."

"I will. What about you?"

A police officer rapped on his window. "I'll call you when I get done with the cop."

Damian ended the call and rolled his window down. "Is there a problem, officer?"

The answer was much more extreme than Damian had thought possible when he looked up to see a gun aimed at his head.

* * *

Paige hung up the phone and looked for the information Damian had asked about. An article on the fire came up on her first try, but nowhere did she see information about the reconstruction of any buildings. Trying a different tactic, she searched for images, listing the street names Damian had given her.

This time several results appeared. One included photos of a new parking garage. When she flipped through the additional photos included in the article, she saw what Damian was looking for. The building next door to the garage was still under construction when the photo was taken. Paige could clearly see the framing of the building, including a stairwell descending below ground level.

The Saint Squad knew they were likely walking into a trap, but was it possible they were putting themselves in danger to rescue someone who wasn't even there? Paige wavered on what to do. She didn't want to call Vanessa. Even if her phone was on, she wouldn't want to risk someone hearing it go off if she was trying to sneak into the office building.

Damian said he would call back, but he had no way of contacting the rest of his squad to let them know what was going on. He also couldn't be in two places at once. If Seth really was at the building near Damian, Damian would have to choose between going to help his squad and trying to find Seth alone.

Paige reminded herself she wasn't trained for this kind of work, but that didn't stop her from grabbing her purse and heading for the door.

She flagged down a taxi in front of the hotel and gave the driver Damian's location. Assuming he wasn't in a position to answer his phone, she sent a text message confirming his suspicion along with the location of the building she had identified.

The lack of a response sent her nerves into overdrive. What could she possibly do that Damian couldn't do alone? She nearly decided to have the cab driver turn around when she saw Damian pushed up against the side of a police car, his hands on the hood and his feet forced apart, the police officer standing right behind him.

The moment the taxi pulled to a stop, Paige tossed some bills over the front seat at the driver and leapt from the car. "Help!" Paige yelled, rushing toward the policeman. "My sister is missing!"

She shouted in English, but the volume and panic she forced into her voice were sufficient to get the policeman's attention. The moment his focus shifted, Damian threw his weight back, brought his elbow up to knock the gun free, and swept his leg out to drop the man to the ground.

In a blink, Damian had the man pinned to the pavement. Damian let out a stream of rapid Spanish. Paige couldn't understand any of it, but from the intensity of his voice, she suspected this hadn't been a routine traffic stop.

The man grunted in response but didn't say anything.

"Get the handcuffs out of his belt." Damian tilted his head to the left, indicating which side she would find them on.

Damian's urgency prompted her to act quickly. She unfastened the snap that held the handcuffs in place and handed them to Damian.

With surprising efficiency, he cuffed the policeman and pulled him to his feet. "Open the back door," Damian said, dragging the man toward the police car.

Paige complied and watched Damian shove the man into the backseat and slam the door. "What are you going to do with him?"

"Leave him here." Damian collected the weapon he had knocked free, engaged the safety, and stuck it in his jacket pocket. "I have to say, your timing was impeccable."

"Glad I could help." Her voice shaky, Paige motioned to the police car. "What happened?"

"Best guess is that someone paid this guy to detain me. I ran a red light, but he didn't have any interest in seeing my ID or collecting a bribe. He pulled his gun before he even looked in the window."

"Then you probably didn't see my text message." Paige pointed at a nearby building. "That building over there has a basement. I found a photo of it while it was being rebuilt."

"What about the others?"

"I don't know." Paige thought back to the photo, trying to remember if she had seen any indications of whether the others had dug basements or not. "I'm pretty sure I remember seeing the one across the street on the edge of the photo, but it had a basic concrete slab at ground level."

She pointed at a nearby building. "What do we do now? The rest of your squad is very likely walking into a trap."

"They already know that."

"But they don't know that Seth may not be there," Paige reminded him.

Damian debated briefly. Logic told him he should go get the rest of his team, but a gut feeling urged him to start his search without them. Remembering the way Vanessa had rushed into the warehouse in search of Seth, he suspected his team was already inside the other building.

"Knowing Vanessa, they've probably already gone in." Damian took his keys and handed them to Paige. "I'm going to check out the basement over there. If I don't come back out in ten minutes, I need you to drive over to the office building. If Seth is there and they get him out, they may need you to drive him back to the hotel."

Paige swallowed. "I'd really prefer that you come out in less than ten minutes."

"I'll do what I can," Damian promised.

CHAPTER 39

"We can't wait any longer," Vanessa insisted, speaking in hushed tones to Brent. "Damian should have been back by now."

"I still don't like you going in first," Brent said.

"It makes the most sense. So far it appears they want me alive. The rest of you may not rank that status."

"I'm going to let the others know we're ready. Wait until I signal before you go in."

"I will." She settled back in the shadows with Jay, studying the side door Brent had chosen for her entrance point.

She knew the others would wait two minutes for her to try to draw Seth's captors away from the basement. When that time elapsed, the squad would enter, Brent and Jay taking the responsibility of protecting her while Tristan and Quinn searched for Seth.

A minute later, Brent returned and shifted into position.

"Be careful," Jay whispered.

"You too," Vanessa said.

Then Brent signaled to Vanessa. Drawing a deep breath as well as her gun, she gathered her courage and crept slowly forward through the darkness. She examined the door, found it clean, and holstered her gun long enough to pick the lock.

* * *

Damian picked the lock on the building Paige had indicated. The business listed on the sign hanging outside claimed it was a women's boutique, one that had supposedly closed two hours earlier.

He drew his weapon and took all the precautions he had learned during SEAL training, checking the doors for wires and alarms, covering security cameras so he couldn't be identified or located remotely.

Inside he discovered exactly what the sign claimed. Women's clothes hung from racks arranged around the room and off hooks on the walls. Purses, scarves, and jewelry adorned the area by the checkout counter.

He checked the main floor, including the dressing rooms and the storage room in the back. Finding nothing suspicious, he located the staircase to the basement.

Cautiously, he opened the door, expecting someone to jump out at him at any moment. The third stair from the top creaked under his weight. He froze, again listening for any indication that he wasn't alone.

All he heard was silence. A lingering floral scent carried from upstairs, but he didn't smell anything clashing with it. He would have expected some sort of cologne, perfume, deodorant, or even body odor.

His training told him to expect the unexpected. Remaining alert, he continued downward.

When he reached the bottom of the stairs, he was alone with a doorway on either side of him. Checking them both for tampering and finding none, he opened the one to the right to reveal another storage room, this one with bolts of fabric and sewing supplies rather than completed clothing.

To his left, he slowly opened the door and found several tables laden with sewing machines, a design table in the far corner, and many pieces of apparel in various stages of completion.

He looked at the floor and saw the most important factor. Tile. This floor was finished. Determined to be thorough, he made sure there weren't any hidden rooms or closets before heading back up the stairs.

* * *

Paige really hated this. She sat in Damian's truck, watching the street in front of her. The waiting was likely going to drive her insane.

The cop car was somewhat hidden behind Damian's truck, and no one seemed to have noticed that the policeman who drove that particular vehicle was locked in the backseat.

A door opened, and she saw a splash of light coming from the building on the other side of the parking garage. A man stepped outside and lit a cigarette. Extinguishing his match beneath his shoe, he walked from one corner to the other, looking down the sides of the building. Even from this distance, Paige noticed the slight bulge at the back of the man's waistband.

She watched as he marched back and forth twice before disappearing back inside.

A sign hung outside the doorway, and Paige strained to read it in the dark. She didn't understand all of the words, but *restaurante* was one she recognized.

Why would a restaurant need a guard? She leaned forward, gripping the steering wheel as another thought struck her. It was only nine o'clock. Why would a restaurant close so early?

She was so focused on the building that she didn't notice Damian beside the truck until he opened the door. Her hand flew to her heart, and she gasped in surprise.

"Sorry," he said in a low voice. "Didn't mean to startle you."

Willing the adrenaline coursing through her to steady, she took a deep breath before asking, "Did you find anything?"

"Nothing. Seth's not there." Damian looked around the area. "Almost a dozen buildings were affected by that fire. I may have to check them one at a time."

"You should start with that one over there," Paige suggested.

"Why?"

She described the man she had seen and her observation that a business that should be open at this hour wasn't.

Damian clicked back into his Navy SEAL mode, all of his focus now on his objective. "Same rules apply. Give me ten minutes."

"Okay," Paige said, but she was talking to herself. He was already sneaking off into the shadows in search of Seth.

* * *

Vanessa ducked down as she entered the door, knowing someone was waiting for her somewhere inside. Security lights overhead illuminated the tiled hallways and a bank of elevators to her left. Knowing the stairwell would be near the elevators, she fought against instinct and turned to her right.

Her footsteps were nearly silent, but the lack of any other sound caused her to keep each step slow and deliberate. She would have to make some noise eventually to draw Seth's captors out, but first she wanted to put some distance between herself and the path to Seth.

She passed a series of office doors, each one with a mounted sign outside identifying the business within. No light was visible beneath the doors, and Vanessa didn't sense anyone in the building. Surely they were here somewhere. Or had they guessed wrong? Maybe Seth really was being held in a laundry room or some other place that wasn't a basement.

No. The video feed had been more than evidence of Seth's capture. It had been an invitation.

She reached a cross-section of the hallway, slowing to give her senses a chance to catch up to her forward movement. The faint scent of coffee and fried meat caught her attention.

Her arms tensed, both hands clasping her weapon. Leading with her gun, she swung around the corner, aimed, and saw a woman standing calmly, facing her, a detonator in her hand. Her hair was longer and darker than in the image Paige had shown her, and her eyes were brown rather than green. Yet Vanessa had no doubt she was facing Andrea Kemper.

"I suppose now would be a good time to tell you this has a dead man's switch. Shoot me and your husband dies."

"Where is he?" Vanessa demanded.

"He's close by."

"What is it you want from me? You've obviously gone to great lengths to get me here."

Andrea cocked her head to one side. "I need you to be Lina Ramir again."

"Lina? I don't understand. How do you even know about her?"

"You'd be surprised at what I know," Andrea said with arrogance. "More surprising is what you don't know."

"Like?" Vanessa prompted. She forced herself to keep her focus on Andrea even though her hearing was tuned to anything that might indicate the Saint Squad was nearby.

"Like the millions of dollars belonging to the Ramir family in the bank." At Vanessa's blank stare, Andrea laughed haughtily. "I bet you didn't even know your name is on the account."

Vanessa spoke the simple truth, reminding herself to take her time and to stay calm. "I don't have a clue what you're talking about."

"I'm talking about more than fifty million dollars hidden in a numbered account in the Cayman Islands, money you're going to get for me."

"I worked undercover for more than a year, and I never heard about this money. What makes you think it really exists?"

"Because I found the account number while working for Morenta. It's the money he paid Ramir for the helicopters he bought the last time you had a run-in with him." She spoke confidently, her hand steady as she held the detonator up higher. "Akil Ramir was captured before he ever got a chance to access the money, but he put a second name on the account. Yours."

"I don't care about Akil's money. Give me my husband alive, and I'll sign whatever you want."

"Of that, I have little doubt. Now give me the gun."

"Not until I see Seth."

"It sounds like we have a stalemate." She gave a cocky grin. "You have less than fifteen minutes to change your mind."

"Why's that?"

"Because that's when the bomb will go off if I don't disarm it." She held her arms out like she didn't have a care in the world. "Your choice."

"It sounds like I have a few minutes to consider my options," Vanessa said stiffly. "I think I'll take them."

CHAPTER 40

Damian opted to enter through a window after seeing the alarm system on the doors because the window sensor was easier to disarm. Unfortunately, it took several minutes longer than he would have liked to pry it open.

He slipped inside, finding himself in the main section of the restaurant. Using the tables for cover, he steadily worked his way through the dining area in search of a basement stairwell.

Being overly cautious, he cleared each room of the main floor as he went, ultimately not finding the stairwell until he reached the final section, the huge kitchen.

Unlike in the boutique, he immediately felt someone else's presence: a strong scent of cigarette smoke, the sound of rubber soles against a concrete floor.

The stairs hugged the back wall, and Damian felt a sense of relief when he saw they were concrete. They were also open to the kitchen so he didn't have to worry about a door at the top of the stairwell. The footsteps stopped briefly before starting again, this time heading his way.

Remembering the element of surprise was on his side, Damian squatted beneath the half wall that separated the stairwell from the rest of the kitchen. His whole body throbbed with the adrenaline now coursing through him. He fought to keep his breathing quiet, to battle against the sweaty palms and the shakiness in his hands.

Flexing his fingers and tightening them again on his gun grip, he counted the steps as the person drew closer. The thought flashed through his mind that this guy could be an innocent bystander, someone who worked here in an honest fashion. Knowing he couldn't take the chance, Damian waited for him to emerge at the top of the stairs.

He sprang from his hiding place, knocking the man on the back of the head. The moment he dropped to the floor, Damian did a quick search to find he had not one gun but two. Taking care not to make any unnecessary noise, Damian relieved the man of his weapons and secured his hands and feet with some zip ties he had in his pack.

Not certain if another guard might be present, he crept down the stairwell slowly. He heard sound coming from close by but couldn't determine the source. This wasn't footsteps; it sounded like metal on rock. It took him a moment to recognize the tapping for what it was: a message.

Deciphering it in his head, Damian felt almost simultaneous surges of relief and frustration. He had found Seth, but now he had to figure out how to get to him safely. When he reached the bottom of the stairs, he assessed the situation.

Apparently the guard upstairs was the only one in the building, but the door was armed with twin explosives. Retrieving a small flashlight from his vest pocket, he illuminated the bombs. One appeared to be rigged to a pressure plate and would go off if the door opened.

The other was much more complicated. It didn't appear to have a timer or pressure detonation system, but after another minute of study, Damian understood. This one could be remotely detonated. Someone had a button they could press, and instantly, he and Seth would die.

He didn't want to die. That thought popped into his mind, along with an image of Paige and the future they could share.

The tapping continued, bringing Damian back to the moment.

"Seth? Can you hear me?"

"Damian?" Seth's voice came through the door. "Careful. The door's wired."

"I see it." Damian described the two bombs.

"You're going to have to disarm them," Seth said. "Start with the one with the pressure plate."

"I thought you'd want the other one disarmed first."

"I do, but you might inadvertently set the other one off while you work on it," Seth said. "Talk to me as you go through the steps. I'll help you through it."

"Good, because I think I'm going to need the help."

Seth talked Damian through the first device, Damian describing the locations of the detonator, the power source, and the various wires.

Several minutes ticked by as Damian studied the wires, retrieving the knife from his pocket to cut the wire that would hopefully disarm the bomb. "Are you sure about this?"

"As sure as I can be without seeing it," Seth said.

"Okay. Here it goes." Damian grimaced, bracing for the unknown, and cut the wire in one clean swipe. His breath rushed out when the light on the bomb went out, indicating it was no longer active.

"One down," Damian told Seth.

"Tell me about the other one."

Damian looked at it closer, discouraged. "It has a twin power source. I don't think I can do this alone."

* * *

Brent stood around the corner and listened to Vanessa begin her subtle interrogation.

"I can understand why you wanted to draw me back into the field, but why did you fake your own death? Was that really necessary?"

"It was the only way for me to get off the radar. My father was watching me too closely, trying to protect me." Andrea's voice turned derisive. "Besides, he didn't approve of my choice in men."

"I gather you're talking about Terrance Gunning," Vanessa said.

Brent couldn't see Andrea's reaction, but the sudden silence indicated her surprise.

"I see you know more than I gave you credit for."

"That may be, but I'm having a hard time understanding how you could let yourself get mixed up with Morenta."

"He was a means to an end. I gave him a way to get to the Saint Squad, and without knowing it, he opened the door for me to lure you here."

"So you're betraying your country for money?"

"A lot of money," Andrea corrected. "Money is freedom. Terrance and I will never have to work again, and we'll be able to disappear somewhere where no one will ever bother us."

Vanessa continued to probe Andrea, and Brent processed everything. The dead man's switch was a contingency he hadn't planned for but one that could be remedied. He knew Tristan and Quinn were headed to the basement right now, and they would deal with whatever explosives they might encounter.

Still standing silently in the hall, he listened to Andrea's phone ring.

After offering a brief greeting, Andrea said, "I found her. Any sign of any of her friends?"

Brent guessed the answer was a negative by her reaction.

"Keep looking. She probably has someone lurking around here somewhere."

Silently, Brent backed away from the hallway. His squad needed to neutralize this woman's partner before he stopped Quinn and Tristan from disarming the bomb. What he wouldn't give for working communications equipment right now.

* * *

His ten minutes were up, but Paige couldn't bring herself to leave Damian behind. She considered that Damian wanted her to go signal his team for help, but what if the distraction caused more harm than good?

She couldn't call him for fear that he was hiding somewhere within the building, trying to find his way to Seth. The possibility of the guard prevailing in a struggle between them was one she could barely stand to consider.

Overwhelmed and confused, she uttered a quiet prayer, searching for guidance and inspiration. An engine revved on a nearby street, and a thought popped into her head. If the man she had seen really was here to guard Seth, then Seth was inside. Maybe he was hurt, and Damian couldn't carry him out by himself.

Hoping for some communication from within, Paige decided to use the only thing accessible to her that would also blend into the sounds of the night. With the heel of her hand, she pressed hard against the center of the steering wheel, honking the horn three times.

CHAPTER 41

"Did you hear that?" Seth asked.

Damian glanced down at his watch. "That must be Paige. I told her to wait ten minutes and then go signal the rest of the squad at the office building."

"What office building?"

"It's where we thought you were being held. They were going in knowing it was a trap, but they also thought they would find you there."

"Is Vanessa with them?"

"Yeah, she's with them."

"I've got to get out of here," Seth insisted. "Go get Paige. See if she can come help you disarm the second bomb."

His stomach clutched at the thought. Bring Paige into harm's way? The bomb could go off any minute. Then he thought of the rest of his squad and how Seth must be feeling knowing he was helpless to protect his wife.

If he didn't reach out to Paige, she might go in search of the others and land in the middle of the trap these people had laid.

"I'll call her." Damian pulled his cell phone free and dialed her number.

"Are you okay?" she asked breathlessly.

"Yeah, but I need your help. The guard is already tied up," he said. "Come down to the basement, and bring the toolbox that's in the back of the truck."

"I'll be right there."

"This had better work," Damian said after he hung up.

"Talk me through this one. We'll figure it out while we're waiting for Paige. I don't want her in danger any more than you do."

Damian flashed his light at the new challenge and prayed this would all be over soon.

* * *

A prayer running through his mind, Brent moved silently, stepping carefully to avoid detection. He caught a glimpse of a shadow falling over the intersecting hallway and, a moment later, saw a man's silhouette. Quickening his steps, Brent peeked around the corner just as Tristan stepped through a darkened doorway.

The man started to turn, but Tristan grabbed him around the throat with one arm, both holding him in place and preventing him from crying out. With his other hand, he injected a needle with a heavy sedative into the man's arm.

A slight vibration of the floor followed as Tristan lowered the man to the ground. A short distance away, Quinn appeared from another adjoining hall, signaling that the area was clear.

"Seth?" Brent's voice was barely audible.

"We checked the basement. He's not here," Tristan said in a whisper. "Maybe this is the wrong place." Motioning to the man on the floor, he added, "Which means I owe this guy an apology."

"No, your instincts were right. This is where they wanted us." Brent quickly filled him in on the conversation he had overheard between Vanessa and Andrea.

"We'll check the rest of the building in case they moved him," Tristan said. "What do you want us to do with this guy?"

"Tie him up and lock him out of sight in one of the supply closets," Brent said. "Jay's still keeping watch outside. Go grab him if you need extra manpower to search. I'm going back to Vanessa."

"What are you going to do if we can't find him?"

"Vanessa said she'll cooperate. Let's hope she won't have to."

Tristan motioned to Quinn. "Go grab Jay. I'll meet you upstairs."

Brent crept back to where he had last seen Vanessa, praying they could find Seth before it was too late.

* * *

Damian heard Paige's footsteps as she rushed toward him. He sensed the moment she saw the bomb. "Is that a . . . ?"

"Yeah. I can't disarm it alone." Damian glanced over his shoulder. "I know it's dangerous, so you can say no, but are you willing to help me?"

The internal battle was evident on her face. Damian had seen the way his squad had often used humor to ease their stress. He attempted his own brand when he said, "At least it isn't a gun."

Paige cocked one eyebrow, but his comment seemed to snap her out of her debate. She moved closer and set the toolbox down beside him. "What do I do?"

"I'm going to have to clip two wires at the same time. I need you to hold them clear so I can reach them without accidentally clipping any others."

"Sounds simple enough," Paige said. She stepped closer and took a look at the jumble of wires. "Maybe not."

Damian dug through his grandfather's toolbox. He found several pairs of wire cutters and determined to thank his grandfather in the very near future for never throwing out his old tools. Closing the toolbox, he pushed it closer to the door. "Here, you can stand on this so you can reach."

Paige stood on the sturdy metal toolbox, using the wall to balance herself. Damian guided her hands to the section of wires he needed her to hold. She followed his instructions, and he struggled to access the correct wires.

"Damian, what are those numbers?" Paige asked. Her voice rose in panic. "Is that a countdown?"

He looked at the detonator, saw the display that had previously been dark, and watched the number forty-six change to forty-five. Suddenly, he faced an unsettling moment of indecision. He might be able to send Paige to safety, but if he did, Seth would die. "Just hold steady. I can make it." Damian pulled back another batch of wires. "Count it down for me."

"Thirty-four, thirty-three, thirty-two . . ." Her voice hitched as she fought for control, and Damian willed his fingers to work faster.

CHAPTER 42

"Thirty-one, thirty." Andrea held up the display, showing Vanessa how much time was left. "It's up to you. We can help each other, or you can become a widow in"—she looked down at the display again—"twenty-five, twenty-four, twenty-three."

"Fine. You win." Vanessa couldn't take the chance. She would have to give this woman what she wanted and trust her husband's squad to help both of them. She lowered her gun to the floor. "Now flip whatever switch that is to turn it off."

Andrea pressed a series of buttons, presumably a disarming code. "That was close," she said, shaking her head as if she were scolding a small child.

"What now?" Vanessa asked.

"Now, you and I are going to take a ride to an airstrip outside of town. Tomorrow morning when the banks open, we'll be in the Caymans and we can conclude our business."

"First I want to see my husband."

"The money first."

Vanessa straightened. "My husband comes with us, or you'll never get the money."

"That's where you're wrong." She drew her gun and aimed it at Vanessa. "You'll help me get this money, or you and your husband will both die."

The look in Andrea's eyes, the telltale glance away from her when she spoke, set Vanessa's whole world on edge. "You killed him."

Andrea looked down at her watch. "He has at least a few seconds left."

***

"Ten, nine, eight . . ." Paige continued her countdown, desperately fighting against the panic boiling inside her. "Damian, hurry."

"Pull those apart a little wider . . ." He slid the wire cutters into place, Paige watching the numbers tick down. Four, three . . .

Damian snipped two wires.

Paige slumped in relief, her breath coming out in a whoosh. Damian dropped the tools and reached his hand out to steady her, afraid she was going to faint. "Are you okay?"

Paige couldn't speak, but a voice from the other side of the door snapped her back to reality. "I'd be a lot better if you'd get me out of here."

"Stand back." Damian took a step back and kicked out one leg, breaking the door in. He quickly used his knife to cut the rope off Seth's wrists.

"Let's go. We've got to get to Vanessa." Seth raced toward the stairs, taking them two at a time.

Damian leaned down and grabbed the toolbox with one hand and nudged Paige forward with the other hand. She felt like her legs were jelly, but she managed to follow Seth into the kitchen. The three of them hurried to the truck, and Paige was surprised when Damian motioned her into the driver's seat.

"You want me to drive?"

"Yes. I have a plan, and we'll need your help." Damian and Seth climbed in beside her.

"I really could use a bit less excitement in my life."

"We'll work on that tomorrow," Damian promised. "For now, take a right at the light."

Paige turned on the engine and pushed on the gas pedal. Making her way down the street, she prayed she would never, ever have to see a real bomb again as long as she lived.

* * *

Brent faded back against the wall, not wanting to consider that Seth might be dead. With Vanessa unarmed and currently standing between Andrea and him, Brent didn't have a shot, nor was he sure if the dead man's switch was still active, assuming Seth was alive.

"Is he alive?" Vanessa asked, raw emotion obvious in her voice.

"There's only one way to find out. As soon as you're done signing the money over to me, I'll tell you where he is."

"Which way?" Vanessa asked, motioning back to the hall where she had come from.

Brent shifted slightly. He would have only a brief opening when they passed him. When he heard Andrea's next words, his frustration rose another notch. "We'll take the private elevator over there. I'm not taking a chance that you have friends hiding around the building."

He had only seconds. If he didn't act now, he was going to lose her. Without any way to communicate with his squad, he wouldn't be able to tell them what to look for, nor did they have transportation to take up pursuit.

He would have to choose. Save Vanessa now, knowing Seth would most surely die, or hope Seth was still alive and that Andrea would eventually let Vanessa go.

He heard a horn honking, once, twice, three times.

It couldn't be.

The sound repeated. One honk, two, then three.

When the same rhythm repeated a third time followed by silence, Brent knew. Code three. He wasn't sure what the signal meant, but it pushed him to act. Leading with his gun, he swung into the open cross-section of the hallway. "Vanessa, down!"

She dropped instantly, Andrea aimed her weapon, and Brent fired. Andrea crumpled to the ground, and Brent rushed forward to secure her weapon before checking to find she didn't have a pulse.

Footsteps sounded in the hall, the evidence of several people running toward the gunfire. Tristan and Quinn arrived first, just as Vanessa was pushing herself to a stand.

Tears running down her face, she asked, "Seth? Did you find him?"

Brent took it upon himself to answer. "He's not here. We don't know where he is."

"She said she deactivated the bomb, but I don't think she did." Vanessa pressed her lips together, and she swiped at the tears on her face. "I think she killed him."

"We'll find him, Vanessa," Brent promised. "No matter what, we'll find him."

More footsteps pounded toward them, and then there was a shout. "Vanessa!"

Vanessa's eyebrows rose, and her mouth opened in astonishment. "Seth?"

She ran into the hall, and Brent watched in wonder as Seth rushed around the corner and swooped down to lift his wife into his arms.

CHAPTER 43

DAMIAN'S KNOWLEDGE OF THE CITY had proved invaluable when the men had discussed their exit strategy. Using Paige's phone, Damian had given Amy a secluded spot thirty minutes outside of Maracaibo for the navy helicopter to pick them up.

Brent's decision to leave Andrea's body behind had simplified the process. Terrance Gunning had remained unconscious until they were nearly out of the city. When he had awoken to find several Navy SEALs staring at him, he had wisely cooperated. Thankfully, this time, the night extraction had gone off without a hitch.

They had also passed off the information to the CIA and DEA about the new drug traffic lanes through Maracaibo, and the Saint Squad was happy to be free of that burden. Now they were aboard the USS *Harry S. Truman* in a boardroom, discussing their next move.

"Gunning isn't talking," Brent said. "Without his confirmation, we have no way of knowing who else might be involved."

"From what I got from Andrea, she tricked Morenta into paying to have the Saint Squad stranded in Canaima," Vanessa said. "He's the one who tried to kill you, partially as revenge for crossing him a few years ago and partially to send a message to Americans that we shouldn't mess with him."

"They still had to have someone from CIA helping them find you in Maracaibo," Amy said. "We know Andrea stayed in South America after faking her death, and Terrance Gunning didn't have access to the information. Plus, he had already dropped off the grid before Vanessa left."

"I know it sounds impossible, but it has to be Warren behind all of this," Vanessa said. "No one else knew when I would be at the airport, and no one else knew Damian went to Canaima to look for you."

"How do you want to approach him?" Seth asked. "We can't accuse him without proof."

"The lack of access by anyone else may be proof enough," Paige offered.

"I agree," Vanessa began, "but I would like to have something more substantial. He could always claim someone managed to tag me before I left for Maracaibo."

"But you said you swapped out your clothes when you got there," Paige reminded her. "We screened everything you had with us in Venezuela and checked to make sure you hadn't been tagged with a marking spray. Everything was clean."

"Then we need to prove no one else had access," Vanessa concluded.

Amy motioned to a bank of three computers on one side of the room. "I could use some help with the search."

"Amy and Vanessa, divide up what you want us to analyze," Brent said.

"You know, for Navy SEALs, it sure seems like we do a lot of desk work." Damian took a seat at the work table in the middle of the room.

"It's not all sneaking up on bad guys," Jay agreed.

"But there'll be plenty of that," Quinn promised.

"You can all speculate on future missions later," Brent said. "For now, let's get to the bottom of this."

* * *

The complete picture was falling into place. A deeper look into Andrea Kemper's file provided an angle Vanessa hadn't before considered. Now only one piece of the puzzle was missing, and Vanessa knew she was the only person who could find it.

She would have preferred to meet Warren at CIA headquarters, where she could be assured that no one would have a weapon besides the security police. In fact, she would have been happy to have even arranged this meeting in the United States. Unfortunately, the money was the key, and there was only one way to prove her suspicions.

With the information retrieved from Andrea Kemper's belongings, Vanessa had already confirmed the existence of the bank account in the Cayman Islands. Now, here she was, standing on the sidewalk two hours after the bank opened.

She looked over at Paige. "You know, you don't have to do this."

"We both know I'm the only person who can do this. If you have anyone else with you, you'll raise suspicions."

"I can go in alone."

"That's not going to happen." Paige adjusted the strap on her purse and shifted it more firmly onto her shoulder. "You need someone to watch the door, and no one would believe you would come here without some kind of support."

She was right. Rule number one was to cover all your bases. She would never go into an undercover operation alone without already having her support system in place.

"If there's any sign of trouble, you call for help," Vanessa said.

"I will." Paige lowered her voice and added, "But I doubt the guys will wait for a phone call. They'll be here before I finish dialing."

"True." Vanessa resisted the urge to look for the Saint Squad. As the newest and least recognizable member, Damian had been assigned a spot inside the bank. Besides being armed with a concealed handgun, he was also wearing a comm unit disguised as a Bluetooth. Quinn had taken a position on the roof while the others were scattered around the area, covering the various entrances to the bank.

Paige reached into her purse and glanced at a message on her phone. "Looks like someone's heading for us."

Vanessa turned to see Warren's secretary, Maryanne Pennington, walking down the sidewalk.

"Maryanne, I didn't expect to see you here." Vanessa stepped forward and gave her a quick hug. "Where's Warren?"

"He couldn't make it. Some big meeting up on Capitol Hill." She reached into a purse-like briefcase and slipped a sheet of paper from it. "He sent me with the information you asked for."

Vanessa took the paper from her and glanced down at the account numbers and percentages that were to be transferred to each one. Suspicions raced through her mind. She had initially thought Warren was the only person to have access to the information that had leaked. When she discovered his secretary had gone through her initial CIA training with Andrea Kemper, new possibilities surfaced. As Warren's secretary, Maryanne was trusted implicitly and could just as easily have been the leak.

Drawing on all of her acting abilities, Vanessa said, "Thanks. I guess it's time to see if this will work." She took a step toward the door, and Maryanne moved forward as well. "You don't have to come in. I can take it from here," Vanessa said.

"Sorry, Vanessa, but you know it's procedure. You have to have a witness when transferring seized funds to make sure the money is going where it's supposed to."

"I know. That's why I brought my assistant." Vanessa waved in Paige's direction.

"Yes, but she's in your chain of command. I'm afraid it will have to be me."

"Okay. If you insist." Her suspicions heightened. Vanessa turned to Paige. "I guess you can just wait here."

"I'll come inside with you." She pointed at a cluster of chairs visible through the window. "It looks like there's a waiting area in there."

Vanessa nodded her agreement. The three women walked inside, Paige taking a seat near the door. A man behind the counter greeted them. "May I help you?"

"Yes, I need to transfer some funds out of an account," Vanessa said.

"Do you have the account number?"

"Yes." Vanessa retrieved the account number she had written on a piece of paper and handed it to him.

He punched the account number into a computer. "Your name?"

"Lina Ramir."

"And your ID, please."

Vanessa handed him the passport that identified her as Lina. The man verified the information and waved her forward. "Right this way."

Vanessa and Maryanne followed him past two desks, including the one where Damian was currently sitting under the pretense of asking about different account types. At the third desk, the man stopped and indicated for them to sit down.

"Mario will be able to help you." The man handed Mario the paper with the account number before returning to the welcome desk.

"What can I help you with today?"

"I need to transfer the money out of this account and close it. Here is where the funds need to go." Vanessa passed him the paper Maryanne had given her.

"I'm sorry to hear we will be losing your business." He pulled up her account on his screen, and his eyebrows drew together. He typed the string of numbers in a second time. Now he looked up. "Are you sure this is the correct account number? My system shows it was closed yesterday."

"What?" Maryanne asked before Vanessa could respond. "That can't be. I checked the balances yesterday morning."

Vanessa looked over at her inquisitively. Maryanne had just confirmed her suspicions. Maryanne had accessed every piece of information that had leaked, and now she had fallen into the trap Vanessa and the Saint Squad had laid. Vanessa's voice remained calm. "How did you do that?"

"That's my job as your assistant—to make sure everything is in order before we travel." The assistant story was clearly for the benefit of the bank clerk, but Vanessa decided to pound the last piece of the puzzle firmly into place.

"Yes, but I didn't give you the account number."

Maryanne's face paled slightly. "You must have had Warren give it to me."

"No. I didn't give it to anyone. The only person who would have it would be the person who was working with Andrea Kemper," Vanessa said. "I have to say, I was surprised to find out that you were the one who recommended Andrea for the Morenta assignment."

"I don't know what you're talking about." Maryanne's voice took on a higher pitch than usual. "I'm just a secretary."

"Oh, no. We both know better than that. As the trusted assistant to Warren, you have access to all sorts of classified information, including the intel about Ramir's bank account," Vanessa said. "And imagine my surprise when I found out you and Andrea were roommates during training when you started with the agency."

Maryanne clenched her teeth, color flooding into her cheeks.

Vanessa stood and spoke to the bank employee. "Thank you for your cooperation." She then reached for Maryanne's arm and pulled her to a stand. "You and I have a lot to talk about."

In the act of rising, Maryanne dropped her purse. She jerked free of Vanessa's grip and leaned down. When she straightened, she had a gun in her hand.

"Where's my money?" she demanded frantically. Keeping the weapon trained on Vanessa, she nodded to the man behind the desk. "Make him give it back."

"And to think I once thought of you as a friend," Vanessa said with disgust. She saw the movement behind Maryanne but deliberately kept her focus on the woman.

"That was your mistake." Before Maryanne could continue, Damian struck from behind, grabbing around her so her arm was forced down and the gun along with it.

Maryanne cried out and struggled against the sudden assault. Vanessa rushed forward, prying the gun from her hand. It fell to the ground as

Maryanne leaned back against Damian and kicked her feet out, forcing Vanessa to jump back.

As Damian tightened his grip to subdue her, Vanessa moved forward again with the intent of securing Maryanne's weapon. To her surprise, Paige was standing beside her, the gun in her hand, the magazine of bullets already free of the chamber.

CHAPTER 44

Just as the thought crossed Damian's mind that this whole ordeal was finally over, the sound of glass breaking rang out, immediately followed by the whistling of a bullet. Blood splattered onto his face and neck, and Maryanne's body went limp and lifeless, a bullet hole now visible in her head.

"Damian!" Paige cried out and grabbed at his arm to pull him down. That slight movement to his left saved his life, a second bullet whizzing by his ear and impacting the wall behind him.

He released his grip on Maryanne and dropped to the ground beside Paige as he shouted to Vanessa, "Get down!"

Screams punctuated the air as other patrons realized what had happened, and Damian spoke tersely into his comm unit. "We've got a shooter, southeast side, upper story."

Seth responded first, his voice tense. "Is everyone okay?"

Damian looked over at Maryanne, whose eyes were glassy and staring into space. He tried to distance himself from the knowledge that the woman was now dead, reminding himself he had to focus on the here and now. "Maryanne's dead," Damian said.

"Vanessa?" Seth asked.

"She's okay." A third shot splintered the desk Vanessa had taken cover behind. "So far."

He saw the terror in Paige's eyes, but he couldn't think of that right now. Whoever was out there had to be stopped.

"Quinn, do you have eyes on the shooter?" Brent asked.

"Negative. The rooftops are clear."

"Does anyone else have a visual?" Damian demanded.

"Negative," Brent responded, followed by similar responses from the rest of the squad.

"It's got to be coming from one of the second-story windows across the street," Quinn said.

Vanessa spoke, pulling Damian's attention back to the woman beside him. "Who would shoot Maryanne? And why?"

"Maybe they weren't aiming for her," Damian suggested, all too aware that he had been mere inches from where the bullet had struck. He heard Brent giving directions to the rest of the squad, each of them positioning themselves so they would be able to corner the shooter.

"I can't believe she's dead," Paige managed to say. She still had Maryanne's gun and bullet cartridge in her hand. "What do we do now?"

Vanessa scooted over to them, relieving Paige of the gun and loading the cartridge back into the chamber. "We wait here. The rest of the Saint Squad will find the shooter. This is what they do."

The thought crossed Damian's mind that once again the squad was about to function without him, this time in order to protect him, Paige, and Vanessa.

Memories of the file Kel had given him to review suddenly came to mind.

"This is what they do," Damian repeated. He looked at Maryanne's lifeless body, at the perfect execution-style shot through the center of her forehead, and a clarity of thought struck him. He spoke quickly to his team once more. "Everyone hold fast."

"What's wrong?" Brent asked.

"I think this is a trap," Damian said.

Brent's voice came over the radio again. "A trap for who?"

"For the people who messed up Morenta's plan." Damian's mind raced with possibilities. "Give me a minute."

Damian shifted to face Paige. "You did the psych profile on Morenta. What lengths would he go to for revenge?"

"I don't know," she said, her voice shaky.

"Paige, think. You can do this. If Morenta is the one who tried to kill my squad in Venezuela, what would he do if he found out they were still alive?"

Understanding lit her eyes. "He'd go after them again to prove his strength."

Damian spoke into his microphone once more. "Brent, I think Morenta is behind this. He could be trying to draw you guys out."

"Quinn, you've got the best vantage point. What do you see?"

"There's an open window in the building across the street. It looks like the shooter is in the jewelry center."

"We know Morenta has been paying in diamonds. It would make sense that he could gain access there," Damian said.

"If you guys try for that building, everyone would be exposed when you cross the street. There's no place to take cover."

While Brent gave directions to the rest of the squad, Damian turned to Paige and Vanessa. "I'm going up to the roof to help Quinn."

"We'll come with you. You may need the extra sets of eyes," Vanessa said.

Damian didn't bother to argue. He took a moment to determine the safest way to the stairwell. Seeing they could remain concealed behind desks and partitions almost the entire way, he outlined their route and found himself praying they would all get out of this alive.

* * *

"Not again." Paige looked at the wires affixed to the door leading to the roof, now experienced enough to recognize the plastic explosives and detonator for what they were. "How could someone have planted a bomb here? Quinn had to have gone through here when he went out on the roof."

"Morenta must have known the Saint Squad was here. Someone probably followed Quinn here and planted the bomb after he was outside," Vanessa said.

"What do you think?" Damian asked. "Is it just a motion sensor?"

Paige knew he was talking to Vanessa, but she answered anyway. "It has that same little black box the other one did."

"She's right. There's a secondary trigger," Vanessa agreed.

Damian spoke into his headset. "Quinn, the door to the roof is booby-trapped. Stay where you are."

"That confirms Damian's theory that this is a trap," Brent responded. "Tristan, how long until you can get in position?"

"One minute."

"Everyone hold on," Vanessa interrupted. "We've got a secondary trigger on this bomb. If our shooter sees anyone coming for him, he might detonate it."

"Copy that," Tristan replied.

"Let's do this." Damian said, pulling his Swiss army knife from his pocket. He studied the wiring, hoping the confidence he forced into his voice would translate into his actions. Less than a minute later, he shook his head. "This has a secondary power source. I can disarm it, but it's going to take at least ten or fifteen minutes."

"By then, whoever this guy is will know something's wrong when none of the Saint Squad try to get to him," Vanessa said. "What's the blast radius?"

"Twenty feet? Maybe thirty."

"Leave it," Vanessa insisted. She tugged on both Damian's and Paige's arms, pulling them back down the stairs. "Damian, tell Quinn to make sure he's at least thirty feet from the door."

Damian relayed the message.

"Why are we leaving it?" Paige asked, struggling to keep up.

"Hurry!" Vanessa said, not taking the time to answer Paige's question. They made it down the first flight of stairs before she added, "That bomb might be meant for Quinn . . ."

"Or it could be for us," Damian said, apparently understanding Vanessa's determination.

They all quickened their pace. They were only a few steps past the next landing when a jolt rocked the building, plaster and shards of wood exploding through the air and down the stairwell.

CHAPTER 45

From his position in the bank parking lot, Seth heard and felt the explosion rock the ground. He looked up to see white smoke billowing from the top of the bank building. "Vanessa!"

"We're okay," Damian assured him. He coughed several times before adding, "But they know we're on to them."

"Quinn?" Brent asked, clearly looking for his status.

"I'm good, and I think I may have a visual on our shooter. Male, dark hair, gray T-shirt, blue shorts."

Seth looked out at the street, which was now largely empty, the local tourists and shoppers all having wisely taken cover. The suspect stood just outside the doorway of the jewelry store, a phone to his ear. "I see him."

"Quinn, do you think you can flush him out of there?" Brent asked. "Let's see if we can make sure this is really the guy we're after."

"Let me know when."

"Damian, can you make it to the bank's rear exit? I want you to back up Seth on the south side."

"I'll be right there."

"Jay and Tristan, be ready. He should come out into the street right between you."

As soon as everyone's positions were confirmed, Brent gave the word. Quinn fired a single shot, hitting the doorway a few inches above the suspect's head. Sure enough, the man immediately drew a weapon. He started to step back into the building, but Quinn didn't give him the chance. He fired a second shot, this one hitting the door and startling the man forward.

The moment he was in the street, the SEALs surrounded him, their weapons drawn. "Be smart and put down the weapon," Brent advised.

For a second, Seth thought he might not understand English. Then slowly, he held his weapon out sideways in front of him and lowered it to the ground.

* * *

"What do you think's happening?" Paige asked Vanessa.

"The guys will take care of whatever's out there. The best thing we can do is stay out of the line of fire," Vanessa told her.

"I can't stand not knowing what's going on."

"Let's go up on the roof, then, and see if we can help Quinn." Vanessa led the way through the dusty stairwell, both women holding their breath the last few yards to keep from inhaling the smoke and drywall dust.

When they reached the rooftop, Quinn was looking through the sniper scope on his rifle at the street below.

"What's going on down there?" Vanessa asked.

"They got him."

"Him?" Paige asked. "There was only one?"

"Yeah, why?"

"Ramir only sent one person after your squad when he tried for revenge a couple years ago. I thought Morenta would have learned from Ramir's mistakes." Paige shifted closer to the edge of the roof and looked down. She saw Brent securing a man's hands behind his back, Damian and Seth standing a short distance away, both of them with weapons in their hands.

The guns didn't look as scary from here, Paige thought. She looked over at Quinn, the sniper rifle in his hands, and she felt only a little nervous to be so close to a man wielding a weapon. She didn't know how it had happened, but sometime over the last few days, she had come to trust these men completely.

"I don't know about you guys, but I'm ready for some lunch," Quinn said, still keeping his eyes dutifully on the scene below.

"Quinn, you're always hungry."

Paige listened to the friendly banter, amazed that Quinn and Vanessa seemed to be able to shift back into a normal existence even though a woman had just been shot to death a few minutes before, a woman who had been standing only a few feet from Vanessa and her. Her eyes stayed on Damian and the men below.

A glimpse of movement caught her eye, and she shifted her gaze to see a man dressed in a plain T-shirt, faded shorts, and a ball cap. The simple fact that he was walking on a street that had up to now been deserted caused her to look closer. Recognition dawned in the same instant the man reached a hand behind his back. The diamond courier from Maracaibo.

Even from four stories up, Paige saw the man's hand reemerge from beneath his shirt, a gun gripped there. "Quinn! There, to your right!"

"Shooter! Damian, your five o'clock," Quinn called into his headset, immediately swinging his rifle toward the new threat. He fired a shot, but in his haste, the bullet went wide.

The men below reacted, instantly keying in on the new threat. Damian led with his gun as he turned. Gunfire sounded below, the squad members diving for cover and dropping to the ground in that instant. Paige gripped her hands together, a prayer running through her mind as she watched for movement below.

The courier was lying on the sidewalk, his gun still gripped in his hand. Brent pulled his prisoner to the side of the street, dragging the man as he stumbled behind him. Seth and Damian had dropped to the ground, sprawling on their stomachs to make sure they weren't easy targets, each man with his weapon aimed and ready.

When the courier lifted his hand to shoot once more, three more shots rang out, and all movement ceased.

* * *

"Any idea who these guys are?" Brent asked, watching as the police took their prisoner away. "He didn't have any ID on him."

"That one over there is the diamond courier we saw in Maracaibo," Damian said, more policemen working that side of the scene. "The marking spray we tagged him with showed he went to Cali, Colombia, so we're sure he's involved with Morenta."

"If we could trace him, why didn't anyone know he was heading here?" Jay asked.

"Someone in intelligence probably knew he was coming to the Caymans, but they didn't know we were here, so they wouldn't have known to tell us," Brent said.

Paige and Vanessa exited the bank with Quinn following behind them. The moment the women were clear of the building, Damian and Seth shifted their attention to them. Seth scooped Vanessa into his arms, and Paige hugged Damian.

No one spoke for a moment. Then Paige took a deep breath and said, "This is why I don't like guns."

"It's okay now."

Paige swallowed hard when she pulled back and motioned to the man the police had led away. "Is that Morenta?"

"I don't know," Damian admitted.

"It's not him," Vanessa said. "That's Rodrigo, one of the top men in his organization."

"How do you know him?" Brent asked, stepping up behind them.

"I saw him a few times when I was undercover. He did a lot of Morenta's dealings for him."

Uneasiness reflected in Paige's eyes. "If that's not Morenta, then he might try to get to you guys again."

"He might want to try, but with his sources in the CIA gone and with one of his top men now in custody, he's going to be hard-pressed to find us," Seth said. "It took him years to find us this time, and that was with a lot of inside help."

"Eventually, I have to think someone will authorize a mission to go get him," Brent said.

"I don't know which one is worse," Paige admitted. "The possibility of Morenta finding you or the idea of you guys going after him."

Vanessa put a hand on her back. "Sometimes it's best not to think about how our guys spend their days."

CHAPTER 46

"You know, I almost fell over when I saw you holding that gun." Damian sat beside Paige on the private jet, appreciative that the rest of the squad had settled in the seating area in the back.

"I can't believe we were allowed to stay a whole week in the Caymans. And I really can't believe the secretary of the navy sent a private plane to pick us up." Paige swiveled in her seat so she was facing Damian more fully. "I could get used to this."

"You're trying to change the subject."

"Yes, I am." Her eyebrows drew together. "Should I be worried that you noticed?"

"Maybe," Damian admitted. He was a little surprised himself that he had learned to read her so well. "What do you think? Are you over your fear of guns?"

"I don't know if I'm over it, but I have a new one that definitely outranks it."

"What's that?"

"Bombs. I'm afraid of bombs."

"That's hardly a phobia. That's common sense." Damian reached over and took her left hand, rubbing his thumb lightly over the ring still situated there. "I wonder if there's any way the government would let me buy this ring off of them."

"Why?"

"It looks good on you."

"Thank you, but I can hardly let you spend your money on a ring just because it looks good on me."

"That wouldn't be the only reason." Damian's chest tightened. He knew he shouldn't broach this with her right now, but it was as though his mouth had a mind of its own. "I figure if you can pick up a gun, maybe you could get used to having one in your apartment."

"Holding one and owning one are two entirely different things."

"I didn't say you'd have to own one." He held her hand up and kissed her fingers. His heart pounded in his chest, and knots tangled uncomfortably in his gut. In a true act of bravery, he forced himself to continue. "I never really thought about what would come after I finished SEAL training, but when I put that ring on your finger, I figured out what I want."

"I don't understand . . ."

Feeling more adrenaline pulse through him than if he was about to step off a cliff, he forced himself to push on. "I'm saying I want you to marry me." When her jaw dropped and she continued to stare, he added, "We can have a long engagement if you want, but I want you to keep that ring on your finger. And I want to know it's there because I gave it to you. I love you."

Wonder filled her eyes, along with the tears. She didn't speak, and Damian felt his nerves go on edge.

"Well?"

Her voice was hoarse, and he could tell she was fighting back her emotions, but the words were the ones he so desperately wanted to hear. "I love you too."

His eyes stayed on hers, and he held his breath for a moment. "Does that mean yes?"

Now she nodded, and her hand reached up to touch his cheek. "Yes."

She tilted her face up to kiss him.

He brought both hands up to frame her face, holding her there as his heart erupted with joy and wonder, the kiss holding unlimited promise.

"Are you engaged yet?" Quinn called from the back of the plane the moment Damian pulled away.

Damian let out a short laugh, realizing Paige wasn't the only person he had come to know and love in a short period of time. "Yes, we're engaged."

"Congratulations!" Vanessa and several of the men called from the back of the plane.

Quinn's comment came a fraction of a second later. "It's about time."

Damian laughed. Only Quinn would think he was dragging his feet. He shook his head and met Paige's eyes. "It's not about time. It's about timing."

"Perfect timing," Paige agreed.

Ignoring the cheers from his teammates, Damian leaned forward once again and kissed his bride-to-be.

ABOUT THE AUTHOR

Originally from Arizona, Traci Hunter Abramson has spent most of her adult life in Virginia. She is a graduate of Brigham Young University and a former employee of the Central Intelligence Agency. Since leaving the CIA, Traci has written several novels, including the Undercurrents trilogy, the Royal books, *Obsession*, the Saint Squad series, *Deep Cover*, and *Chances Are*, as well as a novella in *Twisted Fate*.

When she's not writing, Traci enjoys spending time with her family and coaching the local high school swim teams.